GIFTED

DAVID GEARING

AKUSAI
PUBLISHING

GIFTED

DAVID GEARING

1

_____

Well, step one is to get out of here, and to do that, I have to
devise a plan. I don't know how deep I am and how much
digging I need to do. The only way to move is to slide your hands
along your side and up and across your chest, then flip your hands
over and touch the front of the coffin. It's a soft felt lining and when I
push forward, using the back of the coffin as leverage against my
shoulders, the coffin lid gives way just a little bit.

I need to get out of this coffin. It's dark and stuffy and has that
musty, damp smell of a sandbox.

Seriously, no light and no outlines for my eyes to follow. It's so
dark, I'm not even sure if I'm horizontal or vertical. If it weren't for the
smell of fabric and wood against my nose, I wouldn't even know that I
was in a confined space.

You know, even with everything that I can do, I can't just get
myself out of here. For the first time in a few short days, I'm going to
have to put some effort into this.

And if I'm in a confined space, then I can't panic.

I'm not allowed to.

Because if I do, I'm signing my own death sentence. When you
panic and run out of air, you hyperventilate, the way you do when

you're buried under people at the local public pool at the tender age of seven-years-old and can't figure out which way is up to fresh air.

How you hold your breath and flail your arms around until you just can't find the floor or the surface. You flail and swing and struggle until you end up hitting someone who was reaching down to grab you and pull you out.

Then you cry and hyperventilate all you want because someone is holding you close and telling you it's okay. Your lungs celebrate the crisp cold air going in and out in large gulps, and you shout at your mommy that you never want to go swimming again and, please, could we just go home and never come back because you just want to go home and go back to your safe and sound Playstation.

Just saying.

So that asshole just leaves me to die. This is no way to treat your boyfriend.

With my hands, I search around the insides of the coffin, pressing my fingertips against the wood. My fingers make small circular motions to figure out the size of the coffin. I'm happy I've been short all my life because someone clearly made this coffin for a bigger person than me, which is most people nowadays.

My fingers clenched into a tight fist, I tap against the wood to feel any soft spots—maybe an air pocket or loose dirt—where I can somehow, someway get myself out of here. I wait and listen when my knuckles rap against the soft wooden coffin lid. I wait and listen for the hollow sound, the reverberating wood sound that echoes back into the empty pockets of space around me.

Remember, Teddy, just breathe slowly. Breathe slowly, hold your breath, and let it all get out little by little. Just like your mom taught you, just like your PE teacher taught you in yoga class. All those times I made fun of that shit, and here it is, helping me out after all.

Remind me to send a thank you note to Ms. Lalane.

The trick is to hold my breath as long as possible, so my lungs can use up as much of the air as possible, then let it out. If I can control my breathing, I can control my nerves.

I can control everything. Being buried underground? I can fix that.

No, really, I can.

No noises of emptiness, no hollow air pocket sounds. This might suck, so I kick and listen for more hollow sounds. The tips of my Nikes don't reveal anything: no secret soft spots to help me break through and dig. Therefore, I figure this will have to be done the hard way: I'll have to dig my way out.

Kicking, hard and fast like at kickball in fifth grade, I bend and bend the soft coffin door. It gives more and more, and it's harder than it sounds, kicking a door open and keeping my breathing in a steady stream of Zen-like calm and concentration.

My foot goes back against the bottom of the coffin, then as fast as it can for only two or three inches until it bends the front wooden piece. Over and over again. When I make one last final kick, the cracking wood sound of freedom makes me smile just a little bit. My foot hits soft dirt, and the wet soil smell of the dirt creeps into my nose, and I couldn't be happier.

One more step closer to kill that rat bastard boyfriend of mine.

Okay, maybe we're exes now. I mean for serial, can you still be in a relationship with someone who tried to kill you?

I'm a little excited right now, so I am not controlling my foot motions. I'm just kicking in any which way. And it feels like I have a rubberband wrapped around my chest about thirty times. And through this, I'm realizing that I'm letting more dirt get into the coffin. It's going to bury my feet and, eventually, my face if I'm not more careful. I sigh and realize that this is going to be just as hard as it looks.

I cross my arms across my chest, pulling tightly toward myself because of my limited space.

I hope to me this works.

When I pull my arms across my chest, and pull my elbows outward, the palms of my hands are at my shoulders.

Seriously, I don't know how long I've been in the dirt, but I cannot see anymore. I can't tell where I am and which direction I'm facing.

And I'm just as confused as when I was above ground in my pre-AP calculus class. I reach around and eventually feel the seams of my T-shirt, where the arms meet the shoulders. If I can pull my shirt up and over my head, I can create a cloth mask that might protect my face from the dust and debris I'm about to let in.

Using my fingers to inch my shirt up little by little, my back becomes exposed to the bare bottom of the coffin. It's not cold, but not warm, either. More moist and wet from my breathing and sweating. This is so gross and so disgusting, but I have to do this.

I have to kill Pete Hensley.

By the time my shirt is about halfway up my chest, I pause and swear into the enclosed darkness. Pulling my arms out of my shirt so I can keep pulling it up to finish my mask is not going to be easy.

Think, Teddy, think. How can I do this.

My shoulders pull forward, but it does nothing but stretch out the shirt. My arms are extended outward and forward, up against the front of the coffin, and I cannot move them. They do not want to move, and I cannot pull my arms out of the armholes.

I'm going to die. I'm going to die I'm going to die I'm gonna die I'm gonna die.

No.

Breathe, Teddy.

Breathe and think. Think slowly and breathe calm, long breaths. Just like your speech therapist taught you to do in third grade.

I pull my chest upwards, breathing in slowly. Trying to keep my tummy still and firm, I exhale and breathe through my diaphragm. Breathe slowly and close my eyes and shut out the noises.

Pulling my wrist and fists close to my chest, I realize I'm doing this all wrong. Get the shirt off me first, then put it back on.

Pulling on my shirt at the shoulders, the shirt inches up my back, over my shoulders and eventually off my head. The trail of wet soil marches into my nostrils, and I'm trying everything I can to keep from sneezing right now. Moving my nostrils around, blowing out of my nostrils. Even pretending to sneeze to trick myself.

Does that use up a lot of oxygen or a little?

If I die in here, Pete Hensley, I swear I'll fucking kill you. I'll come back alive and kill you again and again and again. Then I'll bring you back to life, and I'll kill you again.

I've done it before, I can do it again.

Even though no one can see me, I feel beyond stupid and embarrassed with my shirt off. Nevertheless, this has to be done. And though there isn't a lot of room in here, I try a partial sit-up and pull my head through the neck of the shirt. The rest of the shirt hangs just above my brown-black hair dyed burgundy, and I realize, I'm almost there. Part one of my great escape is almost complete.

I swear to God, Peter, I'll fucking kill you.

2

I f I'm really honest with myself, everything in my life has really
  been about death from the day I was born.

You see, when I exited my mom's vagina, I was pronounced dead
on the scene. The doctors call this 'stillborn': when a fetal corpse exits
the birth canal. I don't know what usually happens to babies who are
born dead, and their mothers have to deal with it the rest of their
lives. For all I know, the doctors put them in a little coffin and buried
them in a cemetery somewhere. For all I know, they could be thrown
in the medical wastebaskets and life goes on.

So to speak.

See, I don't know what happens to dead babies when they are
pronounced dead because I didn't stay dead.

My mom tells it like this:

When she was pushing and pushing and crying and yelling
things at no one in particular, my dad was off in the waiting room,
pacing back and forth. When asked if he wanted to be in the room to
watch the delivery and to help out, he politely told the doctors and
nurses, "I don't do well with pressure."

The doctors, they didn't know anything was wrong at first. They
were just concerned that my mom was in so much pain because she

refused to go with an epidural, that little needle that goes into her back and injects all kinds of painkillers so she can just pop a squat and push the little infant freeloader out into the cold world. After about a half an hour of pain, my mom began screaming at the doctor to knock her out.

"Please, God," she screamed out to them, "if you have any kind bones in your body, please knock me out and drug me up." The doctors held my mom still, pulling her shoulders still and pushing her off to the side while a nurse pushed the needle into her skin and flooded her system with nice, relaxing painkilling meds.

After that, my mom told me, everything got a little foggy, and I was finally out into the open and silent. Babies usually cry when they get exposed to the dry coldness of the medical rooms, the white bright lights piercing into the eyes and skin of pale uterine parasites. It's a dramatic moment. Believe me, I understand. I don't even like getting out of the pool to dry up and go to the bathroom inside.

When the doctor checked my little infant body out, he said I was stillborn, not moving and not breathing. My mother, still drugged up and emotional and all that, demanded to see me. She demanded to hold me, and even though the nurses and doctors hesitated, she said, they still placed me in her arms. My body, she said, was still and firm, like a frozen turkey, I guess. But to hear her say it, you would think I was the most beautiful corpse that ever lived.

My mother draped her sweaty hands and fingers and pushed back my downy soft, newborn hair across my head. Wiping tears from her eyes, she said that she pushed her thumb into my tightly clenched, soft wrinkled hands and cried. My eyes were closed, but my mom held me for hours, staring into my face and tracing my cheeks with the tip of her middle finger.

I, of course, don't remember any of this, but I hear this story every year on my birthday. Every three hundred and sixty-five days, I get a reminder that I died.

When the doctors were happy that she had enough of me, a nurse tried to pull me from her arms. The nurses, she tells the story, the nurses had to lie across her feet to keep my mom from kicking them.

She kicked and screamed and told them that she was going to keep her baby and wanted to leave.

Sometimes, she tells the part of the story that she actually tried to leave the hospital room by inching her butt and body off of the bed. Just as she reached the edge of the bed, the nurses pushed her back onto the middle of the bed and took me from her confused arms. Dazed and completely lost, my mom sat in the bed and watched as an elderly black nurse, Nurse Edwina, took me from her arms and carried me to a nearby baby bed cart thingy. And this is where mommy's little miracle story begins:

When Nurse Edwina tried to put me on the baby bed cart thingy, my mouth opened and I inhaled, then exhaled life-giving breaths. My first act as a newly resurrected newborn was to cry and scream and throw my fists around into the air.

It was a miracle as my mom tells it. The way she really tells the story, you would think that the heavens opened up, and I was touched by the grace of God himself, but I don't really imagine it that way.

When I think about my resurrection, I imagine it was something like more relaxed.

Like when I took my first breath, I kick and scream and do the normal baby things, and my mom opens her arms up and the nurses, amazed and shocked and probably horrified by the zombie child in her arms, happily offers the infant to its unsuspecting mother to be the first victim of the baby zombie apocalypse.

Unfortunately, I grew up healthy and somewhat strong and without any lust for brains or peeling skin.

But think about how cool it would be to be born a zombie. For serial.

My sister wasn't born yet. That wasn't until a few years later, in 1997. So at that time, I was an only child, and I was spoiled like no one else. When I pointed to the shelves in the store and saw a toy I wanted and said, "Mommy, buy me that!" I got it. Each and every time.

Still, we didn't have everything we ever wanted, and to be perfectly honest, I was okay with that.

When you're known as the "boy who died", it's like your whole life is Easter Sunday over and over again.

Not saying I'm Jesus Christ, but you know what I mean.

When the doctors checked me out after I announced myself by crying, my mom told me that there wasn't anything found wrong with me. I guess I was just born not breathing and somehow I had decided that I wanted to breathe again. I didn't know that little babies could hold their breath. Maybe they can't hold their breath. Maybe I really was dead. What they could tell was that the umbilical cord was at one time wrapped around my neck, I guess, but the doctors say that's way more common than zombie babies coming back from the dead.

What they can't tell me and my mom is they don't know if that was why I stopped breathing. They just knew that it bent my neck a little out of shape. But I guess I'm okay now.

The doctors allowed my mom to go home after a few more days of watching her and making sure that she was okay. Observations about her behaviors to make sure that she won't try to do anything to herself, or that her body was okay after ejecting a corpse. They told her that I, however, had to stay there for a little while longer. Freaky baby zombie shit just needed a few more tests and way more observations.

My mom decided that she wasn't going to go home and no one could make her go home, so they set up a cot and let her stay in a room and I stayed in the newborn baby ward. Every day she would come see me and hold me and stroke my little baby hairs across my big ball-shaped head and cry and be thankful that I was alive.

My dad was, well, I guess my dad decided that he could go home.

Whether they were done or not with all of my tests, my mom was able to take me home a few days earlier than they had planned. From day one, my mom had tried to stay in the room where the hospital keeps all the babies. Instead of sleeping in her room, she would try to go visit me in mine. Understandably, this creeped out all the other new mothers, and they made a big fuss about my mom sleeping in the baby room. For serial, she dragged her cot into the room and tried to sleep next to my baby bed. The way my mom tells it, they let her sleep in there once, probably figuring that Mom was a little stressed out and needed the comfort of making sure that I was alive.

But there she was the next morning when families came to see their newborn sons, daughters, nieces, and nephews: a twenty-year-old woman in her pajamas sleeping in between the baby beds.

This is my mother for you.

You have to understand, I remember my first few years of being alive no better than you remember yours, so the details are a little shady to me. What I can tell you from all the baby pictures and believe you me, there's a shitload of baby pictures all over the place my birthday celebrations were the biggest on the block. My mom— that kind and giving woman that she is— opened up the entire block to celebrate my birthday. She figured that everyone else should care as much about me rising from the dead as she did.

I don't think that anyone had the heart to tell her that they didn't care. So, they showed her by not showing up.

Still, though I wasn't popular, I was Mommy's Little Angel.

And then my sister was born.

I do remember the day my sister was born because my dad was taking the family to Pizza Hut when my mom's water broke. To hear my dad tell the story the way he used to, you'd think that the car was flooded in and we had to swim our way out.

When my sister was born, there was no emotional drama and no life-or-death situation. Instead, it was the exact opposite of my birth. My sister was born alive and stayed alive. She came out just when she was supposed to, and my mom swears that she was in labor for only a few hours, max.

My parents christened her Vanessa Barratt, and we went home. She did nothing wrong and was born perfectly as she should have, and the poor girl has paid for it ever since.

3

My wet body hydroplanes on the slick floor of the locker showers. Around me, Shane shouts in his wet tighty whities, saying, "Stop looking, faggot." My wet boxers cling and hug my ass, and every time I try to put my hands on the wet ground, I slip and fall. My hands won't stay firmly on the yellow-tiled floor of the shower, so my chest and shoulders hurt from bouncing off the shower over and over and over again.

I look up to protect my face from the needle-like water and the potential pain of fists and feet. And the wet outline of his dick is just so right there in front of me. I can't not stare, but I try to hide it, maybe look at his face and his eyes, see the anger and hope he's done pushing me back down. And instead, his wet chest glistens in the water pouring down his body. His body, sculpted from the years of weight training classes and hours of playing football, well, that piece of artwork is the real motivation why I got caught up in this mess.

Shane's bare foot touches my cheek and presses my face down into the cold wet ground. The water does enough to distract me from the smell of musk and bodyspray and sweat.

And of course, the jocks had to turn on the cold water when they threw me into the showers. Though this, in my case, might be a good thing.

"If I fucking catch you staring at me again, I'll kill you. Do you understand me, fag?" says Shane. His foot pressing on my face pushes my lips out like a fish.

All I can do is try to nod my head up and down. The sides of my wet face rubbing against the sole of his foot must have creeped him out, because Shane took a step back, wiped his foot on the ground and said, "Good" before he and his buddies get dressed and leave for sixth period.

The others stop their laughing just long enough to gather into a circle and put their clothes back on. I watch, waiting for all of them to leave. When the coast is clear and the only sound is the echo of water slapping against the puddles on the floor, I decide it's safe to move.

I slide myself out of the shower and try to stand up, grabbing the silver metal grips of the shower knobs, and pull myself up. Just to be nice, I turn off all the showers and carefully exit the shower. My body is still soaking wet, my fingers wrinkled like little prunes and my boxers are skin-tight hugging every private part of my body, leaving nothing to the imagination. Not that I'm really small down there, but I don't need everyone to see this, you know?

"Barratt?" the coach shouts across the locker room. "Barratt? You in here?"

I stay quiet and try to swing my arms around to dry them off. I don't have any towels here since I don't take showers voluntarily, and there aren't any towels for anyone else to use. The showers, I always thought, were just for show and after football games. At least that's what my imagination likes to tell me.

My shirt is just coming over my head when Coach Staggs comes around the lockers and stares at me. Now keep in mind, at this point all I have on is my shirt, which is wet and, thank God, black with a picture of Nirvana's front man Kurt Cobain shoving his face at you, so my body isn't going to be too out there. However, I'm still in my wet boxers. I'll be honest, I had considered just taking them off and going commando to keep my pants dry. With Coach in the room, let's just say I'm happy that I didn't decide to take them off.

"Barratt, what's going on?" Coach just stands there, leaned up against the lockers and watching me not getting dressed because I'm too in shock.

"I was put in the showers. They called me names."

Coach whispers, *Dammit* to himself. He says to me, "Do you want me to write them up for you? Was it a fight?"

The thing you need to know about Coach is this: he coaches our football team and the only reason why he's asking is because he wants to make sure that Shane is available to play in Friday night's game.

"No," I say. With my eyes still on him, I reach out for my pants and decide that he's not going to leave me alone long enough to take off the boxers and go with Plan A. "No, it wasn't a fight. No, you don't have to write them up."

Coach smiles, but tries to hide it with a grim, scrunched up forehead. "Good, well, let me know if those boys give you any more trouble." He says all of this walking away, "And hurry up, you're going to be late for class."

VERONICA LEANS up against my locker, her foot on the bottom locker and her shoulder up against mine on the top. "What happened to you?" she points her pink press-on nail index finger at me and my damp shirt.

"Don't ask," I say. I motion my hands for her to get off my locker.

"Tell me who the bastards are," she says.

"It was nobody," I tell her. My head is buried in the center of my locker, and even though it is not so deep, I can squeeze my entire head in there. With my books and the metal locker baskets holding my Sharpies and highlighters.

"Bullshit," says my sister. Vanessa turns around and looks up and down the hallways, now mostly empty since everyone is either in class or hiding out in the bathrooms. "It was Shane again, wasn't it?"

"It might have been," I say. "I don't know."

And Vanessa grabs the back of my head in a sisterly, loving way, and she slams my locker shut. Still holding the back of my head, she says to me, "You're going to stand up to him or I'm going to do it for you, little brother."

"You're the younger sibling," I say.

And she tells me, "Then fucking act like it." She lets go of my hair, and the skin on my skull pulls back to its normal tightness and location.

When my sister walks down the hallway, she fucking owns the place. She's not exactly one of the popular kids, but she has always been known by all the guys at school. She is what the boys politely call "an easy lay." And while I usually argue with anyone who says that in public conversation, I'm always inclined to agree.

You see, Vanessa has a way with men that most women are ashamed to use or admit to having used.

As Vanessa walks out of the hallway into the outside courtyard, she turns around and waves at me, in my direction, and winks.

Vanessa doesn't wink. She never winks at me, anyway, and so I glance over my shoulder. Right behind me, is Leo I-forget-his-last-name, a wrestling junior who is much faster than his orangutan body would lead you to believe. Naturally, this is my sister.

Outside in the courtyard, two teachers and one of the hall monitors are pulling Vanessa off Shane's jacket. Shane's cheek is red, turning purple. It will be a bruise come tomorrow morning. Only one teacher is pulling on Shane's jacket.

The other two are trying to keep Vanessa down on the ground. She's screaming out, "I'll fucking kill you! No means no, you rapist! No means no!" over and over again.

That's my little sister. Nothing short of insane.

The rest of the students wandering the halls chuckle and encourage the insanity of my sister. One of the boys in the courtyard, he yells out, "Rapist!"

Another one screams out, "Why can't you take no for an answer!" Another one shouts out, "I'm pregnant because of you," and this draws a bunch of laughter from the kids and one of the teachers.

The hall monitor, he extends his arms out to the side and his arms are wide. Like football field wide. He used to be a linebacker, the kids say. He used to be a washed out football coach for the little league teams when he got out of high school. The type of man who couldn't keep his dreams alive, so he lived vicariously through the lives of other people's children. That's a whole different kind of sickness right there. "No kids of my own, so hey! Can I borrow yours for a little bit?" Secretly wanting to say, "I just want to teach him football" and "Make him succeed where I failed", and beg on his knees. "Please, please, please? I just need to know I'm not a failure."

My sister is being dragged away from Shane's cowering body, shielding himself from my sister's insanity and absurd insults. She's screaming at him, "It's your baby, Shane. It's yours!"

And as they drag my sister back to the office, I follow along. Like a car chasing an ambulance on the street, everyone clears the path and I follow along until Mr. Webster steps in front of me.

"Can I help you son?" he says.

This asshole in cheap gray suit and mismatching blue tie with a green shirt has sat and listened to me cry and whine about how the other kids are beating me up, and he can't even take the damned time to remember my name.

"I'm Teddy, sir. Theodore Barratt. I'm her brother," I say and point my finger at the raving lunatic in the office. She puts on a great front for the rest of the school to see.

"It's not necessary that you be here right now," says Mr. Webster. He smells like Old Spice old, a scent that reminds me of my grandfather's old leather chair I wasn't allowed to sit in. Ever.

"But I'm her brother." I gulp. I say, "Sir, I just want to make sure she's okay." I try on a baby sad, whimpering face and say, "I can't believe that she's pregnant, sir."

Webster turns around and his six-foot-three tall frame, draped with a dark charcoal gray suit, shields my view of the office. "Go back to class, Mr. Bartlett."

"That's Barratt, sir," I whisper under my breath and go to the bathroom to wait out the rest of the day.

By the clock on my cell phone, the seventh period bell will ring soon when I hear my sister's heavy footsteps on the bathroom tile. "Teddy, come out, come out wherever you are," she says. She takes one-step and pushes in the front door with her foot. Then another step and I can see her shadow quickly approaching the last stall. My stall.

"In a second," I say, high-pitched and girlish. I flush the toilet and walk out, still trying to fake zip my pants fly.

"Don't try that bullshit with me," Vanessa points out to my crotch. "Your pants are button-fly." She smiles. "Are you ready to go home?" she says.

"Yes, but I have to go to eighth period," I say. My backpack slings over my shoulder and the weight of the books pull me off to the left and into the counter. I don't fall, but it's so easy to forget how heavy textbooks can be.

"You're beyond ridiculous," she says. She turns around, not facing me, and walks step-by-step to the door. "Did you see how I kicked some ass out there?" she says. "I'm being sent home and probably written up because of you." Vanessa comes closer and messes up my hair with her hand. The smooth side of her nail, it scratches against my scalp. It feels good, until I realize that she's destorying my style.

"Will you cut it out?" I say. I shove her hand away from my head and say, "You're messing it up."

"I'm not messing anything up." Vanessa gets right into my face, her nose barely touching mine as she says, "Maybe your problem is you want everything so perfect, so neat and tidy, that you're afraid to stand up for yourself. Heaven forbid you cause any waves, Jesus Christ."

Her hands go up into the air like she's praising God. And she looks at me, her face drops first, then her hands as they fall to her hips. "You're being stupid, and everyone knows it, Teddy. That's why they pick on you."

"You don't know why they pick on me," I tell her. "They call me faggot and wimp and pussy and baby and all that shit."

"Oh for crying out loud, Ted, it's not because you're gay," my little sis says. "It's because you let them."

"Fuck you," I shout at her. My voice echoes off the yellowy-grimy tiled bathroom.

The silence and the buzz of the fluorescent lighting above us silently becomes a noise in my mind.

I look at my sister and the bitch says, "What the fuck ever." She looks at herself in the mirror and fixes her hair with her hand until she seems pleased with her reflection. Then my sister says, "Well, I'm going home and you can come along if you want," she says. "I'm sure I can pull something for you if you need it."

"No, I have a test and it's way too much of a hassle to make it up," I tell her. What she doesn't know is, I don't have a test.

What she probably knows is, I really want to go for a whole another reason.

As my sister opens the door, a freshman stumbles forward, his hand still on the door. He sees me, then my sister, and freezes. He freezes and puts his hand on his pants and literally has no idea what he is supposed to do.

And of course, Vanessa, not missing a beat, she grabs the freshman's chest and looks down at his pants and says, "The bathroom's all yours." Looking at the crotch and taking a step toward him, she says, "If you need help with that, do let me know." Her red lips part into a smile that bears her white teeth, pearly porcelain white, to this poor, poor freshman. As she leaves, she shouts out to me, "See you at home, Jesus."

4
───────

I can barely hear myself in art class, which is possibly the most relaxed classroom in any school in any state. Our assignment is to create a self-portrait, but divide it into smaller pieces using sharp, geometric shapes and lines. Ms. Campbell, our art teacher, says that this is a complex assignment, but I don't believe her. To be perfectly honest, her assignments are crap, but interesting and easy.

My self-portrait is myself sitting in a chair, playing video games. The view you see me as, is from the front, as if you are the television and I am playing my games staring right at you. The controller in my hand is oversized and black like a traditional Xbox controller. My tongue is hanging out slightly over my lips, a little quirk I do when thinking really, really hard. The rest of my upper body, my shoulders and face, is pulled forward. My feet, extended out and thrown into the screen. Total forced perspective.

Ms. Campbell steps behind me and I can sense the stale, dusty smell of paint and glue from behind me.

"Hi, Ms. Campbell," I say. My eyes stay on my artwork. I move the ruler, pulling it through and across the drawing, finding a way to somehow draw a straight line right across my head, through the forehead and down across the cheek so only the top left third of my head is on this triangle.

"This," Ms. Campbell says in a gasp. "This," she says again, stepping around me and points at the pose of my left foot. "And this," she says again, pointing to the line that intersects my hairline. "This is so beautiful." Ms. Campbell's bare, ringless hands clutch themselves near her chest and she takes an admiring glance across the piece.

"Thank you, Ms. Campbell," I say, chipper and smiling big. If I had to pick a favorite teacher, I would have to choose Ms. Campbell. I mean, she *always* compliments anything I do.

"Teddy," she says and rests her hands on the edge of the paper. Her eyes never leave the piece or the movement of my hands as I try to make more lines with the edge of the ruler. "Teddy, this is fantastic. I wish I had an advanced art class," she tells me. Ms. Campbell tells me, "Your sense of control of the details is amazingly real." Her eyes are beaming pure joy and inspiration when she says to me, "You've got a gift." She pats me on the shoulder and continues her tour of everyone else's work.

Looking around the room, you see most of the girls are on their cell phones texting someone else, probably someone else in the classroom across the way. There are some of the girls grouped up together, blocking Ms. Campbell's view of them as they gossip about someone or something, trying to block the teacher's view while one of them puts on her makeup in the middle of class.

And one of the girls looks at me, giggles, and waves with her fingers over at my direction. The girl's name is Sammy, and I don't like her. There's nothing much to like about her, actually. From the trailer-trash-and proud personality to the white T-shirt stretched so far over her huge breasts that it has stretch marks to the giggling way she says "LOL" out loud in everyday conversation, she's a total and complete annoyance.

So of course, she wants to talk to me. Like a cat, these people always seem to know when I don't like them and don't want them around.

"Hi," says Sammy. She giggles in embarrassment, then brushes her hair out of her eyes. This act makes no sense because most of it is held back behind her head with an elastic scrunchy. The hair has been dyed so many colors I don't think she knows what her real hair color is anymore. "So, I was wondering," she says. She leans in over close to me and looks from side to side like this is some kind of clandestine meeting, a secret covert operation that will determine the fate of freedom in the United States of America. "Are you gay?" she says, following it up with, "That's just what I heard, and I totally don't think you are, but you know, it's not like you can tell just by looking at anyone."

"Draw your own conclusion," I tell her. I don't acknowledge her sitting here. I don't look at her, and I try as much as I can to block out the fake Britney Spears knockoff perfume she bought at Walgreens.

"So you are!" she says. Sammy puts arm around my shoulder and laughs, pulling me in tightly. "So you should meet up with some of my friends, cuz they are gay, too, and well I think you're totally adorable."

"I didn't say I'm gay," I echo back to her.

Then she pauses, stares at me as I draw a final line to close off the isosceles triangle on my drawing. "Wait," she says. "You aren't dating anyone, are you?"

I don't want to answer, but my mouth is on autopilot when I answer back, "No." I answer back to her, "I'm not gay." Closing my eyes, I tell her, "Can you please just leave me alone?"

"Awesome," she says. "You should be my new bestie!" This annoying cow of a woman, she hugs me again and I wince because I might have to burn this shirt. The stench of that perfume is that bad.

"I don't want to be your bestie," I say to the back of her nappy head. Sammy walks away, swinging her ass back and forth like a dog that has just won himself a biscuit. Sammy didn't hear me, doesn't want to hear me, or is completely ignoring me. I might as well have said nothing at all.

And now the rest of the school is going to start to think I'm gay. Great. Wonderful.

"What the hell are you doing?" says Ms. Campbell. She's standing next to Richard, who is painting the word 'fag' on the back of Donny's shirt.

"Dude," Richard's friend Donny says to him, "it better say 'beast' when you're done or I'm going to kick your ass."

"Get out of here, Donny. To the office. Now." Ms. Campbell yanks the brush from Richard's hand and puts it back in the supply closet, not even trying to wash off the paint. "Richard, wash your hands in the sink and go to the office, too." She points to the door, where both of them are laughing. "I'll send the referral in a minute."

"I didn't do anything," says Donny, but he ducks his head down and leaves the classroom anyway. As he exits out the door, someone shouts out to Donny, "Gay homo!" and they laugh.

Everyone in the class except Ms. Campbell. Every single student laughs except me.

It's not that I don't want to laugh, it's that I am not sure that laughing is going to accomplish anything right now. For serial, I'm kinda tired of everyone just throwing around the word like it means nothing.

Ms. Campbell sits down at her desk and the white glow of the computer screen reflects off her glasses. The glasses must be for reading because she doesn't use them otherwise. If I had to take a guess, Ms. Campbell is only about thirty-five, maybe up to forty years old and not unattractive.

As a matter of fact, she looks something like a normal person when she's in the classroom. You could even say she looks like a regular teacher, her loose pastel blouse paired neatly with a flowing paisley skirt that hangs off her body in a desperate attempt to flow in the air-conditioning fans. The colors, of course, match and don't match at the same time. Opposite sides of the color wheel to provide the most amount of visual "color conflict", she says. As Ms. Campbell describes it, the purpose of art is to provide people with a way to think about what we learn and what we do.

Thinking about her words, I pick up a blue color pencil and begin shading in some of the triangles and geometric shapes. I go for various shades and darknesses, going heavy on some of the triangles and light on the big ones, then small ones. I take an orange colored pencil and trace, then shade in, parts of my face that fall in the geometric shapes. One quarter of my face is a hard, darkened orange that makes me think of tanning bed tans and mandarin oranges. The lower jaw is a shade that's more peach than orange, it's so light.

And the two conflicting colors, they describe the piece so well that I can't help but hold it up in front of me and admire my own work.

In English class, you learn that many of the writers didn't dare admire their own work. It seems to me that the only way to be successful is to be dead and think that your work isn't worth anything, but to keep on doing it anyway. If I were to believe that, maybe I should shove this off to the side, bury it in a box somewhere, and go kill myself with hemlock or cyanide.

Where do you get hemlock and cyanide these days anyway?

Ms. Campbell comes over to me and stands next to the table. As the fake fluorescent lighting pierces the paper fibers and carries the waves of color to my head, Ms. Campbell completely ignores it and says to me, in a close, quiet whisper, "I'm so sorry about that." She leans in a bit closer and says, "I just want you to know that I'll write them up and make sure that they get in serious trouble." Her hand pats me on the back, like I'm in need of a pep talk, and she says, "Just so you know, you're safe here."

"For what?" Trying to play it cool, I put the pencil down quietly, almost too calmly, and I tell her, "Why apologize to me?" I feel rage.

And Ms. Campbell looks at me, God bless her artistic little heart, and she says, "Oh don't worry, honey. It doesn't matter at all to me."

5

I spot my first reddish-orangish-yellowish leaf on a tree when I step off the bus after school. My sister, already home, didn't want to come back and pick me up, so it was off to the bus I go.

It was the normal noisy ride home. The other kids drawing on the seats and on each other. The boys shouting stuff at each other and girls telling the boys to be quiet. Gender warfare because of all the sexual tension. Boys want to fuck girls, girls want to make out with boys. And probably fuck them, too. I don't know.

I do know that I get off the bus and I don't have to worry about that stuff anymore. Instead, I'm left with my thoughts and the wind bringing the cold weather along with it. My favorite time of year, autumn is. Trees begin their descent into hibernation, and people begin burning maple and hickory wood. It always makes me think about Thanksgiving dinner and the sweaters we have to pull out because the dry air cools down enough to chill your bones.

The streets are narrow and dark, full of potholes that make my mother swear when the car bumps over them. Most of the houses around here are one story and built so close to each other that we can sing along with the songs our neighbors play too loud.

About a block away from home, I realize that I don't have my house key.

Dammit.

The key hangs from the lanyard on my wall at this very moment. And it's the worst feeling in the world, when you realize you don't have something, can see it in your mind, and have no idea what you can do without it.

Seriously, it fucking sucks, but happens way too often.

My mom once described me as being someone who lived life in his head. She used to say that one of the reasons why I'm such a great artist is because my mind is so active and so vivid that it creates its own reality.

"Mom," I want to tell her, "this is true for a lot of people. It's called psychology."

Still, it makes me feel special from time to time. Not short bus special, but warm-fuzzy special. It's always nice to have someone notice you, but my mom sort of overdoes it.

Vanessa better have the damned door open. She had better be home. The door had better be locked.

Or. Um, or. Or.

Or, I don't know what.

But I'll think of something. It's what brothers and sisters are for, right? Tormenting each other?

The streets are mostly empty in my subdivision. Most of everyone here has a job, or two jobs, to survive. My mom is no exception. She's still at work and it's my turn to cook dinner. And no, I don't know what's for dinner just yet.

Maybe I'll just watch a cooking show until something inspires me.

The only things that sit in our carport are the multiple oil stains on the cement. No cars, no sign of them being there. Which means Mom is at work and my sister is I don't know where.

This is fantastic.

I hold my breath and hold the door handle. Please, God or Allah or Yahweh or whatever you want to be called, please let this door be open.

I pull on the handle, twist it to the right and it locks up. No movement, and I'm stuck outside.

And suddenly, goose bumps take over my forearms and the hair stands up on its ends. I begin to shiver and I realize that I'm already getting colder with the thought of being stuck out here.

She knew I was coming home. I don't even know why she has the car in the first place. She's only sixteen. Vanessa should not be driving alone in the first place. At least in most families. When my mom and dad divorced, what was left of my family decided that we all needed to be able to drive and use the car whenever we wanted because my mom would be busy working all the damned time.

The downside to that plan was, my sister would be taking the car all the time. She would be gone doing who knows who and coming back with a smile on her face at the end of the night.

At least she has fun, I guess, though I couldn't tell you who her friends were.

I rest both of my hands on the door handle, gripping tight. Please God, don't leave me out here in the cold. I don't want to die out here alone.

And I twist the handle, smooth and quick, and it jiggles a bit and the damned door, this stupid door that should be open. It's locked. Closed and locked.

I let out a growl into the fall-almost wintery air. "Damn you, Vanessa," I say.

I check my backpack again. Nothing in there, or in the front pockets. Nothing in the side pockets for pencils and markers and stuff. Nothing, nothing, nothing.

I check my pockets, pulling them out so they look like rabbit ears. Once again, a whole lotta nothing.

Seriously, Vanessa, I'll kill you.

And when I shove my pockets back into my pants, something scrapes my right leg. Just a second ago, I had nothing in my pockets. What the hell?

Like an idiot, I shove my hands into both pockets, pushing the rabbit ears back into place inside my pants. And there it is. The key and the lanyard and everything. And though I know it wasn't there at first, here it is in my hands. I'd call it a miraculous coincidence if it didn't seem to happen to me all of the time.

6

My mom used to call me one of the luckiest men alive. My sister calls me a magician, my dad called me a weirdo, and the rest of the school calls me a freak. I couldn't tell you when it started, but I can say that me and strangeness, we're special friends.

When I was about four years old, my family owned a light orange tabby cat called Puzzle. The name came from me, and when my mom gave me the special task of naming the cat, I said, "I don't know. The fur looks like puzzles." The dark orange lines curved and swirled across his back and sides, giving my four-year-old self the impression that his body was really just patched together using giant puzzle pieces.

I loved that cat, even though it didn't love me. I was the substitute mommy for it. What I mean is, Puzzle only came to me when my mom could not be found. Puzzle never learned to like babies, so he left my sister alone, and my dad hated cats. I was left the object of its affection by default. Good ol' default.

Now plenty of people say that their animals are strange, but seriously, I had never seen a cat that drank with its paws. The way Puzzle drank his water was rather unique from what I can tell, though I've looked it up from time to time, and I guess it's not all that uncommon, too.

Anyway, Puzzle drank his water by licking the water off his paws. At first, we had always thought that he was fishing in his water bowl. That was one of his other weird habits: he drowned his mice and toys in the water bowl and then offered them up to us. My mom said that he was trying to give us a gift, contributing to our food. Unfortunately, we don't eat cat toys.

I, however, didn't want to disappoint poor Puzzle, so I always thanked him by scratching underneath his chin and pretended to eat the wet toy that he left for us on the edge of the kitchen floor. Each time. Every time.

My mom thought it was cute, but really, I just didn't want to hurt his feelings.

When those times arrived that Puzzle didn't have things dying in his water bowl, we noticed that he was still dipping his paws in the water and pulling it out. Watching further, we watched Puzzle take his paw to his mouth and his grayish tongue and lap up the water from his paw. Then, dip his paw back for a second drink. Not once did I ever see this cat drink from the water bowl the way we are taught when we're little. Nope, Puzzle hunched over his bowl, tongue lapping up droplets of water in the wet rhythmic *slap-slap, slap-slap*.

Puzzle stayed with us for about three years before we learned that she had cancer. At the age of seven, I got a crash course in the dying process and I watched our cat deteriorate. We had to pick him up and take him to his water bowl. Puzzle, never having drunk the normal way before, had to be fed water through a syringe, and we all took turns feeding him until one day, when Puzzle got up by himself, there was blood on the floor.

My mom said that meant he was too far gone, and the cancer had taken over his insides, making him bleed. For a seven-year-old to understand what that meant, well, let's just say it led to quite a few dreams of being eaten up from the inside out.

When I turned eight, my mom found Puzzle lying in his cat tree, motionless and dead. My mom broke the news to us as soon as we got home. Puzzle, a relatively small cat for his breed, was placed in a large shoe box my mom had for her boots, and we buried him off into the woods near our house. I cried so much that day and that night that I tried to stay home from school the next day. It worked. I got to stay and my sister had to go to school.

I still think she hates me for that.

Anyway, all of this sounds normal, but the weird part was a week later. I drew pictures of Puzzle all the time, put him in stories and made up little ways that I could always remember him.

Well, one morning at our doorstep, I heard some mewing. I opened the door and saw a little kitten, which couldn't have been more than a few weeks old, sitting at our door and mewing for who knows what. Without telling anyone, I grabbed the poor little guy and carried him back to my bedroom and hid him under my bed.

I was eight, how was I supposed to know that he wouldn't stay still under there?

When my mom came into the room to tell me it was time for dinner, she saw the kitten's tail sticking out from underneath the bed. I couldn't deny it any further when the new kitten chased one of Puzzle's favorite toys out from under the bed, pouncing on it for one last kill.

My mom let me keep him, but only because I had asked.

That night, we let the new cat, which I named Tigger because of his stripes, wander around the house. And then it hit us. All this time we thought our cat Puzzle was the weird one. That is, until that day when we watched Tigger drink from his water dish. And guess how he drank?

You guessed it. He dipped his front paw into the water and politely licked the droplets from his paw. He did this two or three times until he was finished and then went to the cat tree to lie down and sleep.

That cat stayed with us for five years until we moved out after Dad and Mom divorced. I missed Puzzle so much, and here we were, with another cat that had the same habits as Puzzle. This newer kitten that couldn't have been older than a few weeks, was right back with us. Like we had Puzzle back all over again.

I'm telling you, it's strange.

But not stranger than this one time when we were going on a family trip. I got angry with my dad that we couldn't go into the pool at this motel we were staying at. We were in the middle of driving across the Great State of Florida on our way to Disney World. I wanted to go swimming, because if you know Florida in the summer, it's always a good time to go swimming. So I put on my swim trunks and grabbed a towel and my dad says to me, "Teddy, where do you think you're going?"

I was young, probably about five years old, when I said, "I want to go to the pool."

My dad approaches the door, closes it firmly and says, "No," and goes to sit down. He told me no, but I didn't want to hear it. I was cooped up in the car for five hours, it was hot outside. I wanted to go into the pool. But, I wasn't allowed to. My dad forbid it.

That afternoon I sat on the bed, flipping through pages of a magazine my mom got me, the types with kiddy crossword puzzles that are way too easy for anyone and the pictures where you have to pick out all the differences between the first one and the second one, my mom gets into the shower to cool down.

What we hear next is the popping of metal against the plastered wall and my mom screaming out to us, "William! William!"

My dad gets up and knocks on the door, then opens it. My mom is standing in her towel, almost undressed and her face looked like she ran through a sprinkler. It turned out that the showerhead flew right off of the pipes and stuck inside the wall. My dad was unable to turn off the water and the motel room flooded.

For serial, true story.

Somehow, I still got my pool. Sure, it was a shitty pool, but it was a pool.

For serial, though, those are just the big things.

There was that time when I really wanted to win a free shopping spree in this toy store at the mall and ended up winning even though it was the only contest I had ever entered. There was that time someone almost hit me when I was crossing at the crosswalk all legal like, and I ended up almost getting hit by this one dude. Then I shouted out to him that I hoped he got in an accident.

When he turned around the corner, his car spun out and he hit a house. I got my accident.

There are lots of things that I get. I like to joke with my mom that it's really because "My god is an angry God," you know, that old shit you hear about the Old Testament. But, for real? It could be true.

I mean, the Lord works in mysterious ways, right?

7

Because no one in this house knows how to knock before barging in, my mom pokes her head into my room and surprises the hell out of me. I won't say what I was doing, but it would have been nice if she would at least knock first.

My mom's head turns around the corner from the doorway, peers at me with her great big smile, and says, "So where do you want to go to dinner tomorrow?"

My mom's hair is pulled into a ponytail that reveals her amazingly high European fashion-model cheekbones and sad gray eyes. When she's done up, she looks absolutely amazing, but in her bright red polo shirt uniform of her banking job, she looks tired and flushed. I have my mom's eyes, actually, those tired gray eyes with thin long lashes that I secretly love having and hate having at the same time. When my mom had friends or neighbors over for coffee and such, they pinched my cheeks and said what beautiful little eyes I have. They rubbed up the top of my head and said that they would kill for eyelashes like those.

When I was five, I had nightmares of old women coming to take my eyes.

The rest of my mom's body follows her head inside my room. She sits down on my bed. Her eyes watch me watch the intro video of a computer game, a massively addicting online role-playing game, because I need something else to do while she's in here.

"We can check out that Italian place you like, you know, Luigi's?" my mom says. Her voice is soothing and calm and fake excited. Her sentences sound like questions, that faux upswing in her voice, when she says, "I know you liked that place when you were younger. You just loved their spaghetti and meatballs."

"Loved, mom," I say. On the screen, a blue orc with upward pointing tusks slams his burly club into the head of a high elf. The orc then receives a sharp arrow to the head from a distant tree.

"Well, you know it's your birthday, so I wanted to make it special," she says to me. "I don't know why I bought you that video game. It's way too violent."

"That's just the intro video, mom. The rest of the game is just little sprites bashing at each other. No blood," I say. The game, contradicting me flashes into a play-by-play sequence of a human man with long blonde hair pulled back into a warrior's ponytail pulling up a sword from a rock, then hacking his panther enemies tornado-style.

"You're lucky I love you," Mom says. She gets up, puts her hand on my head and bends over at the waist to kiss me on the cheek. "You know I love you, Teddy."

"I love you, too, Mom."

My mom stops at the doorway of my room again and puts her hand on the eggshell white wall. "So does Luigi's work for tomorrow?"

"Sure," I say.

"Are you sure? I can change it if you want." My mom's face goes from tired to worried, her exhausted, slightly curved smile suddenly pointed downwards. "There's that Greek place downtown, or we can just do something simple at home. Ice cream cake and...and," and her voice trails off into thoughts about what we probably don't have in the fridge at the moment.

What she meant to say was, "I really hope that Luigi's is okay because I wasn't planning on changing my plans anytime soon."

"Yes, mom," I say with a smile I really don't mean. But appearances are important and I want to make her happy. For everything she's done for me, I need to make her happy.

"Yes, what, Teddy?"

"Yes, Luigi's is good," I say. My eyes return to the computer game and I load my first character, a young human female named Ellees.

"Okay, good. So tomorrow, I'll pick you up from school and we'll head right down there," my mom says. My mom's eyes go back to their dark-circled tired look. "Sound good?"

"Sounds good," I say. My door closes with a click.

When I close the window for the game with the left click of my mouse button, the screen shrinks down and I'm back to the social networking sites, Facebook and Tumblr. Both are where I go to find out more about what I need to know about being gay. Saraday, South Carolina is not known for a whole lot. Mostly a lot of freaky weird stuff that happens here. A fire that burned down the oldest town. Car crashes and missing old persons. What it's not known for is its tolerance. It's still too Confederate for my tastes, a place where the Stars and Bars still flies above every local bar in town. That red flag and blue stripes that say to anyone here, "We're Southern and we're proud. Oh, and membership only."

What I open my webpage up to is an IM from Dark_Boi96 that reads "Hows school?"

I type back, "It was OK. Same shit different day."

He types back "LOL" and I click open my My Pictures file and pull out DarkBoi96's picture that he sent me. It's him, shirtless and wearing his hat to the side. His hair is long, probably cut with a straight razor because it zags all over his face, making a feathered mess around his head. His eyes are dark and blue, inviting me to stare longer and harder and mysterious enough to keep me talking to him over and over again.

I type back to him, "What's new with you?"

"Nothin cutie," he types to me.

I can't help but to smile.

"Aww," I type back. I type out a semicolon and an end parenthesis, giving him a sideways winking smiley face.

"So when do I get your pic?" he asks.

I type out "Never" and delete. Then type it out again, then delete.

Rinse and repeat, before I go into my opened My Pictures file and drag out a picture of a redhead boy, short face and cute smile. Pale as hell, but his blushing cheeks make him look innocent and adorable, sort of how I wish I looked right about now.

I right click Copy and then Paste it in our IM box.

"Here ya go," I type and press enter.

The picture goes almost instantly and he says to me, "Hawt!" He sends another picture and a message that says, "Anyone tell u that u r totally cute?"

I lie and type back, "Yeah, all the time."

He types to me, "We should meet up." He types back, "Do you have Skype?"

And I type out back to him, "No, my sister is in the room, so I can't really do that type of stuff."

And the IM window flashes blue and orange with a new message. A pic of DarkBoi96 in the bathroom mirror. His shirtless body glistens after just getting out of the shower, wet and shiny. A white towel drapes just below his navel, and if I squint real hard, I can tell that he trims pretty close.

My mom knocks on the door this time and my natural reaction is to leap out of the seat from nerves. "Dinner is done," her muffled voice announces through the open door. I click the IM window closed and say, "Okay, I'm coming."

8

M r. Webster's voice comes in loud and clear through the TV announcements in the morning, nearly shouting into the headset microphone that he's wearing. He says, "We must be more respectful toward the posters and announcements in the halls."

No one is listening when Mr. Webster continues with his announcement, "It has come to my attention that the posters for the new Diversity Club have been torn down and every day they were put up. This is very disrespectful and unnecessary. Every club has a right to exist on school campus, and all voices have a right to be heard." He looks off camera and nods.

Mr. Webster shifts his head to another corner of the room, like he's in the newsroom and someone whispers to him, but still loud enough for the microphone to pick it up, saying, "Where are you looking?" Mr. Webster's eyes shift back to the camera and he's staring back at us, his face cold and firm like it could have been chiseled out of rock. "No more taking down posters, guys. I expect better from our Pirates."

Today was a good day despite it being a Pep Rally day. Our basketball team is playing our local rivals, White Pine High. Their colors—white, silver, and black—just happen to coincide with the colors I'm wearing today. Just saying. My white shirt, silver watch and black jeans go nicely with a slightly warm fall day, but the others jocks in the hallways. Well, they don't really seem to understand that clothes are just clothes.

"What the fuck, Barratt?" says Ivan. His basketball jersey hangs off his super skinny body, kind of like curtains in our living room. His shorts barely hang off his ass and extend below his knees. All five foot ten of him stands between me and my chem class.

"What are you talking about?" I just stare right ahead at his chest. It's not too terribly defined, not like Shane's. Probably more flat than concave.

"What's with this?" he says and he points at my shirt. "You're wearing their colors?" he says to me. His hands push me into the lockers and the sharp handles press, then cut, into my spine.

"It's what I had clean," I say. "Come on."

"Hell no," he says. "You come to this school wearing our rivals' colors?" Ivan shoves his hands back on my chest, shoving me into the lockers again. This time, my hand slap against the lockers echoes down the hallways and announce to everyone not in their classrooms that I'm about to get my ass beat.

"Fine, I'll change," I say.

"Yes, you will," he says. His face is close to me, and he's looking down to me, down the bridge of his nose. His eyes nearly cross as he says to me, "You change soon or I'll come looking for you later."

"Deal," I say. I extend my hand to shake on it, but Ivan slaps my hand away with his fist, slamming it into the lockers beside me. Another embarrassing echo of flesh and bone against blue painted metal.

"Show some school spirit, Barratt," he says. When he walks away, the teachers just watch him leave the hallway and say and do nothing to him or me. They watch his skeleton, wax-like frame walk away. This man, he does what he wants with impunity. That's one of our new SAT words this week in Mr. Ress's class.

I wait for the bell to ring and everyone to get into their classes before I budge. My face is hot and I don't have to look in the mirror to know that all the blood is rushing to my cheeks and my forehead. My tear ducts itch and I am not going to cry. I am not going to cry at all.

Don't give them the satisfaction, Teddy.

So I rub my eyes and the bit of slick, salty tears that erupts gets wiped away, first onto my knuckles of my left hand, then onto my white shirt.

When I kick myself off the lockers, the entire hallway is abandoned and I'm alone. It would be easy to break down, cry everything away, but I'm nearly eighteen years old. I don't need to cry. Boys don't cry, isn't that what we're told?

I clench my fist, curled up nice and tight, shaking tight, and I pull it back as far as my shoulders will let it go. I spot out a safe place to land my fist. No scratches or sharp protrusions that might scrape up my knuckles. The locker hasn't been used all year, so it still is completely empty, which means nothing up against the door, nothing to hold it in place. Looking at the locker door, it looks softer than the others, a safe place for my fist to go into it and bounce back.

I pull my fist back and clench my jaw tight against my upper teeth. This is how it's supposed to look like, right?

I check out my desired spot on the locker and release my hand. I release it and I'm ready to brace for the impact before my hand just stops. All momentum exhausts itself from my muscles and I'm already feeling tired. My nervous wet noodle arm drops to the side.

Next time. I swear.

To my left is a half-torn poster for the Diversity Club, barely hanging onto the white-painted brick walls with a patch of tape. Underneath the poster is another pink one with black writing. I pull the hanging announcement poster, telling everyone that the next meeting is today during lunch in the Art Room. I fold it neatly in my hand and read the pink paper underneath. It reads in sharp, angular and angry black letters: Stop! This is why we need a GSA.

GSA: Gay Straight Alliance. The place where people go who are gay or support gays. The joke was that everyone there is gay or will be. A dating circle where the not-so-closeted go to co-mingle.

For the rest of the day, I keep my eyes to the blue carpet in the hallways. I notice dark blue stains from spilled drinks and the darkened wads of ABC gum. I notice small trails of ants that lead from one locker to the other. Down here, it's easy to get lost in the details, to lose the big picture.

That picture being me being really, really upset and sad and about to fucking go off on the next asshole to touch me.

Except I won't, and I know I won't. But I want to. I just...can't. I wasn't raised that way and I can't even hit a locker.

I don't have to dress out for PE today because today happens to be what we call a B day. Our principal divided our daily schedule into different partitions, an A and B day. That's if we don't have any scheduled pep rallies or presentations.

Our A days are really just every class period we have that is an odd number. Periods one, three, five, and seven all fall on that day. Zero hour lands on this day as well, even though it's not technically an even or an odd number. At least that's what our math teachers argue.

On B days, we see the even numbers. My schedule is a little bit tougher on B days because I end up getting all of my core academic classes those days. English projects, American History projects, and Chemistry projects are all due on the same day. If I didn't know any better, I'd say they all pulled out their schedules and checked each other for projects and assignments.

Seeing that there is a science lab report due on Wednesday, the English teachers decide that Wednesday is also a good day for us to read five chapters of some Nathaniel Hawthorne book. The history teachers figure that all of their worksheets will be due that day so we can take our test on Wednesday.

It's their way of screwing us over, because, you know, the real world works that way.

At the same time, everyone is going to want to have their projects and assignments due on the same time. Because every lawyer and engineer and doctor is going to have to see every patient and client at the same time, deliver the same prognosis and create an entirely new and interesting solution to a problem at the same time to all clients.

Because that's what really happens.

But it must, because our teachers wouldn't lie to us, and those self-righteous bastards must really think that we only see their classes all day.

But it doesn't matter, really. It doesn't matter because at the moment, all I need to do is get through the day so I can go get spaghetti and meatballs.

But first, a quick stop to check out this club.

I sit down at one of the giant wooden tables, hiked up on metal poles to about waist height, and take out my lunch bag. I brown bag it almost every day now, since my mom doesn't really have thirty dollars to spend on lunch every week for me and my sister. My sister has a job, or so she claims, but her babysitting money isn't really enough to give her lunch and everything she could ever ask for. I peer down at the tuna sandwich with thickly diced pickles. My mom knows that I love a little crunch in my tuna sandwiches, and I just smile. Inside is a note on a pink Post-It that says, "Happy Birthday! I love my miracle baby so much." All of this is written in a big black Sharpie heart.

The note goes directly into the trash. I open my mouth and take the first bite, all bread and a little bit of mayo. If I close my eyes, it might actually taste like something edible.

I'm startled from the cellophane sound of a grab-sized bag of chips that hits the table in front of me. "Do you like sour cream n' onion?" says this boy in front of me. His eyes are a light blue, his hair light brown and curly and short. His braces take up most of my eyesight, but his smile is sincere and full of hope.

"Who doesn't?" I say. I eye the bag of chips and take another chomp of the sandwich.

In the art room is a grand total of five kids, including me. The art teacher is I don't know where right now. Hopefully coming back soon to lead this meeting.

"Well good. It's yours," he says. "I'm Allan." Allan extends his hands and looks me in the eyes. His voice is soft and boyish and I wonder if his voice has even cracked yet.

"I'm Teddy." I grab Allan's hand and he pulls me to stand up.

"It's so very nice to have new members. Nice to meet you, Teddy. Welcome to the Diversity Club."

Smiling is the only thing you can do when you're put on the spot.

"Let's get this started, girls," says Allan. His grip loosens on my hands, turning my palm slimy and nervous wet. "I appreciate those of you who attended despite the threats and awkwardness in the halls. It's not easy to come to this meeting knowing that the rest of the school seems to hate our posters."

The group chuckles to itself, all four of us.

"Today I think I want to bring special awareness to National Coming Out Day, which usually falls around our fall break. I want to make a bigger deal of it this year because, let's face it, we need to get tolerance back into the hallways," says Allan with the wit and voice of a politician. His eyes bring a blue fiery passion to the speech. Maybe he isn't a freshman.

"I would also like to welcome," Allan pauses and looks at me, his smile and head nodding me to stand up, "Teddy, is it?" and I shake my head. "Teddy! Go ahead and stand up and introduce yourself to the group."

And what do you say to that? He already announced my name. I stand up, wave to only half of the group since I'm so nervous. I shove my hands into my pockets and my shoulders wave from side to side, spinning at my waist. The group of boys and two girls here are nothing too threatening, but I wasn't even sure I wanted to be here.

"Maybe he's just a little shy," Allan says. He stands away from the whiteboard and comes over to me, where he towers of my little five-foot-six frame. Glancing at his body, I'd say he probably did track at one time in his life. "I'm sorry to put you on the spot, Ted," he says.

I try to hide my face from his piercing glance as he checks to see if I'm okay.

"Well, we're glad you came, and we're always glad to have new members, isn't that right?" Allan says then he starts his own applause. The rest of the group—all four of them—clap at us and the door opens, revealing the bright sunlight of the outside fall sun.

In comes Ms. Campbell with a white Styrofoam tray. Peaches

slide around one of the pockets, trying to escape from being eaten. What looks to be a dry chicken sandwich, a whole wheat bun that's half brown and half stale-white, and a pale yellow chicken patty.

"Oh good, we have a new member," she says. Ms. Campbell puts her food down on a desk and wipes her hands on the smock she wears pretty much twenty-four seven. Her mouth full of freshly chewed chicken sandwich, she says to me, "Teddy! I knew you'd come sooner or later." She winks and returns to her food. "I'll be back here if you need anything."

As Allan goes on and on about having a small celebration in honor of Coming Out Day, he winks at me and volunteers me to hold his colored markers as he draws mock ups of posters or buttons that we could-slash-should make in honor of the occasion. He draws out a circle in black, then in white letters, he erases "Come out, come out, whoever you are."

I raise my hand, "Shouldn't that be 'whomever'?"

One of the girls, short brown hair and a pink polo shirt, raises her hand and speaks before anyone else can call her name, "Look at this school, Teddy. No one will know the difference."

"I will," I say, but apparently not loud enough for anyone to hear it.

"We'll see what we can do," says Allan. He eyes the picture of the circle of the mock up. Putting his hand to his chin while still holding the marker, he says, "We may not have enough room for the 'em'."

Another boy stands up, his brown hair tussled and pink at the edges. His clothes are little too tight, boasting the name a store in the mall. Somehow, the pastel blue short-sleeved shirt tries to get away with "athletic department" along his left side. He raises his hand, but only partially, bent at the elbow and he says through his moppy hair, "None of this is going to matter if we aren't making this school safer." Mop Head stares at me, then blinks and shifts his eyesight back at Allan. "No one will want to wear those stupid buttons if we're just going to get our ass beat over it." Mop Head blinks, shifts his gaze toward me. Burning a hole right through me, his eyes just beg for my vote.

"He's, um," I say. Or try to say. What really comes out is more of a mixture of vowels searching for consonants.

"Teddy, did you have something to add?" says Mop Head.

"Well, we know that the kids here aren't exactly accepting," I say. "I mean, the kids pick on others smaller kids and they'll throw them in the showers and such."

"Like what happened to you!" says Mop Head. His hands display me and my withdrawn posture in front of the entire group.

If I could crawl under the desks or turn invisible right now, I'd be okay with that.

All I can do, though, is nod and sit back down near my lunch bag. Inside is just a small can of diet coke, which my mom never packed, but I stole anyway. I pop the tab open and look at the rest of the group.

Maybe I made a mistake. Maybe I shouldn't have come. Now everyone will think I'm gay. They'll think that I'm a faggot and can't wait to get into their pants. Because that's what we all do if you were to believe MTV and the radio and all the rumors.

The way Allan leads the rest of the group, the girls who sit nearly snuggling with each other while the boys argue about what exactly the phrasing should be on our next poster and whether the club should be a "diversity club" or an official gay straight alliance.

The bell rings before much more can be accomplished, and I sling my backpack over my shoulder and ball up my brown bag of lunch. My last class is chemistry, so I figure it would be a great time to take a quick nap and not think so damned hard. Maybe we'll have a lab.

"Ted!" Allan shouts over my shoulder. My hand freezes on the door, upright and about to push out. His Vans make plastic slaps against the white tiling of the concrete room. "Hold up," he says. I turn around and say nothing. This should be rich.

"I wanted to apologize for earlier," he says to me. "I think we can probably get an em in there somewhere. I mean, just cuz we're gay doesn't mean we have to speak like Neanderthals." Only the left side of his mouth turns upwards into a quirky smile, confident and flirtatious.

"Thanks," I say. I stare, at him or through him, I'm not sure. The lighting in the room is frozen on us, giving me a headache, but it pales in comparison to the outside fireball of the sun. Thing is, he's not moving much either. He either doesn't want to move, or is waiting for me to make the first move.

For serial, I'm not okay with this.

"Um," I search for words. "Thanks again. It was interesting." I pause and escape into the bright sunlight from outside.

9

The truth is, in high school, it's next to impossible to date anyone in this town. It's hard enough because everyone knows your business.

This means that you have no chance in Hell of dating anyone, anywhere, if you are gay and not exactly out.

The boys who are available are so far out of the closet that they are giving make up tips to the cheerleaders. These are the boys who are wearing Daisy Dukes on the weekends or, if God really wants to punish you, jean shorts cut off at the knee, but rolled up in thick rolls across the thigh. The rumor that gays are fashionable is taken way too out of context.

Small town boys are not fashionable. Gay men in large cities? They know how to dress.

I am what you would call in the closet and classified as a twink. I'm young and fairly good looking, but I don't flaunt it in everyone's way.

Not that I judge those who do. It's just, if I was born with testicles, I think I should act like it, you know? It's gays like that that give us a bad name.

It's these things I think about when I sit in the back of my psychology class. Today's topic is the idea of stress, what Mrs. Tyler calls "cognitive dissonance." She writes on an electronic white board that connects to the teacher's computer to show slides and allows us to write on it with large colored styluses. This is what we call a SMART board. Sometimes it's a dumb board when it decides that it doesn't want to work for the day. On the board is a T-chart, one side marked as "actions" and the other side marked as "thoughts".

I raise my hand. "So on the thoughts could be 'believes in equality', but the actions side could be 'treats everyone unequally'."

Mrs. Tyler says, "Good job, that's one example." Her handwriting is a mixture of print and cursive, something that confused us the first time we read it all. "What else?"

No hands go up into the air, so I just shout out an answer. "Someone who kills a person but believes that killing is wrong."

Mrs. Tyler nods and then scribbles that into the T-chart. "So what does this mean we have to do?" she says. "What happens when we act against the beliefs that we hold?"

The class doesn't say anything until Mrs. Tyler points to the board, up top at the title of the chart.

Together, the class reads, "Cognitive dissonance."

"Good," she repeats, "cognitive dissonance." She sits down on her desk and crosses her feet at the ankle. Mrs. Tyler wears the unofficial uniform of all female teachers: fancy looking blouse and either nice dress pants or a skirt that extends to the ankle. She chooses the pants. If she really tried, I bet she's really attractive.

Mrs. Tyler runs her hand through her hair, gray hair with streaks of white and black throughout, and lets out a sigh. She takes a deep breath and then begins the inevitable lecture. "Fine," she says. "Take notes."

The rest of the class digs through their notebooks and backpacks. The noise of papers crinkling and tearing and clasps of binders snapping makes it next to impossible for Mrs. Tyler, who has clearly had better days, to continue teaching. But, true to her nature, she does it anyway.

"When the human mind realizes that someone is doing actions

that conflict with his or her belief system, there is stress. The mind begins to wonder why he or she is acting in this way, and there are two actions that have to occur in order for the stress to stop. She can either stop doing the action and recognize that it's wrong, or she can change the belief system and make an excuse or reason for doing something. If a vegan is forced to eat meat, it's probably going to change the way the vegan views the whole meat is murder thing. If a man believes stealing is wrong but steals from his company, that man is sure going to make some kind of concession about it all."

A boy shoots his hands up into the air.

"Yes, Rick?"

"You mean they have to make popcorn or candy or something?" he says. The others laugh.

Mrs. Tyler's mouth frowns, and she lets out another sigh. I have to bite my lips because the need to laugh tempts me to join in with the others. "No, he or she needs to make an agreement that the victim, in this case the company, is doing something wrong and deserves it. Maybe they are an evil company. Maybe they need to be punished for a perceived wrong. Maybe they just won't miss the money because they make so much anyway."

The bell rings and we're dismissed with a wave of Mrs. Tyler's hand. The herd of high school seniors rushes the door and filter out two by two. Me, I'd rather wait it out and let them be the ones who get hurt.

"Are you okay?" my teacher says.

"Ya, I'm perfectly fine," I say.

Mrs. Tyler's mouth purses together, then says, "You seem a little distracted."

"I'm not distracted," I say. "Tired."

"Tell me about it," she says. Small talk isn't going to work with me, lady. I hate small talk.

"What do you think about today's lesson?" she says, picking up papers and pencils and pencil erasers from the floor.

"I thought it was interesting," I say. "Kind of pointless, but interesting."

"Nonsense," she says. "The point of the lesson is to help you solve problems. If you are unhappy with a situation, then you have two options. You can change it, or you can change your thinking and accept it."

"What if you can't change it and you don't want to change your mind?" I ask. "Like, what if you can't do anything about what you think, and the other people won't let you change the situation?"

"That's the problem with youth," she says. Mrs. Tyler sits on her desk and folds her hands across her lap. "Students at this age are rarely ever ready for change, not in their thinking. You have an idea of what the world needs to be. Some of you are right, but the world isn't ready for you. Not yet." Mrs. Tyler looks at the clock and then grabs her bags. "The trick, Teddy, is to get everyone else to change their minds."

10

The Halloween banners have just been put away yesterday, and yet the people still stand out in front of the stores with their bells and red metal buckets, asking for money. The local grocery market, Owl Foods, is the only market in the area. When I described Saraday as being small? I meant fucking microscopic.

Inside is the darkened lighting that is customary of a store that has just changed to natural lighting. Those economical companies that try to save on electricity bills by reducing the lighting and making it shift from light to dark again, so you keep thinking that the sun is being blocked by fast-moving clouds. Beyond that is just a tidy little store, packed with foods with bright labels and starburst signs that shout at you how much everything is.

Broccoli! Ninety-nine cents a pound!

Yams! A dollar and nineteen cents a pound!

Buy me! You need me! I'm healthy for you! Boom! Boom! Boom!

What I'm really in here for is an energy drink to keep me from wanting to pass the fuck out during dinner. And my sister, well, Vanessa is here for the stock boy at the end of the aisle.

When we first met him, he introduced himself as "Um, Peter" and he wouldn't keep his eyes on either one of us. The whole time, he was trying to dodge the awkward glances of a teenage girl. A sure sign that someone isn't into you is when he tries to go help a woman looking for the perfect avocado across the aisle.

Also helps when he hears his phone ring, but no one else doesn't. Or that time when he left my sister talking to herself while he picked me by my sleeve and took me to the potato chips. I guess my sister wasn't that mad about it because she was smiling and nudging me on the trip back. If you're ever sitting in the passenger side of a car, please don't nudge the driver constantly while he's trying to drive. It scares the hell out of him. Especially if he's a teenager just learning how to drive.

The cool freezer of the alcohol and mixer aisle always makes me wish that I brought a sweater whenever I come here. The air is so refrigerated that it comes off into the rest of the store as mist, like special effects from a haunted house ghost story. It's when I reach out and grab the lemon-flavored fizzy one that tastes like Mountain Sprite that Vanessa comes around the corner.

"Did you see Um Peter anywhere?" she says. Vanessa doesn't look at me or even through me, but around me. She's really hot for Peter. Still. After she apparently practically asked him out, and he said no. At least that's what she told me.

For being dumped, Vanessa made a really big, almost happy deal about it.

"No, I didn't see Um Peter anywhere." I read the label content, looking for something without high fructose corn syrup because, you know, I gotta watch my figure.

"That's a shame," she says. Her eyes still survey the entire store, like she can somehow scan x-ray vision through the shelves packed with cellophane potato chips and whole wheat bread.

Vanessa is wearing a black skirt that cuts off just above her knees and a pink shirt on it that just says pink. The 'i' is really a sparkly heart. Extra credit if you figured that was somehow pink, too.

"I never rememberize his schedule, you know?" says Vanessa.

"Ya," I say with a smirk. "I never rememberize it either. It's like his schedule changes from week to week or something."

Vanessa hits me with her small underarm purse. "Shut up, okay! It's a real word. I heard a teacher use it."

"Is that so," I tell her. "Did you want one, too?"

Vanessa says *no* and grabs me by the shirt collar. My shirt is buttoned down, gray with a small pocket on the side. I was never a fan of the polo shirts myself, and though I'd rather be in a T-shirt, my mom always swears that I dress up for my birthday. This time, she let me wear the red one with these black pants with a gray pin stripe. It looks a little old fashioned, fancy zoot suit style, but I like it.

"So we need to, um, look for ice cream," Vanessa says. She pulls me along and my feet hit each other as I'm trying to keep up with her pace. Her eyes and head turn and scan every aisle, and I'm pretty sure right about now that she doesn't really need any ice cream. Then, she spots what she was really looking for. "Peter!" she says.

And Um Peter is putting frozen foods in the big glass freezer. His hands are covered with oversized gray gloves insulated to keep his fingers from getting frostbite or whatever. He is of course in his typical maroon vest and white buttoned down shirt, sleeves rolled up to show his forearms with just a slight bit of dark hair near his wrists.

"So Peter!" she says and puts me in the front of her, a human shield. The glass door of the freezer is right in between me and Peter, and it fogs from the different temperatures on both sides. "Peter, you remember my brother Teddy," she says. Vanessa nudges me along in syllables as she re-introduces me to someone I've met and talked to over and over again.

"Um, ya, I think we met," he says. The foggy glass door closes shut, revealing Peter's new haircut. I guess you could call it a haircut. His hair, longish up front and shorter near the back, makes him look like some Hollywood up and coming screamo rock star than a stock boy in a local grocery store. His hazel eyes and brown hair flash at me and he says, "You guys are pretty dressed up. Going out tonight?"

"I'm glad you asked," she says. Still holding her opened hand against the small of my back, she nudges me forward but I refuse to move. "Today is Teddy's birthday." I can hear the smile in Vanessa's voice from behind me. Her tone sounds like a bragging question, loud and clear for the entire store to catch on.

"It's not a big deal, really," I say. I wave it off with my hand and shrug. I'll be honest, I don't remember Peter smiling so much. I like his smile.

"Well happy birthday," he says. "How old are you?" Pete's hazel eyes, big and round, invite me to keep staring, searching the corners of his eye sockets.

Wow, that sounds creepy.

"I'm on the edge of seventeen," I say and grin.

"Nice," he says. "Stevie Nicks fan?" Peter takes off his gloves, shoves them in his pockets.

"Just like good music," I say. "And Rock Band." I blush.

"Love Rock Band!" he says.

"You should come over and play some time," says Vanessa. She pulls me closer to her and wraps her arm around my neck. "Teddy here is like a music genius. A little bitchy when he sings, but he's really, really good."

"You mean, pitchy," I say. I brush my hair back with my hand only to realize that my hair isn't long enough to go anywhere. "Don't we have to go?" I say. "Mom is waiting for us." I want to put my hands in my pockets to keep from shivering, but I can't because I wasn't smart enough to grab a basket while shopping.

Instead, I stand there and shiver, shifting my balance between my left foot and right foot back and forth. As if I'm not looking like a big enough dork, Vanessa sways back and forth with me.

"You know, if you aren't busy some time, you should give me a call," she says to Peter. Vanessa takes out her cell phone with the one hand that isn't wrapped around my neck and shoulders.

"Yup," he says. "I got it." Peter smiles at me, and I'm not sure if it is or not, but he seems to wink at me. "I'll text you when I get off work," he says. Then looking over his shoulder and across the empty hall he says, "I gotta get going and finish this load." He waves his big pale hands at us. Vanessa grabs my shirt collar again and pulls me down the aisle. "Happy birthday, Teddy!" he shouts at me down the hall.

Then, Vanessa stops pulling and hands me her purse. "Here," she says. Her purse is heavy for something so small and sparkly. Black sequins stitched into the side, and it feels round and lumpy in my hands.

"What the hell do you have in here?" I ask.

"Take some money out of it," she tells me. She says, "Go get in line, I'll be right back."

"But Mom is waiting," I say and point at the door. It's a balancing act to keep the energy drink can and her black sequined purse in the same grip.

"And I'll be right there," she says and shoves me along. "Now go."

Common sense dictates that we don't actually walk backwards because we don't have eyes behind our heads. If I was going to hit something, I don't actually know, but I needed to keep my eyes on Vanessa and Peter as long as I could. Without being suspicious, of course.

Which I guess is hard to do when you won't turn around and walk like a normal human being.

Seriously, Teddy?

At the end of the aisle, I turn around and go back to the soft drinks and grab another energy drink. This one is orange flavored. If Vanessa is going to pay, I'm getting my money's worth.

Vanessa catches up with me just as I'm going through the first set of self-sliding doors. "Why do you have so many tampons in there?" I ask. "They're so big," I say.

"Don't ask questions to something you don't want to know the answers to," she says.

You know those moments you wish you just didn't say something, but you couldn't in that very moment? The phrase Mom uses is "mouth vomit." Well, I proceed to say, "So, do those things hurt when you put them in?"

"Why are you so curious?" she says. And with a big grin illuminated by the setting sun, she says, "You do know they are for the front door, not the back, right?"

11

The storm clouds rolled in faster than I had remembered them in a long while. The funny thing about living in Saraday is, you could always watch the rain come closer and closer to the front door of the house. A curtain of raindrops, or like watching one of God's sprinklers gradually turn your way. The curtain just barely blurs the view down the narrow, light gray road. It's a few miles out, but it's like looking through sheer silk, the way the rain blurs and bends the reality just beyond.

And my mom knows how to ruin a beautiful car ride through a perfectly cloudy day. She starts with the same old story over and over again. "I can't believe it's been seventeen years ago today that you."

"Died?" I say. I can't keep my smile hidden from Mom. I know I'm probably going to Hell for a few things, but enjoying this moment is going to be totally worth it.

"I was going to say the day you were born, Teddy." Mom shrugs her shoulders forward and says, "You are the only one who hates your own birthday." Her hands grip the wheel and tighten so hard the vinyl on the steering wheel screams. The rest of the car smells like mom may have been smoking on her rest breaks again.

I sniff the air, making as much noise as I can to let her know that I'm on to her.

She shakes her head and rolls down the window.

Message sent.

Vanessa is sitting in the cramped backseat, texting someone, which is clearly hinted at by the fact that her thigh vibrates and her face glows bright blue every few minutes or so. "So where are we going, exactly?" she says.

Outside, the wooden houses turn into green, sparse forests and then to dirt roads and pastures as far as my eyes care to look.

"I thought about your suspension, Vanessa, and I'm not going to ground you after all," my mom says.

"You're kidding," I say. If I can turn my head just right, I can catch a reflection of Vanessa in the backseat.

Vanessa puts the phone down, just as dumbfounded as me, and she says with her bright pink lip gloss, "Wait, what?"

"You were helping to protect Teddy, right?" Mom says to the mirror, the reflection of Vanessa's mouth, open and dumbfounded.

"Um, ya," Vanessa says. Her eyes looking into the side window reflection looking back at me, they blink twice in slow, staccato blinks. "Of course," she says.

"Then I guess I'm just going to take the car," Mom says.

Not sure if she's joking or serious, I turn and look over my shoulder, but the seatbelt holds me pinned to the chair.

Vanessa snaps her fingers. "That's the mother I know," says Vanessa. "Whatever," she says. She plugs her ears with the blue headphones buds and stares out at the blue gray sky.

"I know you had a good reason, honey, but it's not okay that you start fights. And you better not be pregnant, young lady," says Mom to no one in particular since Vanessa stopped paying attention. "There needs to be consequences for your actions."

Vanessa looks up at the back of my mom's shoulders and nods, then stares back outside. We both know that arguing is counterproductive. If we argue with her, we must be thinking that she's stupid. If we don't argue with her, then we admit we are guilty.

Honestly, we're screwed before the conversation even starts.

For serial, I hate women sometimes.

Because I'm obviously a weatherman and studied meteorology at school, my mom asks me, "Teddy, was it supposed to rain today?"

And I say that I have no idea. The clouds outside are dark and fluffy. They move slowly through the sky toward the hills to our east, toward the Low Country. I point outside. My sister smiles and hides her laughter in the background.

"I hope we'll be okay," she says. The drive to Luigi's is only a twenty minute drive, but the after-school and after-work rush hour stands between us and another sit around a table hearing about how I almost died and then didn't.

The rest of my mom's words are drowned out by the revving of an engine. An orange Ford Mustang charges past us, like it's white-rabbit-late for a tea party somewhere.

Staring at the car, then looking away into the green pastures, I say, "I hope he gets into an accident."

"That's a horrible thing to say, Teddy," says Mom. She grabs my hand. "Are you okay?" she says. Her eyes leave the road as she tries to study my face.

Completely on to her, I smile, showing my teeth in a goofy grin. Hide everything, Teddy. Don't show her that I don't want to go. She wouldn't want to see it. She can't know it. I can't ruin this for her.

Yes, that's right. For her. This is the first time in years that I didn't allow myself to be checked out of school early, taken out of town for my birthday. I didn't go because my sister was too busy getting suspended and fighting.

What I told my mom was, "I have a final in chemistry, mom. I can't miss it. The teacher isn't letting us make it up."

When that didn't work, I told her, "Mom, I'm already on the way to perfect attendance. I don't want to mess that up."

Finally, she relented. This year, she was threatening to take us to Disney World in Orlando. The trip, she said, would do us good. Would get our mind off of our stress.

What she really meant to say was her stress.

But when the bank didn't give her the time off, she came into my room and stood in front of my television with her eyes about to burst like a dam. The first droplet of sadness leaves her eyeballs, and she says to me, "Teddy, we might have to change our plans for your birthday," she says. Wiping her tears away and pretending that she has to be strong for me, Mom says, "I think we might have to keep it a little bit smaller this time."

When I ask why we need to stay in town, she says, "I can't get the time off. Someone already requested the days off and I'm supposed to cover her." My mom gives me a big, exaggerated hug, and she checks my eyes to see that I'm okay. Each of her eyes, they scan mine to see that I'm holding back my tears. She wants to know that I'm not heartbroken about this.

"We'll just have to make do, Mom," I say and pat her on her back. By the way, when you feel your own mother's bra strap, it's extremely awkward. My hand leaves her back and rests off to the side, pushing against my bed's mattress to keep me sitting up.

That was two weeks ago.

Today, my mother holds my left hand and rubs it with her fingers and says, "I love you."

And I rub her hand with my thumb and say, "I love you too." And as misguided as she is, my mom is my biggest cheerleader. She gave up her marriage and made so many sacrifices for me. How can you not love a martyr?

"Mom!" my sister screams behind us and her fingers point ahead through the windshield to the line of cars ahead of us. A row of double red lights means that we aren't going anywhere. My mom sighs, looks at the clock and she says, "Well, we're probably going to miss the reservation. I hope we still get our table."

I grab my mother's hand. "We'll be fine."

My mother wipes her nose and nods.

When I roll down the passenger's side window, a breeze of cold wind caresses my face and blows my mom's hair back. The wet smell of cut grass and swamplands rushes in. God, I love that smell.

"This just in, this is Theodore Barratt reporting for WTEV. It looks like we're in for quite a storm," I say with my hand holding in an imaginary headset and microphone up to my head.

"Looks like it," Mom says. My sister is caught up in her teeny bopper bullshit in her headphones.

"Have you ever wondered what it'd be like if lightning struck like that close?" I say, pointing off into the distance at some pine trees along the interstate.

"No, I can't say I have," says my mom. Her head is stretched as far as her short neck will let her go. Scanning the long line of waiting cars, she says, "Maybe we should just turn around and get us an ice cream cake somewhere." My mom grabs my hand with hers and looks at me. She says, "Is that okay with you, Teddy?"

I don't think when I just say, "Sure. That works." The words, "more tears" and "not sad enough" fly into my brain and flutter around. Do I need to put on a better show? Show her that I care about as much as she does? Maybe more?

"Are you sure?" she says again. She squeezes my hand tighter.

But I can't fake it. "Yes!" I say. "Of course. Mom. Just go already. Look, you can turn around right there, between those cars." I point over at the long shoulder of the road, where there seems to be enough room for us to at least pull off and finagle into the off ramp over there.

My mom nods and says, "Yes." Trying to convince herself she repeats back to herself, "Of course, fine with me." She rolls down her window and takes a long breath. Then, taking in a long breath to herself, making her chest rise in a big "calm yourself" type of move, she checks behind her to make sure the coast is clear.

My mother steers the car off the side of the road, then into the extended asphalt place where you're not really supposed to be driving, but you do anyway because it's your last chance to get to the off-ramp.

My sister screams. At the same time I jump and I'm blinded and deafened. The trashcan-banging sound of thunder and lightning striking simultaneously echoes deep into my ears.

"Is everyone okay?" my sister says. She hides the panic in her voice with four or five "Oh my God"s.

I'm rubbing my eyes and trying to see what's going on. When I open them, the only things I see are blue dots and squares blocking most of my vision. When I blink, the blue dots turn bigger and smaller at the same time, dilating.

"Mom!" Vanessa screams into the open cabin of the car. "Mom! Are you okay?"

I rub my eyes harder and faster. If I rub fast enough, maybe I can rub the squares and circles away. When I blink to refocus my eyes, I get red dots. Purple circles. Blues and colors mixing together.

My sister's elbow keeps hitting me in the shoulder and I shove back.

"I'm trying to help Mom, you idiot," she says.

I rub my eyes and my sister's elbow pushes me against the door again.

"Mom," she finally says calmly. "Are you okay?"

Rubbing my eyes, I turn to look at her and blink three times and pray for luck. My sister's head is pulling away as she returns to the backseat. Sitting down, Vanessa takes a few deep breaths and fans her face.

What I see is a blurry picture, gradually coming into focus.

The image I see is my mother grabbing her elbow, which is red and blistered.

"I don't need to see a doctor," she says. Trying to cover her elbow but not touch it, my mom says to us, "Let's just go home."

When we get off the interstate, my sister and I get a good look at the cause of the accident. Up against the side concrete walls the construction workers use to barricade off drivers, well, there was the orange Mustang. It turned into a giant metal accordion of a car, pressed up into almost half its original size. As we drove downward, following the off ramp back into town, my sister points out the car to us. There's a stain of dark liquid coming from somewhere beneath the car.

"Is that the car you said would get into an accident?" she says.

My sister coughs, almost chokes. "Is that blood?"

"I think that's the car," I say to her. "I told you he would get into an accident."

My mom, she says nothing. Eyes straight ahead to the road, silent.

"No, you said you hoped he would get into an accident," says Vanessa. She presses her head tight against the roof of the car as we travel downwards. "Slow down, Mom, I want to look."

My mom, she says nothing.

"Never mind," says Vanessa. "It's pretty bad." Vanessa looks at me, "You killed him."

12

The nice part about being in the dark is you don't really lose any of your eyesight when you have your shirt tied up around your head.

Don't get me wrong, you don't gain anything either, but there's not loss of any of your senses that completely incapacitates you for the first couple of seconds.

My nostrils fill with dirt from just outside this coffin and the faux fruity lavender of the laundry detergent. Grabbing my shirt, and like it's going to do anything important, I kick at the bottom of the coffin as hard as I can. With each kick, my eyes squint and squeeze so hard my tear ducts tickle.

And more and more dirt flies in. More dust clouds inside and if weren't for the smell, I would think that I'm actually getting wet, it's so cold. That awkward wet feeling you get when something really touches you, it makes me crave sunlight. I want to bask my wet pants legs in the sun.

I get an instant image in my head of my coffin filling up with dirt and it piling down my chest and suffocating me. Though I don't see any light anywhere, this image in my head is as bright as daylight. That perfect movie of my own death by asphyxiation.

Breathe, Teddy. Breathe.

And I shovel my hands downwards, flexing my legs like a frog as much as I can. Push the dirt downwards and off to the side. Get the piles of cold, moist dirt further into the bottom of my coffin. Space is limited. On either side I have either two centimeters or two inches, I can never tell. I was never good in geometry and estimations. During contests at carnivals where we had to guess how many marbles were in the pickle jar, I guessed fifteen hundred, then five hundred, then settling on five. Yes, I was stupid.

The important part is not getting suffocated by the dirt, but it's all about not using up all of my own oxygen. It's about being economical with what I have left in here. Maybe more air comes in from the lightly packed dirt. I don't know because I can't smell it. I can't feel it against my skin since my head is covered in a T-shirt. My arms are pressed up against the wooden coffin, which is hot and sweaty from my own perspiration and sweat and worry and frustration.

Okay, maybe kinda wet from my tears.

Why bother even getting out of here? Maybe Peter was right to put me in here. Maybe he should have done it much sooner. Not like he couldn't have killed me.

Maybe I deserve to die.

My sister? She might be dead because of me for all I know. My mom? She's probably dying inside. Losing her poor, poor Teddy. Poor defenseless Teddy. Poor freakishly mutant Teddy. Poor baby who died and lived and died again. Dust to dust, if you'll pardon the pun.

My toes have to be bruised, if not bleeding. The shoes cramming against my big toe and my even longer second toe, it hurts with each kick, but it's do or die. If I don't get out of here, I suffocate on carbon dioxide with nowhere to go. I don't move and I rest in peace.

Can't think of that. I must breathe slowly. Calmly. Breathe. Think Zen, Teddy. Think yoga breathing. Smooth in. Smooth out.

And kick.

I kick again and more dirt comes in through the cracks. As I kick and kick and kick, I get more and more frustrated. What if I don't get out? What if everyone is dead when I get out? What do I do?

Who will love me?

I kick. I kick and more coffin splinters at my feet. I kick again.

More splinters. More dirt.

Push the dirt down.

I could just as simply get myself out of here with my powers, but they seem wonky. I can't focus. No relaxed wanting. All I want to do is panic and freak out. I could will myself out. I could, trust me.

I really could.

But Life. Well, life seems to have a different plan for me.

I kick more.

I'll fucking kill you, Peter. I'll kill you dead.

I love you, Peter.

13

My mom insists that we don't visit the doctor when we get back to the apartment. My sister and I, we were to too afraid to insist that she go and too afraid to argue. We didn't want to push her into hysterics all of a sudden. Then we'd never get back home, and we'd never get the ice cream cake.

That whole drive home was in complete silence. My sister back into her cell phone, changing songs in her headphones. Even her headphones sounded quieter, maybe afraid to disrupt the awkward silence of your mother almost dying on the interstate.

My sister and I let her go to bed when we got home. She insisted we had to blow out candles and sing, but my sister being the pushy little bitch that she is, she told my mom that she promised she would sing to me. She promised that I would get plenty of ice cream. She promised we would clean up, and I just sat there. I sat there and hated everything.

I thought about the dead man in the car, the imaginary blood all over the windshield and driver's side airbag because I didn't really get to see the accident.

Have you ever noticed that no matter how bad something gets, it's never as bad as it is in your head?

In my head's accident, I see the car's hood flipped up into the air, landing next to the body of the car. I see the man's dead arm, hanging lifeless from the open driver's side window. I see the man who is not breathing, what's left of his heart and blood scattered all over the interior. What used to be black vinyl is now a ruby-marbled painting.

What I see are cops all over the place, reds and blues flashing and circling the place. I see the people writing a report, in the space that says "cause of death," it says "Teddy's wish."

I shudder and clench my stomach. What if?

My sister Vanessa takes Mom's bedroom door and closes it slow and quiet. It bounces as it closes and then she turns to me and my sister says, "Let's go outside for a bit."

At a cool seventy degrees outside, it's a perfect time to eat ice cream. The lights are coming on in the street and the nice people of the apartment complex are walking their dogs in pairs.

Sometimes the dogs are pairs. Sometimes the people are pairs. Either way, no one is as alone as I feel right now.

Everyone is alive and happy and not alone.

The apartment complex is really a series of three-story high buildings with a strange yellow stucco color that looks like faded baby vomit. Three pools are spread out between the buildings. This gives us all a bright, bitter surprise as chlorine come sto wake us all up in the mornings when they treat the pools.

Even now, this afternoon, there's a trace of chlorine and pool water wafting down the road, mixing with the sogging wet smell of humid air.

The ice cream we settled on came from the thirty-two flavors store that opened up near Wally World. My sister just hands over money and grabs the white quarter sheet cake, the one with the flowers and the clown on it. The clown is plastic and not made of candy so after we get out of the door, she opens the cake and takes the clown into her dainty girly pink hands.

"We don't really need this creepy little guy, do we?" she says.

The clown ends up in the black trash bag in the green trashcan near the door.

"This looks better already," I say and we get into the car. My mother sat in the car, waiting.

"I trust you," she told us. Handing us money she remained silent and holding her elbow.

We ate off of the fine china of plastic forks and paper plates and sat on the trunk of her car. With the two of us together, the back tires flattened out quite a bit, dropping the car down at least three to four inches. Or three to four centimeters. I dunno. From where we sit, we can get a great view of the sun setting over the horizon to the west and giant deciduous trees to our east.

"This isn't bad," I say. "Not mint chocolate chip, but not bad." I shovel another piece of the cookies and cream and vanilla ice cream cake combination my sister picked up.

"Sorry," she says. "I can take it if you won't eat it."

As a dare, I lick the spoon and plate and the top of the ice cream. Vanessa laughs and goes back to her phone.

"Who the hell are you texting now?" I ask her.

"How does it feel to have killed someone?" she asks me.

"And this night is over," I tell her. I put the paper plate on the back of the car and hop down. "Good night."

"Get your ass back up here," she says. Vanessa grabs my wrist and pulls me back onto the trunk. "Come on, I'm sorry," she says. "Please?"

I have nowhere else to go and she knows it. "You win this one," I say.

"But seriously," she says and my heart begins to beat faster. Fight or flight response. I don't know if I want to know where this is going. Vanessa looks at me, swallows another mound of white ice cream and brown cookie chunks. She looks at me, blinks, and then says, "So how did you do that?"

"Do what?" I say.

For the record, yes, I know what she's talking about. Let her work for it.

"Do that thing, with the car, with the man, with the face." Vanessa says after putting more ice cream in her face, "How did you murder him?"

"I did not murder him," I say. "I didn't do anything."

"You do a lot of stuff you don't actually do," she says. At this point, no one is looking at anyone. Instead, we both watch an older couple walk their gray and black poodles. The one closest to us, with a small fluffy tail full of tight curls, it sees us and jumps toward us, pulling the leash so tight that he's walking on his hind legs to get to us.

The old couple, they smile and pull the dog backwards. The poodle forgets us when sees a leaf blowing along the black parking lot.

"I know," I say. "I thought it was just me who noticed those things."

"You know?" she says. "That time we had a bunch of birds hitting our backyard patio door, was that you?"

"I don't know. I think so." I shrug. "I was just angry at dad. I wanted him to hurt since he was leaving us," I say.

"But you know, if we didn't have that new screen door, the birds might have actually broken that door," says Vanessa. "And all that blood," she says. She stares off directly in front of us. Like she's studying the light brown sugar brown Cadillac boat parked across the lot from ours but not, she says, "I can't believe Mom managed to clean all of that up."

"Did I tell you I tried to tell that story at school once and Mrs. Jessop said I had a wonderful imagination before she sent me to the counselor?" I tell her. It's much funnier now than it was then.

"Remember that time your teachers kept quitting?" says Vanessa. Her questions are more like statements, not rising up at the end like normal asking questions behavior.

"Yes."

"And the time the faucet at the motel room that one time blew off?" she says.

"It was a showerhead," I say. "And yes, I remember."

"And remember that time," says Vanessa.

And I tell her, "Yes, I remember." I remember them all—flashes of images and blood and cats and people coming into and out of my classroom. These all flash into my mind like an on-screen movie flashback. I see them all and I wonder, just how much of this did I actually do? "Hey Vanessa," I say. "Does that mean that I hurt Mom?"

"Fuck!" says Vanessa. She holds her hand to her mouth and looks at my ice cream. My sister grabs my back and rubs it. "I don't think so," she says. "I mean, it was a freak accident, right?"

"And having twenty-some birds crash into your window isn't a coincidence?" I say. "I don't know that coincidences exist anymore."

"And how could you have hurt Mom? Why would you hurt Mom?" Vanessa says. She balances the white paper plate, now soggy with melted ice cream in a big wet spot in the middle of the plate, on her lap. "You couldn't have known," she says.

"But what if I did know? What if I knew I could do it? What if I wanted to do it?" I ask. These questions and more just come pouring out of my mouth. What my mom calls word vomit.

"Well, did you?" she says.

And I open my mouth to talk and say something, but I can't make anything come out. I can't speak for her or for me and I don't know anything all of a sudden. My mind is blank and whited out.

"See?" says Vanessa. "Nothing to worry about." Vanessa smiles and picks up the paper plates and lays them flat together on the other side. "So I was wondering if I could ask you something," she says. And as she finishes the sentence, her phone buzzes in her lap and glows bright blue back at us. "Oh, speaking of which," she says.

Speaking into the phone and leaving me wondering what she was going to ask, she says to someone else, "Hey you!" Then, "Ya, we have plenty of ice cream cake here. You should come here and help us finish it off." Vanessa looks at me, listening to someone else talk her ear off, and she finally gets her chance to say, "So our place is on your way, then? Ya, we're at the corner of Walker and Sunset."

She nods like the mysterious caller can actually see it.

"Great!" she exclaims and claps her hands together. "Good! I'm glad you can come." She winks at me with a big smile, then my sister says, "We'll see you soon."

The phone shuts off when she pulls it away from her face and Vanessa shoves the phone into her pocket.

I raise my eyebrows and wait, tapping my foot on the bumper of Mom's car. "You were going to ask me?"

Vanessa looks at me as blank as her apparent memory. "What?" she says.

"Ask me? You airhead. What were you going to ask me," I say. I point at her pocket with my fork and say, "You said you were wanting to ask me something."

"Oh!" Vanessa says. She pulls her ass closer to the edge of the trunk. Her eyes open up, as does her smile, and she says to me, "So, what do you think about Peter?"

"Peter?" I say. Not where I thought this was going to go. "I guess he's okay. He's a pretty cool guy, I mean. If you're into that kind of guy." I look at her and she's nodding and smiling. I say, "Don't you think that Peter is a little too old for you? He's like, what? Twenty?"

"Nineteen," she says. "He's not that old." My sister holds her hands out in front of her and counts. "I'm only one year younger than you," she says. "So he's only," and she counts on her fingers and mouthing the numbers at the same time, one, two, three. "He's about two years older than you." Vanessa shrugs. "That's respectable."

"I guess I don't see what you see in him," I say. "And I don't get why you're asking me. You never asked me about any of the other guys you hang out with."

"I don't hang out with Peter," she says and pokes me with her fingernail right into my side. "That's the difference," she says. "Here," she says and takes my plate. "Let me get the birthday boy another slice."

"No, seriously, I'm good."

"No, I insist," she says. "Besides, I need to come back out anyway and bring him one."

Vanessa's eyes draw a line to a shadow walking down the long driveway that bisects the apartment complex. This road is barely long enough for two cars to drive past each other in opposite directions, but with a tall shadowy figure walking down the way with the setting sun and rising moon lighting the backdrop, it's an eerily romantic setting.

Romantic as in nature-loving and 1800s romantic. Like that guy we had a test on in English, Thoreau and what's his name who wrote those poems about lakes and flowers. Not romantic as in flowers and hearts and that shit.

"I'll be right back," says Vanessa with a smile and I'm left to greet Peter when he emerges from the shadows like a suburban Batman in street clothes and longish brown hair.

Okay, not like Batman at all.

"Heya there, Teddy," says Peter. He extends a hand out and shakes mine. "How was your birthday?"

"Non-existent. No dinner party," I say. "I don't want to get into the rest."

"Ouch," he says and holds something up to me. "This is for you," he says. A birthday card in what could be a baby yellow if it weren't for the odd bluish fluorescent lighting above from the street lights.

"You can open it now if you want," he says and then looks around. "Where's your sister?"

"She went to go get more ice cream cake," I say, but tuck the card underneath my leg. "I'll open it later inside when I can read it."

Then awkward silence.

He looks at the tall buildings, the three stories of apartments stacked on top of each other and I watch his ears as he turns his head.

When Peter turns to look at me, he smiles and I smile and I have no other ideas about what to say rather other than, "So, how was work?"

Peter smiles. "It was okay. I think I want to quit," he says. "My boss is a bitch and I'm tired of the crap." He eyes my leg and the card underneath it, then he sits up back on the car where Vanessa sat. "So you don't normally have parties, do you?"

"Usually for my birthday?" I laugh. "It's a long story, but ya, my mom likes to go throw a large party every year. Usually it means we go on trips and stuff this year, but my mom couldn't get the time off."

"Ya, I noticed you were here this year."

I can't not blush.

"You noticed?"

"Well ya, before you and your mom leaves," he says, "I noticed that you guys usually come and stock up on snacks and car trip stuff. Pretzels and drinks and stuff."

I nod my head and smile. "Oh, ya, that."

"I just noticed that you guys didn't come pick this stuff up this time," he says. "I figured you were staying home, or I didn't know what day it was."

"And just how long have you been noticing this?" I ask.

Peter shifts his body weight away from me. He says, "I guess since I was sixteen. I've been working there for about three and half years now." Peter's eyes gaze up at the sky and his mouth moves silently, so small that I can barely read what he's saying to himself. "Ya, about three and a half years."

"And you figured it out that soon?"

"What can I say?" he says. His shoulders climb up his neck in a drawn-out shrug. And just as I realize I'm confused as all hell, Vanessa's high heels click down the stairs to announce her entrance. I swear that's why she wears those damn things.

"You're here!" she says. Vanessa offers the bigger piece of cake to him and hugs his ribcage with her free arm. "I'm glad you could come," she says.

"Thanks," says Peter, holding up the cake to acknowledge the offering. "But shouldn't the birthday boy get the bigger piece?"

My fork is already pulling a small, melted piece of cake and ice cream away from the slice she brought me. "Oh, no, this is already my second slice," I say.

"Third, actually," says Vanessa. "How was work?" she says to Peter.

"Same shit, different day," he says. He puts a dainty piece of ice cream in his mouth and it pulls tight. His lips purse together and he licks with just the tip of his tongue a small droplet of cream trying to escape.

I eat faster, more ice cream in my mouth, more cake.

"You know I was thinking about getting a job, but my mom says I can't get one until I'm in college," I say. "I wanted to apply at the store where you work, or at the bookstore when I turned sixteen, but my mom said school is more important."

"That's good advice," he says. Peter points his cleaned fork at me and says, "I wish I did that. I wouldn't still be working at that hellhole at nineteen."

"Are you going to school?" my sister asks.

"Well, I'm in the community college, but that's nothing special. Like high school two-point-oh," he says.

"When Teddy goes to college, he wants to study art or animation or something," she says. "What do you want to study?" my suspicious sister asks.

"Not sure," he says. Peter puts another piece of soft white cake into his mouth, and his lips make a heart-shaped circle as he swallows it down. "I guess I want to study communications and try to get into radio or business." Peter shrugs. "I mean, something like that."

"That's pretty cool, isn't it, Teddy?" says Vanessa.

And I was blind. I couldn't see it coming and I'm a completely clueless dumbass. I know what she's doing.

Now I just have to decide if I'm offended or not. I mean, I guess I don't object.

Peter's mouth swallows another piece of cake and I really don't object, I guess.

It has been decided. And I wonder how it feels to be that cake right now.

And I realize I'm really, really happy that I'm sitting down at the moment.

"I'll take that," Vanessa says, and she takes the empty paper plates from us. "Was it good?" she says.

Peter nods.

"Good," she says. "Let me throw these away for you."

As she disappears behind me and up the steps to the apartment, I think about what's in the card. I think about what he might have written or wanted to write. I wonder what really happened between Vanessa and Peter and if he actually knows what's going on.

And this poor sucker, he scoots off of the trunk and turns around, his hands in is blue jean pockets and he looks at me with his hazel eyes and pale skin. His bangs hang in front of his forehead and the edges trace the lines of his eyebrows.

"I think I'm gonna go," he says to me. "It was cool hanging out with you," he says. "We should do it again some time."

I nod and I am speechless. My smart ass self has nothing to say. Nothing at all. All I can do is wave and nod and mumble something that sounds like "Yes."

"Well," says Peter. He approaches me and then pauses. His eyes look at me directly in the eyes and he says, "I'm a hugger," and he opens his arms wide. "I hope you're okay with that."

I can definitely be okay with that.

But what I really say is, "Okay."

I hop down from the car and open my arms up. Peter's large embrace grabs me and my cheek is pressed against his chest. Not muscular, but still comfortable. His long-sleeved shirt smells like a cologne musk, but more inviting. More calming. I breathe it in and take a long breath out. We could have been hugging for a year I was so out of it from this embrace.

"Well, buddy," he says. "I'll see ya around. I hope you like the card."

And when he turns around, he does so by rotating on his heels. With a little flourish of his feet, he takes exaggerated, dancey steps as he walks away from me. The air around my head still smells like his musk. I watch his body disappear back into the shadows. In the small amount of time we spoke, the sun had completely set, and the moon was almost nearly out. Up above the tree line and the apartments was a dark blue bruise of purple and black and real blue sky.

And when I turn to go around into the house, Vanessa is standing at the doorway, the curve of her body flattening out against the side door frame.

"So how was it?" she says. Her face is still and her lips are pressed tightly together to mask her pleased little smile.

I say nothing and take each step of the stairs in a wedding march pace. Step, pause. Step, pause.

When I get to the top, Vanessa's face says she wants an answer, and she folds her arms so her huge breasts rest just on top of her forearms and elbows. "And?"

And as I walk right past her, I say to Vanessa with a smile, "Thank you."

I MAKE sure that my door is shut tightly and quietly when I check it for the second and third time. To block out the sound of whatever my sister thinks I'm doing in here, I turn on the television to some music channel and let it play a little louder than normal.

That should keep her busy for a while.

I bounce on the bed as I fall backwards, the birthday card from Peter in my hands. My bed is still twin-sized and big enough to hold my short little frame. The rest of my room isn't really anything to look at. The floor is hardwood, which was my mom's minimum requirement for any house we moved into. The walls are the typical eggshell white and barely covered with a few comic book posters and drawings of mine. All of them are inspired by the mutants and heroes of World Wars. It's how I first began drawing, was reading the comic books and seeing the lines and the colors. It wasn't long before I realized that the curved lines that formed this ninja's legs were just too easy to pull off that I could do it, too.

Then, line after line, I added more and more. I added a belt, a mask, and little ovals for the eyes and before I knew it, I had drawn a whole ninja. Sure proportions were completely off and I had no idea about anatomy, but dammit! It was a ninja.

This was when I was eight. I have been drawing ever since.

All of those memories evaporate into nothing when I take the card in both of my hands and hold it up above my face. I don't want to blink because I'm afraid I'll miss something, a detail that would tell me that I should have known she was setting me up with him from the beginning.

My finger pries open the envelope, and I run it along the edge of the card, ripping the card enclosure clear off.

What happens next decorates my body with glitter and confetti. I'm too surprised to actually do anything to it, but the metal glitter and colored paper feel funny and soft against my bare chest. I don't dust it off me, but let it stay. It's not bothering anyone right now.

On the outside is a cartoon panda, huge Buddha belly and all, waving at me while he sits in a clearing in a rainforest. In bright yellow letters, outlined in blue and green, the panda says, "Happy Birthday!"

I open the card to find a picture of a scene that takes both sides of the cards. The panda is from the front of the card is joined by about five or six more pandas wearing shirts from all over the globe, popping out of the treetops and from the long grass, shouting out "Happy Birthday". In big black letters, it says, "I hope you are ready for the panda-monium!"

At the bottom of the card is Peter's message to me: "To Teddy, Happy birthday buddy! Love, Peter."

I close the card and open it again. I don't see the pandas or the birthday wishes when I open it this time. Instead, I see the way he wrote his letter P, the letter T. I see the word buddy and the word 'love' and I close the card.

14

According to my list, we are almost out of bread, peanut butter, butter, and Reese's peanut butter cups.

Don't judge.

Earlier this morning, before school, I scavenged through the cupboards to find out what we might need so I can go to the store and pick things up for Mom. After all, she's like busy and stuff.

Don't judge.

When the bell rang, my heart began to race as far as it could in my little heart. I could have died a million times, from a million heart attacks at that moment. When the bell rang, I think I was actually happy for a change, and not just to get home.

The bus ride had to have been one of the longest bus rides home. Today, I noticed just how many students take the public school bus system. I also noticed just how many people take band and play big brass instruments.

This boy, Jessie, his baritone was carried on a metal rolling rack, the type you use for rolling luggage across the airport from terminal to terminal.

Now, if you haven't been on a school bus in a while, let me break it down for you. The bus has maybe an eighteen-inch clearing between the seats. The mini-tubas are about two feet across. Jessie must somehow practice magic on the side, because he managed to take a massive black vinyl tuba case down the entire aisle, kids' backpacks and feet and all blocking the way.

I'm telling you. Magic.

Then there were the kids with the oversized backpacks that don't use their lockers. Then those kids that were too busy talking to their friends to realize that they needed to get off. What I'm trying to say is, when you're in a hurry to go shopping, the rest of the world turns into a bunch of fucking idiots.

Finally, there came the time when I could get my first foot off the bus, then the second, and I'm free, only a mere twenty feet from the parking lot of my apartment complex.

As I take a step and passed the office, I recounted all the things I needed, careful not to forget them. If I don't write something down, I'm prone to actually forgetting them, only to remember them when I get home.

For serial, if I don't write on my hand, I don't remember shit.

The spare car is there when I get home and I'm already hoping that Vanessa doesn't have to go anywhere.

When we all decided that we were all driving because of Mom's work, we signed an agreement that we wouldn't take the car to work. Seriously, there is an agreement. I could show it to you, but my mom placed it in the fire safe in case anything happens.

And of course, only she knows the combination. But someday, I'll get in there.

Opening the door, I shout out Vanessa's name and wait for the echoes to reach back to my own ears.

Nothing. I scream her name once more. Nothing returns to my ears.

This is a good sign. Almost too good to be true.

To my right is the key rack where we put up all the keys to everything we own, house and cars and gate keys to our grandmother's house.

Seriously, if anyone were to break into our apartment, they can rest easy knowing that everything we need to keep protected—the big expensive, and big ticket items—are just right there. Just keep pressing the red self-locking mechanism to find the car and you're in business. We might as well hand the keys over to strangers.

I grab the keys so fast they don't even have time to jingle. My backpack is still loaded over my left shoulder, but only as long as it takes me to get the door open and toss it into the backseat. Sitting in the driver's seat, I check all of my mirrors and go through all the warnings my high school driving instructor told me. An ex-football coach for the high school, he decided to open up a driving school that was licensed by the state. My mom, figuring that it was easier to do it on our own time, paid the guy to teach me to drive.

Because nothing makes you want to follow the rules of the road more than a super tall gym monkey who gets off yelling at boys. But maybe that's just me.

But there's something wrong. I check my face and hair in the mirror. If I'm going to go out shopping, I always believe I should look my best. It's important, you know, to make a great first impression anywhere you go.

Last week, though, I'm not sure I believed this. But for some reason, I just wasn't happy with my hair.

I sigh and figured this can wait a few more minutes.

Back inside the apartment, I go to my bathroom and wet my hair down completely in the white sink. I can just see it now, my head bouncing off of the faucet and a giant gash opens my brains in the convenient white porcelain of the sink. Red and white scattered all over the place.

I close the door with the toe of my foot to minimize any surprises that might kill me and stick my head back into the sink. My hair feels a little sticky from the water and product I threw into it earlier.

Dammit, I probably used too much.

When everything feels slick and my fingers resist sliding right off my strands of brown hair, I dry my hair with my sister's towel. I'm pretty sure she won't notice.

My reflection in the mirror reminds me of a rock star who just woke up from a cocaine and drinking binge. My damp hair looks the way cartoon characters' hair looks after a bomb explodes in their face. You know, without the grayed out and dirty skin.

Let's see here. Every detail must be perfect.

I take out a little blue plastic ball and twist open the flat, silver lid. With my middle finger and ring finger, I smear out a dab of the white gunk and pull it through the front of my hair and push everything back.

If there's anything I hate, it's feeling of all of my hair is stuck to my head.

Then I shape each chuck of hair as best I can. I try pulling everything up, then pulling it down. I push off to the left and realize that I've trained my hair to do the same thing for so long, I can't get a different style without devoting hours to this.

I don't know how much time I have, so I just let it dry the way it is and let my hair fall as it may. Maybe I'll get points for that look that says, "I just woke up. Look how sexy I am!"

Or something.

In the length of time it took for me to walk from the entrance to the bread aisle, the lights in the store have faded twice and brightened once. Their new eco system causes me more headaches and light-headedness. The light and dark changes quickly, making me wonder just how long it might take for someone else to bump the front of their face or chest into the sides of aisles. To knock over glass bottles of wine and liquor. To just drop to the floor because of the disorientation.

For someone to scream because they think they are losing their own eyesight.

Or something.

It's when I have already collected the bread that I realize I'm never going to be able to read the list on my hand. Though it's in black Sharpie, there is no possible way I can keep reading it and collecting everything in my arms.

I should have grabbed a basket.

My steps are slow and deliberate as I lament not having a cart or a basket to put everything in. That was one of our new SAT words this week, lament.

And it's about the time I'm trying to grab the natural, smooth peanut butter that a red handheld shopping basket slides across the cement warehouse-like floor. I look up and Peter is taking quick steps to approach me. His hand motions to the basket.

"You look like you forgot a basket," he says.

I hold up my hand to him. "Ya, I think I wrote down everything except to grab a basket."

Peter grabs my hand with his and pulls it closer to his face. He squints his eyes. Then, pushing and pulling my hand closer and further away from his eyes, he says, "You need butter?"

"And stuff," I say. I relax my hand and let him do whatever he wants. Really, it's okay.

"Let's go get your stuff, then," he says. Still holding my hand, he pulls me to the back of the store, where the meat displays and cooling refrigerators are. Around the corner, a lobster climbs over his roommates and up the glass walls of the aquatic glass case.

Down the way, women are reading the packages of meat, comparing prices and weights, and looking at coupon books to see what they can spend next.

And Peter, his grip lightens up just enough that my limp hand slips right out of it and I slow down, coming to a near stop.

"Don't you have to work?" I say out loud. What I say to myself inside is, "Shut. Up."

"Ya, but I'm helping a customer," Peter says. "You're a good distraction from what I'm supposed to do right now."

"Glad I could help," I say and Peter turns to me and smiles. He says nothing, but his smile and the way his eyes seem to smile, too, they say all I need to know.

"Do you have a preference about your butter?" he says.

"What are my options?" I'm not watching the butter or the coolers that display them in bright fluorescent lights. I'm not even paying much attention to the people around me. My basket has apparently been in my hand all this time and I didn't even know.

What I could tell you, though, is that Peter's jacket flaps away from him when he walks, and his shoes have red and white stripes up the side of the black vinyl treated to fool you into thinking that it is real leather.

I could tell you that Peter is wearing a bracelet of some kind, but his black jacket is covering his wrists.

"Why do you wear a jacket?" I ask.

"I work in the freezer and have to stock the vegetables and meat and stuff," he says. "It's so fucking cold in there." He holds it up to him and pops his collar up. "Why, you like it?"

I answer with a smile and I'm pretty sure blood is rushing to my face to make me blush.

"Unsalted," I say.

Peter's face goes still until he says, "Oh! Butter!" He picks the store brand, a piss yellow and blue box, and tosses it into the basket. "What next?"

My palms are so sweaty right now that I'm not sure that I can read it, so I just say, because it's the closest thing to me, "Milk."

"That's easy enough," he says. Grabbing my basket from my grip, he pulls me to the glass doors of the refrigerator displays. He opens up the milk and grabs the one percent, putting it in the basket.

I, of course, just let him do what he wants. No, really, it's okay that he does the shopping for me. It's good to have help from a professional. Or something.

"And anything else?" he says.

I hold my hand up to Peter and he squints at my palms. The heavy black lines that used to be there are now replaced by the fainted ghosts of shopping list past.

"I see," he says. Peter's hazel eyes look into mine, and I swear they dilate as he says, "So I guess this is it?"

I nod and, still holding my basket, Peter just starts walking to the front of the store. I'm walking behind him, taking smaller steps because I don't know how to say thank you for the card. I don't know how to say that I got the glitter all over my body and it took two showers to wash it all off. After that, it took another whole rinsing off to wipe the rest of the glitter down the drain. And though my mom didn't appreciate it, I want to say thank you.

These are the thoughts in my head, and the words, "Love, Peter," written in black.

The words, "Thank you" appear as bold red letters in my brain over and over again.

"Hey Peter," I say. Let's give it a shot. "Hey, I wanted to say something."

And Peter stops walking, pushing himself up against the wall of cereals and he holds his index finger up to his mouth, the universal sign of "shut the fuck up".

"What the hell is that?" I say. Peter grabs my shoulders and pushes me into a box of Cookie Crisp and rattles the metal shelves behind me.

"Shut up," he says. Putting the finger on his mouth again, turns his head over to the corner of the aisle he points down on the ground.

And there at the end of the aisle in the walkway to the registers, are the soles of someone's feet lying face down.

Peter walks slowly, tip toe, to me and puts my basket on the ground, slow and deliberate and takes my hand. His mouth says, "This way" without making a sound. And as we take our first couple of steps toward the back of the store, the black plastic handles fall down into their resting position, slapping the basket and echoing into the store.

"What the fuck was that?" says someone with a gun up near the front of the store. I mean, I can only assume that he has a gun at this point.

"Where the hell do you think you're going? Get the fuck down!" screams someone from behind us.

Peter, his hands up in the air, and I, scared shitless, turn around and get a look at the would-be robber. His face is covered with a black wool mask and his thick, burly body is covered by a puffy orange jacket. He holds a gun at us with both hands, overlaying each other to keep it still and steady.

It doesn't take much convincing to make me follow your orders to begin with, and with a gun, I'm virtually guaranteed to do whatever you want to do.

Peter, on the other hand, gets slowly on his knees and still faces the robber. His hands stay up into the air, reaching for the sky, as they say, in cartoons, and he doesn't lie down. He doesn't follow orders.

I'm behind him so I don't know if he's fucking with this guy or if he's just scared frozen solid.

I hope it's neither, but there is nothing I can do about it now.

My heart has probably stopped and started and sped up and slowed down I don't know how many times. My palms sweat ink and smell sweet from the hair product I apparently did not wash off when I was done in the bathroom.

The man with the gun, he approaches Peter and puts the gun against Peter's temple. "Get. The. Fuck. Down!" he says. Pushing the barrel of the gun into Peter's skin further, turning it white from the pressure, he says, "Don't look at me!"

Peter follows the orders. Moving slowly and carefully, he pulls his hands down in front of him and rests his face against the ground.

I think I hear sobbing, but being this close to the dirty, tiled floor, it could be anyone. They used to say that Native Americans would listen to the ground to hear animals or enemies on the move. By tracking the sounds and where they were coming from, the tribes would know where to hunt or where to hide.

Listening to the ground, all I hear is people crying and gasping and telling each other that everything is okay.

With my ear that isn't pushed to the ground, I hear registers opening and receipt tape printing.

Then, a voice shouts out to the store, "Let's go! We got it!"

And the man with the gun, the one who really wanted to kill Peter, he backs up in slow steady steps and then pockets the gun between his pants and his shirt.

I hope he fucking trips and shoots himself.

I hope he bumps into something and dies from bleeding out.

I hope he suffers hard.

When the man is out of the aisle, I lift my head up with my neck, resting my face on the backs of my hands. Peter's feet don't move in front me, but his legs shake. Probably from nerves.

The way I feel right now, I think I need to go to the bathroom. The way Peter feels right now, I can't tell. He won't move.

"Pete," I say. I push on his back with my fingertips. "Pete, they're gone, I think."

Peter sits there and stares off to the side of the aisles. He could be counting all the coins and change under the shelves, but he's probably not.

"Pete?" I say.

And Peter says nothing as he stands up. He dusts off his pants and shirt and looks at me. His eyes are empty as a computer screen. His eyebrows and face is emotionless when he says, "Are you okay?"

"I was going to ask you," I say and I give him a hug on instinct. "You had me scared for a minute there."

"I just," says Peter, and he stops, looking for the right words down the aisles. "Froze."

I go down the aisle and grab his basket and walk to his side. Pulling on his jacket, I say, "Let's go check on everyone else."

We waited for the police to arrive and calmed down as many customers as we could. The managers held up the registers and announced over the public announcement system that everyone needed to stay calm.

The PA system, it told us that the police will be there shortly to take statements. If anyone needed to go, it told us, then we might have to wait for a while.

So of course, some people just walked out and left their groceries at the registers. Lots of go-backs, Peter called them.

Peter grabbed a couple of sodas from one of those refrigerators by the registers and hands me a Dr. Pepper. "If I remember correctly," he says, "this is your favorite." From watching me shopping for the past few years, Peter had memorized my favorite drinks and snacks. He knew what kind of milk I always bought, and he even figured out my favorite flavors of ice cream.

When the police arrived, they let most of us go when we wanted.

The manager announced on the PA system that they only needed the descriptions from a few people. The rest of the witnesses, it said, can have a wonderful day and thank you for shopping at Owl Foods.

Ya, wonderful day.

I'm at the register and taking the receipt from the lady when Peter taps me on my arm. "Manager says I can leave," he says. "I'll walk you home," he says.

"Awesome. Will you put the groceries away, too?" I ask.

"If you want me to," he says. "I have nothing else to do today."

We walk to our family's car and Peter laughs to himself and says, "I didn't realize you didn't walk."

"Ya, I thought I needed more than this," I say and realize immediately I came with a list on my hand. I knew what I needed, and hope that Peter doesn't realize that I'm just lazy.

"I see," he says. He leans up against passenger side door and says, "How did you stay so calm in there?"

"I'm used to bullies." I close the trunk of the car and shield my eyes from the afternoon sun overhead. "I guess a bully is a bully is a bully."

Peter looks at his feet, or the ground, I can't tell. Kicking something away from him, he says, "I'm sorry about that."

"About what?" I rest my but against the car right next to him.

Peter shrugs and kicks more escaped pieces of asphalt away from his shoes. "I don't know."

"It's not your fault," I say. "It's okay. It's over." Turning to face him, I touch his jacket and say to him, "Thank you for the card, by the way. The glitter was an interesting touch."

Peter smiles and says, "Thanks. I had some extra lying around and it just screamed panda-monium."

We both laugh and then there's that awkward silence between two people who don't know what to say next.

And Pete is the first person to break the silence with, "Thank you."

"For what?" I say. "You got me the card."

Peter turns his head to look at me, closing one eye from the bright

South Caroline sunlight above us, and he says, "For looking out for me." He moves the rest of his body toward me and says, "I saw the gun and I just freaked out."

"Are you going to be okay?" I ask.

Peter stares back at the ground, kicking more pebbles and rocks. He takes what seems like a year to answer my question. "Yes, I'll be fine." When Peter lifts his face to look back at me, I'm not convinced his answer is true.

I give him another hug. "I promise you'll be okay," I tell him. Rubbing his back, I say, "I promise."

And though I'm not sure if it's just the moment or what, but I feel his chest press hard against mine, then deflate to release tension. No tears. No sobbing. Just a massive release of every thought and nervous tension.

"You know," I continue, speaking into his ear, "you're welcome to come over and hang out if you want."

Peter's heart beats pretty fast against my chest, but he says while he releases my grip, "No, I should get home. I need to go to my parents' house today. And I barely got any sleep last night."

And for a second, not so nice images flash in my head of what he could have been doing.

"Ya," I say. "Me, too."

"I'll see you tomorrow though?" Peter shoves his hands into his pocket as he begins to walk away from me, toward the side roads. "We should catch a movie or something."

And I think I just made a date.

Wow.

15

M y room smells the way you would imagine the inside of a
paint can would smell. My mother has been busy again.

Vanessa kicked my door open, so hard it bounced off of the wall
and back into her hips as she walked into my room.

"You know what?" she says as she rests herself on the floor. She
scatters her nail polish, polish remover, and a bag of cotton balls on
the floor around her. There, she sits and extends her feet directly in
front of her, the back of her knees touching the floor. This appears to
be a unique gift among women.

I couldn't do that all these years of P.E. I can't do it now. I couldn't
do it three years ago and I'm convinced it's a sign that I'm not
supposed to be able to bend that way.

"I've been thinking," she says. Her fingertips unscrew a skinny
nail polish cap and dip the brush into the red sparkly liquid. "I think
we should try a hypothetical."

My brain makes the necessary adjustments and interpreting
Vanessa's unique language skills. "And do what, exactly?"

"You know, with your," she says and stops to look around. The
brush has a round glob of ruby red sparkly nail polish on it, only

millimeters from her toes, holding still. Then in a whisper, she finishes her sentence, "your powers."

"I never said I have powers," I tell her. On instinct, I get up and close the door. My mom really doesn't need to be hearing this. "These are just, I don't know. Coincidences." I nod as I say this. Half to convince her, half to convince me.

"Ya, right," she says. "You've already killed people and like, summoned birds and shit." Her brush slips across the tip of left foot's big toe. Vanessa's tongue hangs out of her mouth as she does this, a sign that she's thinking a little too hard about something this simple.

"Summoned birds?" I say. "You've been reading again, haven't you?"

"Pfft," she says. "We both know I don't read." Her concentration rests solely on her feet and nails. Her brush goes into the glittery red glob and she slides the brush against her toes again.

Where I'm sitting, on my bed, I just barely start to smell the polish sliding into my nostrils. What I think when I smell this, I think about paint thinner and rubbing alcohol.

"I don't have powers." I cross my arms to let her know that I'm serious.

"Yes, you do," says Vanessa. She blows on her toes. Bending over from her waist so her shoulders are only about six inches or a foot away from the floor, she says to me between puffs, "We should give it a try. Test things out."

"And how do you figure we can do this?" I ask.

My Gamestation has been on pause since Vanessa came into the bedroom. There's no point in trying to play anything while she's in the room. Behaving like a two-year-old that's an only child, she demands attention with stomps and irritating questions. What she does with her voice when she's being ignored should be outlawed against the eighth amendment. That's the one with the cruel and unusual punishment, right? I should have paid more attention in history.

"We could, I don't know. Try to kill something. You're pretty good at that."

"Fuck. You." Both of my middle fingers join in.

I'm not a killer. I swear.

"I'm not killing anyone," I say. "Next idea."

"Okay then," she says. Vanessa keeps her leg unbent, straight out in front of her and then unfolds her other leg to the side, forming a ninety degree angle. Both feet out in front of her, she bends over and begins painting the right foot. "We could do something nicer then." She stops to look up with the tip of her tongue hanging out of her mouth. Then, she says, "Can you make money?"

"Make money?" I ask. "And how can I do that?"

"The lottery?" she says. "Yes, the lottery! We can win the lottery."

"How?" I say. "We're minors, dumbass. New idea."

"No, no, hear me out!" she says. She rests the nail polish and the brush-slash-cap on the wooden floor beside her and she says, "What if we get Mom to buy one. Like you can do your thing and make Mom buy one, and we can be rich."

It could be the smell of the nail polish getting to me and suffocating my brain, making me drunk or high or whatever, but she sounds convincing, maybe she is actually making sense. This isn't like her, so I decide to seize the moment.

"Hey, Mom!" I shout into the hallway.

No response from downstairs, so I shout again.

"What?" my mom screams up the stairway. "What is it?"

"When was the last time you played the lottery?" I ask. "Just wondering."

"I don't know, Teddy." There's a little pause before she yells back up, "That's a weird question. It's been a while, I guess."

"I don't have any money to waste on that crap," she says to me.

Turning on my computer screen, I type in "South Carolina lottery" in Google and see that the South Carolina Education Lottery site says the jackpot is about one hundred twenty million.

"Holy shit," I say to Vanessa. Pointing to the screen, I tell her, "We want to win this." I look at my sister, who is finishing up her nails on her toes, and say to her, "Vanessa, what if we won a hundred-twenty million dollars?"

"Get the fuck out," she says. Vanessa stands up, walking on her heels to keep her toes off the ground. Straight-legged balancing act that she is, she comes over and rests on my shoulders. "Do your thing, Teddy."

And I close my eyes. Looking at the screen again, blinking, opening my eyes and closing them, I think about winning the money. I try to picture my mom getting a large check in person, the type of check that takes two people to hold. On it reads the words "Congratulations", and "$120 million", and "Laura Barratt".

Vanessa's voice pulls me from my concentration. "Oh my God!" she says. "Oh my God! What did you do?" she says. Vanessa points at my nose and she says, "You're bleeding."

I use the closest piece of clothing on my floor and wipe my nose. The thick red liquid smears on my blue shirt are blood alright.

"That can't be good," I say.

My sister, the eternal optimist that she can be when she really wants something, she says, "Does that mean it worked?"

"I don't know," I say. And the thought of being millions of dollars richer makes me smile an ear-to-ear kind of smile. I can't not smile and I say, "Do you have a dollar I can borrow?"

"Sure," says Vanessa and she walks on her heels to her bedroom and back. "What's this for?"

I fold the dollar so it doesn't look so formal. Keep this informal so Mom doesn't know what's going on.

"I think we need to test this out."

"Hey, Mom!" I say. Walking down the steps, I see Mom sitting on the couch, reading one of those harlequin romance books, the types with the big muscle guys with long hair and tanned bodies, always gripping some damsel in distress in a seductive dress that shows way too much cleavage. "Mom!" I say. I hand out the dollar to her. "Can you buy me a lottery ticket?" I ask. "Please?"

Mom finishes the page and rests it, opened, against her chest. "What now?"

I hold the dollar in her face to show her I'm serious. "Please? As a birthday present?"

"Since when do you want to gamble?" she says. "You know the chances of us winning are really, really slim."

The way she looks at me, I know that Mom is going to do it anyway. She has never been able to tell me no, a fact that I'm not particularly proud of. It's not easy to admit that I don't deserve something, and even harder to act on it.

One time, my mom wanted to fly me to Grandma's because of the holidays. That same winter, I had failed two classes with F's. What she didn't know, that the report card didn't show, was that I had under forty percent in each of those classes: math and P.E. I just didn't care about those classes, and I couldn't be bothered with the unnecessary bullshit of the teachers.

Besides, the teachers hated me. At least that's what I told my mom.

Regardless, she was just a click of her mouse away from buying me tickets to Florida. Because she loved me and wanted to see me happy. Those tickets? Well, they were just for me. My sister was condemned to stay with the family all that time.

I never took the tickets. Partly because I didn't want to take something I didn't deserve, and partly because Vanessa threatened to kill my computer if I left her alone with Mom.

I believed her. She's that crazy.

"Please?" I say again, waving the dollar in front of her face. "I'll even put in the money. Just one play. I promise." I cross my heart and hope to die.

My mom, she doesn't think that part is very funny, but takes the money and shoves it into her pants pockets. "I'll go after work tomorrow."

"You can't!" I tell her. "I think the drawing's today. Like tonight today. I think we should go now. We don't want to miss out on one hundred twenty million dollars." I think for a minute and tell her, "Besides, we're out of snacks for school."

"Fine," she says. "Do you and your sister want to come along?"

"I don't know, let me go check," and no sooner that I can turn around does my sister come running down the steps. Freshly painted nails be damned.

"I'm ready to go," she says. My sister is biting her bottom lip, so she isn't bursting into hysterics. The excitement is about to make her nearly literally explode.

VANESSA and I refuse to sit up front so we can talk and whisper in the back. The closer we get to the store, the closer my sister starts to rub her palms against her hands and she looks at me. "How's your nose?" she says.

"Teddy," my mom says. Her eyes stare at me through the rearview mirror. "What's wrong with your nose?"

"Nothing, Mom," I say. "I bumped it on the floor when I fell off my bed."

"Oh honey, you need to be careful," says Mom.

I hit Vanessa in the ribcage with my elbow. "Shut up, stupid. You know she can't find out," I whisper to her.

Vanessa nods, putting her finger to her mouth and whispering, "Shh."

At the customer service counter, my mom gives me the slip and lets me bubble in the numbers. I can only choose numbers between one and fifty-six, so I bubble in random numbers. I already used my quote-unquote "powers" so maybe there's no harm in being random.

"What are you doing?" says Vanessa. She's hovering over my shoulder. "Shouldn't you be using my birthday or your birthday or something?" Vanessa is on her tiptoes as she says, "Use the number seven! No! Not sixteen, what's wrong with you?"

"I wanted to use number twenty-four, since it's the number of my favorite Pokémon," I tell her.

"You're a fucking nerd," says Vanessa.

My mom takes the ticket and my dollar bill and approaches the counter. My sister and I, we figure that it might be safer to not be around the ticket, so we go to the soft drink aisle. I drag my sister's hand down the aisle and stop at the end, near the meat freezer. "You think this is going to work?"

"I don't know?" says Vanessa. Her left eyebrow is raised, right one down. "I mean," she says, looking excited for both of us. "Yes!" Vanessa grabs my hand. "Yes, it will work."

"You're right," I say. I have hummingbirds in my stomach, trying to fly through my chest and back up my throat. "But what if it doesn't work?"

"Shut up!" my sister says. She pretends to slap me across my face and says, "It will work. You have the power." The way she says it, the calm mysterious voice she tries to use, Vanessa makes me sound like I'm a mystic or a medieval sorcerer. Maybe in a past life?

"Just think," says Vanessa. She puts her arm around my shoulder and motions her arm to display the entire store in front of us. "We can have whatever we want. We can buy anything at our whim. If we want it, it will come."

"You're mixing some stuff up, I think," I tell her.

Vanessa puts her right index finger against my mouth and says, "Kindly shut up." Her eyes gaze outward as if she can watch the clouds pass over us, and she says, "Imagine, the world at your fingers."

"Fingertips," I say.

"That's what I said," she argues and then looks at me. "If I'm the only one who believes in these powers, then you're in trouble," she says. "I mean, what if I have to do all of the thinking for you? Imagine the possibilities." Vanessa's eyes gaze at the imaginary clouds above us again. "We could be powerful."

I grab an orange Fanta off the shelf, the twenty-ounce kind, and a diet Coke for my sister. "You've got issues," I say.

On the way home, my sister refuses to talk to me or to anyone else. Instead, she stares outside and smiles. Her head doesn't have to be transparent for me to read her mind. I know what's she's thinking, and it scares me.

How could I possibly get everything I want? Is it really possible? I mean, really, really possible?

What if I could do it? All I had to do was wish and think and "poof!" it's there?

I put the thoughts in my mind. Doing the math, I think about the interest rates and try to calculate how much we could make if we invest it. What could we make if we just spent sixty million and kept the rest and lived off the interest?

My economics teacher used to tell us that money is always worth more now than in the future. Something about inflation. Maybe we should take the cash up front, but that only gives us sixty million right away.

Dammit.

My brain puts together a shopping list of details. Looking outside, two- and single-story houses pass by us. I calculate their values in my head, thinking that I could live there. Or I'd want a house with an upstairs balcony right off of my bedroom.

Maybe I'm thinking too small? Maybe I should get a car first? What kind of car could I get? Should I get?

When I look at my sister, she glances back and rubs her hands together in the evil genius kind of way and smiles at me. In her mind, we've already won and just need to claim the prize.

In my mind, I'm handing over money to people and practically swimming in brand new video games for my Gamestation.

In my mom's mind, we already lost.

When we get back to the apartment, my mom tells us to grab some groceries and we follow her, one-by-one, like ducklings, into the house. We each carry a brown bag of groceries because my mom refuses to use plastic. Years ago, when I was in third grade, we learned that our plastic bags would get destroyed and animals would suffocate trying to eat out of them, or live in them. I forget which.

My mom took it to heart and began a rather aggressive recycling program in our house. We had a blue basket for paper goods, a red basket for trash, and a white basket for bottles. That went on for about a month before the city sent a letter to us explaining that we don't have a municipal recycling program.

That same day, my mom shoved everything into the white plastic bags and left it outside.

In defiance, she decided that we were only going to use brown paper bags and never plastic. It was the least we could do, she told us.

LATER THAT NIGHT, I sat at the computer completely ignoring the reading assignments. I couldn't read *The Scarlet Letter* right now because of money. The possibility of money, or the possibility of losing money I didn't win yet. However you want to look at it. To my sister, it was money that was already ours.

I was less optimistic.

"Did we win yet?" my sister says. Resting her pillow on my floor, she sits down on the pink heart that is the ass of her pants. My sis hugs her pillow against her chest and looks at me like a little child lost in a supermarket. "Have we won yet?" she says.

"No, not yet," I say.

"When do we win?" she asks.

"When the numbers are announced," I say. I click refresh on the screen and stare at last week's numbers. Right now, anything is possible.

"And when is that?" she says.

"After eleven, I think?" I say. I throw my pillow at her. "Now get out of here, I'm reading."

"Reading what?" she says.

"Scarlet Letter."

Vanessa points to the closed book on my desk across the room from me. "You are not reading," she says. "Your book is over there."

"What I meant to say was," I say and pick up the book and sit right back down on the computer chair, "is that I was going to start reading. I need to get a few chapters done tonight because I have a quiz."

"I'm suspect," she says.

"Suspicious," I tell her. "Now get out."

"Fine. I'll be back at eleven oh-five." Vanessa's pillow drags on the floor as she leaves, her big feet slapping against the wooden floor. I turn off my computer monitor and lay down on my bed to put up appearances. The faster I can make her believe that I'm reading and doing homework, the faster I can get rid of her.

When the door clicks, I put my book down on my chest and close my eyes tight. My imaginary self is in the parking lot of Owl Foods, hugging Peter. I'm sniffing his cologne and his jacket. The dust of the back storeroom. The lukewarm breeze that warmed us up after lying on the cold floor. What I'm feeling right now, is a tightness in my pants and I'm pressed for time. The clock says that Vanessa will be back in here in about ten minutes, and while I'm fast, I'm not that fast.

Reading about a puritan whore will make me feel better. Maybe.

The first line goes into my brain over and over again, but just bounces off. I can't focus. Or don't want to.

Fuck it, I'll just check Spark Notes, and I get up out of my bed and turn on my computer monitor again.

I type in "s-p-a-r-k" into Google before I hit backspace and delete everything. Instead, I click in the box and type out South Carolina Education Lottery and click the link. Let's just see, shall we?

And in the middle of the website are the words "Drawing for Wednesday" and I read the numbers.

We were two numbers off, but that's not too bad, I think.

My door opens and Vanessa barges in, not knocking because we never knock in this damned family.

"I thought you were reading," she says.

"I was reading, but it was time to check the website. I point at the screen and Vanessa looks over them. Did we win anything?" she says. "You aren't acting like we won one hundred and twenty million dollars."

"That's because we didn't." My nose tickles and I sniff to keep something from falling down.

"We didn't win anything?" she says. "Your powers suck."

"I don't have powers," I remind her. Pointing at the screen and looking at the ticket on my desk, I trace the numbers and count. "But we are two, maybe three, numbers off."

"That's gotta count for something," she says. Taking the paper from my hands, Vanessa reads that back. "Look," she says.

And right there on the back of the ticket says that having some of the numbers means we still win, just not a hundred and twenty million dollars. Tracing the line across, I look at our numbers. Having only four numbers out of the seven, I stand up and say, "Holy shit!"

My mom listens to us scream and shout as we jump downstairs. I'm skipping two or three steps at a time, leaping down the steps and into the living room. My mom is watching the *Late Tonight Show* or something, and she looks at us, sipping a glass of red wine.

"How did you do?" she says.

"We won ten thousand dollars!" I say.

Vanessa takes the slip from my hands and, pulsing and shaking from the adrenaline, she holds it in front of Mom's face. "Teddy did it, Mom! Teddy won us ten thousand dollars!"

16

That awkward moment when you realize that your dad might be shopping for a child who isn't you.

I refuse to go much further beyond the food court when I bear witness to my father walking out of an Aeropostale store with a bag in hand. Being thirty-nine is too old to be wearing hoodies with numbers and brand names on it, isn't it?

When he left my mother, Dad never said anything about where he was going. That part, I had to figure out for myself. When I was little, it was usually Asia or Europe or some place in Africa. My favorite movies back then were the action movies with a man who has nothing left to lose, out to save the world or kill the big mob boss who killed with family. The man who somehow knows how to street brawl or use AK-47s because it is apparently a useful tool to have in corporate America. In the deepest fantasies, Dad was running out of buildings with a black tank top, wrapped in bullets and weapons the way Christmas trees are wrapped with lights, guns firing off in every direction aimlessly and deadly. That's my dad.

Correction. Was my dad.

Now, "This is my dad," I say and point over to the store's entrance. My dad is at the mall, looking around and checking his watch. We are watching from behind, at a wooden stand with a Greek man trying to sell Peter a bag of Doritos and nacho cheese. "Just take the damned bag," I say. I throw my fist full of change and maybe a few dollar bills that I didn't remember having and pull Peter from that stand to the water fountain.

"Are we going to say hi?" Pete asks. The bag screams as Pete tries to rip it open.

"No," I say. "We can never talk to him ever again."

"I haven't talked to him a first time," Pete says. He shoves more chips into his mouth when he sees just how amused I am not right now.

"We don't talk to Dad," I tell him. "Ever."

"Even on your birthday?" Pete asks.

"Yes, even on my birthday. Or his birthday. Or Vanessa's birthday. Or Mom's birthday." I look over at him and me just talking away is all I can do to keep from punching him right now. "As a matter of fact, he left me about a few weeks before my birthday. Said something about how it wasn't fair and he needed space. His idea of space was about two hours away from here and disappearing from our lives."

Not that I fault him, if I had to live with me, I guess I'd move away far, far away, too.

"That's harsh, man," says Pete. He rests his hand on my deltoid and squeezes it. "Come on," he says and grabs my hand. "Let's go eat."

When I stand up from the fountain and put my right foot in front of my left one, this little boy in a blue and gray striped shirt hits the both of us and turns around. "Watch where you're going, fucking fags!" he says. His middle fingers put the end punctuation on that sentence.

I don't even need a good reason, or a bad reason. No reason at all when I put one foot in front of the other, faster and faster until I'm putting my hands around this fucker's neck and squeezing and punching. Whether I'm hitting the floor or his skull or his shoulder, I couldn't tell you. That phrase, you know, when they say you see red?

Ya, I saw blood.

I couldn't hear Pete's yelling at me, or the adults trying to pry me off of the little shit. His face was I don't know where while I kept hitting and hitting and hitting. Maybe it was the sight of seeing my father, maybe it was Peter's questions about going to talk to him. Maybe it was just the homophobic bullshit.

Maybe it was everything and nothing.

Peter's hands wrap around my head, and try to pull me off. Another man I can't see has my hands and arms pulled up and around my head, locked in place.

My red and hot face stares at the little shit and he pretends not cry. Wiping his face, he says to the adults around him, "I didn't do anything. He just jumped around the corner and hit me."

"Fuck you!" I shout and Peter hits my head.

"You're not helping, Teddy, shut up."

And the man from behind me, his grip lets go.

Me, unexpected, I fall to the floor, landing on my hands and knees. Looking up, I follow the brown leather shoes to the pleated khaki pants to the brown reversible leather belt to the red and green plaid long-sleeved button-down shirt to the soft, fat-filled face of my father.

"Hi, Dad," I say. "Fancy meeting you here."

This man in a black suit, white shirt, shoves his face between me and my dad and he says to us, "This is your dad?"

My dad, reluctantly I'm sure, says everything is okay, and the crowd disperses.

Peter, he's holding my hand as hard as he can, pulling me back. I think he's maybe afraid that I'm going to let go again, try to beat the living shit out of the rude fucker. He's right to be afraid right now.

I'd rather go to jail right now than have to deal with this shit.

"Teddy," says my dad. He takes his glasses off of his nose, wipes them on his sleeve, and puts them back on. "I can hardly believe it was you." The little fucker with the middle fingers comes to stand next to my father. "This is Elias," my father says.

The little fucker waves at me.

This little shit, he couldn't be more than about maybe ten years. Give or take a year.

"Go to hell," is my only reply.

Peter pulls me backwards, steps in front of me and extends his hand to my father, saying, "Hi, Mr. Barratt. I'm Peter, a friend of Teddy's."

"Barratt?" says my dad and looks at me, kneeling down. "She didn't let you keep my last name?"

"I think we need to go," says Peter, and he pulls on my shirt hard.

"Stay," says my father. I swear I see Peter flinch when my father puts his hand on Peter's and keeps it still. "Stay for a while. We can talk. Have lunch," he says.

"I think we have to go. To, um. Dinner. I think. Right, Teddy?" says Peter.

"No," I say. Standing and dusting the dirty walked-on floor off my pants and palms, I say, "I think we have enough time for us to stay and talk."

And Peter's eyes, both eyebrows climb so far up his forehead that I can't see them behind his cute brown bangs. He says nothing for the first time in a long time. Everything about him apparently lets go, as his hands fall to his side, letting go of the last part of my hand and clothes.

Did you know that in order to be an investigator for a public office, you just need a high school diploma and a college degree? Did you know that in most cases, you can get away with a degree in criminal justice in about two years' time?

Ya, guess what my father was doing all this time while he was not in my life?

According to my father, the entire process is a lot easier to do than you'd think. Or at least than I'd think.

All of these things he tells me while I'm holding an Icee against my hands and knuckles. Every time I try to drink some of it, Peter stops me and reminds me that it's supposed to help keep the swelling down. My knuckles look like brown and blue sandpaper, or wood.

The way they feel right now, I want to just put my whole hand in a cast to keep from moving. Just the act of flexing my hand makes me feel the rest of my forearm skin pulling up and down.

All of my tendons and muscles move with a single twitch or thought.

I'm an idiot, but it felt so damn good.

"So," I say. "If you're an investigator and all, why didn't you come find us? Come find me and, I don't know," I say. "Bring us presents or a card or something?"

"I don't know what to tell you, Teddy," he says. "I," he says. Putting his lips together, bringing them into his mouth and turning white, my father says, "I wasn't looking for you because I was." He pauses, looks across the mall's second floor and through the glass elevator tube that's in front of us. My father says, "Busy."

The little shit, however, is bouncing from store to store. My dad... um, father...handed a wad of cash to the fucker and let him wander around the mall at will.

Oh, to have a dad instead of a sperm donor.

Peter stands by my side at every moment, asking me if I need another napkin for my dripping Icee. "Sure, fine," I say and let him go fetch me more napkins from the food court. The drying water on my hand makes me feel itchy and irritated.

Where we're standing, is in front of the Orange Julius cart. Behind me, I notice that Guess is having a sale on shirts with a bird, or dog, or something splattered in black across the chest. The air is thick and floral, smelling like one of their beauty counters threw up all over the store.

"Teddy," says my father. "How is your mother?"

"She's fine," I say.

"Good," says my father. He offers up the money for the fruit smoothies and takes ours off the wooden cart. "And your sister? What's her name?" he says.

"Vanessa?" I ask. "She's okay. She's a girl and a teenager, so crazy as hell."

My father laughs at my words like I'm supposed to be telling a joke. I don't respond or laugh back to him. My goal is to make this whole process as painful as possible.

"Who's the brat?" I ask.

"He's my son."

"Great, so I have a step-brother?"

"Yeah, he's a great kid," says my father.

"Where's your wife?" I ask. I sip my smoothie and look around.

Peter pops around the corner with a handful of napkins and a worried look on his face. His puppy dog eyes, framed by his bangs, make me want to kiss him right here, right now.

"I'm not married, Teddy," says my father.

"Hey, Peter, did you know that the little shit with a big mouth is my father's son and he's not married?" I say. I try my best infomercial voice when I say, "That's right. I have a step-brother. Better set another place at the table for those holiday dinners with the fam, right?"

"Teddy, this isn't really necessary," my father says.

"Teddy, don't," says Peter.

And I say, "And just how old is the little shit, anyhow?"

My father points his finger at my face and says, "Do not talk about him that way. You don't even know him, you spoiled brat."

And that's it. Game over.

"Answer my fucking question, Dad." I want so desperately for him to feel the pain, the frustration.

If anything, I would love to see this asshole cry for the times I saw my mom cry. For the times I cried when I was little. For the times I had to be consoled by Vanessa because I didn't know where Daddy was. When my own sister didn't know who our dad was, or even care, because she was never close to him.

And my father, his mouth just opens up and spills it all out. "He's about twelve years old. I had him with Cynthia about a year before I left your mother. He was the reason why I left and I wasn't sure that I could have two families at the same time so I had to pick one and I chose her I hope you aren't mad at me, but I didn't know how to tell your mother that I had cheated on her and I really didn't want to be around that family because I was never treated fairly."

At this point, he throws his hands over his mouth and he looks from side to side. His jaw is struggling to move despite the combined force of both of his hands pushing his mandible up and closed.

Pete says slowly, "Wow, you're talkative."

I'm biting my tongue so hard I can almost taste blood. I can't laugh or smile right now. He can't know it's me. But this is so much fucking fun. I bite harder into my tongue, the coppery metallic taste of blood slides against the tip of my tongue.

And I notice, besides the self-inflicted wound in my mouth, there isn't any blood anywhere. Nothing drips from my nose. Maybe I missed it, I think and tilt my head downwards to check the floor.

No tiny circles of crimson. No splatters of blood. Nothing warm and slick down my upper lip.

But I am doing this, aren't I?

Peter snickers and tries to mute his laughter at the sight of my father gradually relaxing his grip on his jaw. The look on his face goes from tensed-up worry to the gradual relaxed look of "everything is okay" and then he opens his mouth again.

"And so what I really wanted to tell you was that I couldn't be there in that house because no one ever really treated me fairly because I didn't almost die once, and you did."

My dad's jaw just won't stop moving, and his tongue is working so hard he's forgetting to swallow. Morsels of white, foamy spit come out of his mouth, land on the floor and his shirt as he keeps on talking.

"I felt like I had to almost die too if I was going to get any attention from anyone and it was sad I couldn't even be a good father to you or to Vanessa because I was too busy hating my only son and the only way I could get away from that was to leave the family and start another one all over again except I couldn't get married again because I didn't want to be a complete failure again and now Cynthia is mad at me too because she knows that I won't marry her ever and I think she might leave me for another guy and I'll never see you or Vanessa or Elias or anyone."

My dad puts his hands out the way a gymnast puts her hands out to stick a difficult landing. He pauses, and Peter and I stare at each other, unsure of what he's going to say next.

The words he spouted all at once, they're running through my mind. Sprinting from neuron to neuron and synapse to synapse.

"Great, so even you fucking hate me," I say. "Fuck you anyhow. I hope you rot in Hell," I say as I walk away. "Come on, Peter."

I walk away against the shouts from my dad to stay there and talk. He's calling my name, louder and louder. First shouting "Teddy", and then "Theodore" and finally "I love you" and no matter what he says, I don't turn around. I can't give him the fucking satisfaction.

"Are you okay?" says Peter.

And you know what? I hate when people ask that question when they know damn well what the answer was. If I was okay, I wouldn't feel the need to leave and make a scene doing it. I wouldn't have had to walk away from my father-slash-sperm donor and hide back all these tears that just want to dive out of my tear ducts.

I wouldn't want to punch each and every happy family that shops at the mall looking like a Hallmark card.

"Yes, Peter." I humor him by saying, "I'm perfectly fine." Storming away and looking forward, straight ahead and away from the distractions of the for sale signs and the happy people or cute boys and cute girls. Looking straight ahead, I say, "I shouldn't have said that."

"No, maybe you were right to stay and talk to your dad, Teddy. You didn't know it would work out that way. I mean, you had no idea he would be an asshole and get oral diarrhea." Chasing behind me, Peter's feet are taking long strides to keep up. "It isn't your fault, Teddy."

And I know it all is. What Peter doesn't know is, I think I might have killed my dad, and I won't know until later.

Everything, my dad leaving, my dad's death. My broken family. My fault. All of it.

17

We never went home. That would have been too easy.

Well, okay, we never went to "my" home. Instead, we to Peter's home, or apartment rather. His apartment looks to have been decorated by those people who put together Target ads in the Sunday newspaper. Prints of French movies or advertisements with that forties' flair decorate his walls judiciously. One print per wall. What you smell when you walk in is some kind of winter air freshener that makes me think I'm suddenly hungry for pumpkin pie.

Peter's use of furniture is sparing, but it has potential. I'm glad he got the gay decorating gene. There is only a knee-high table at where I'm guessing the dining area is and the behind a half wall, half partition is where he sleeps, judging by the queen-sized bed that looks more comfortable than anything I've ever slept in.

"Very nice," I say.

The kitchen just so happens to share the same space as the dining area, so Peter only needs to take three steps to drop his bags, grab a glass from the cabinet, and fill it with water.

"How are you?" he says.

"Will you stop asking?" I say. "I was fine when we left. I was fine when we got into your car. I was fine on the way here. And I'm fine now."

And Peter just grins at me. "Good."

Peter rests his glass of water on the counter and grabs my waist. As of yet, we have never, ever touched beyond our hug in the parking lot before Peter almost nearly got shot. His hips are pressed against my hips and I'm thinking about baseball. I'm thinking about women. I'm thinking about how much I don't want to mess this up.

I'm failing at all of this.

"So tell me about yourself," I say. "Where is your family?"

"They live in town," he says. Peter's eyes smile back at me. "I just couldn't wait to get away from them. It's so hard being gay in a Irish Catholic family," he says.

"I know what you mean," I say.

Good, Teddy. Make small talk and hope that he doesn't notice that you have no idea what you're doing here.

"Your sister and mom seem like they understand and accept you. My parents never really did. To this day they tell me that this is just a stage," he laughs. "When I came out, my parents raised hell and wouldn't let me do anything with anyone. If I had any friends, my parents would be concerned that they were gay, too. Maybe they were making me gay." Peter leans in next to me like he's going to tell me a secret, but still speaks out loud, "Nothing beats having to confess you're gay to a priest at the age of fifteen."

"Wow," I say.

"That's not even the worst. My dad made me join the family business of digging graves."

"You're a grave digger?" I ask. "But you work at Owl Foods like all the time."

"I do both to keep track of my money. Make my family happy and afford this dumpy place," says Peter.

"It's not that bad," I say.

"You're too kind," he says and looks at me, leaning forward.

"What are you doing?" I say.

Peter says nothing to answer my question and leans in. His lips touch mine. They quiver and flex against my mouth. When his face pulls away, his hazel eyes open up, and he stares at me. "Sorry," he says. "I've wanted to do that for a while."

And this time, it's me not actually saying anything with my words. I grab the back of his head and pull it closer to mine, his mouth against my mouth. I find his upper lip and I kiss it. At first Peter moans something that sounds more like laughter than pleasure.

"Whoa there, cowboy," he says. "Don't rush anything." Peter takes my hand and leads me to the bed. He sits down and pats the bedspread next to him.

When I sit down, I cross my hands across my lap and stare at him. This isn't going to happen. As much as I want to, this probably isn't going to happen.

I mean, what if it hurts?

Peter grabs my hands with his and puts his fingers between mine, palm to palm. He pulls our hands up and looks me straight into my eyes. Not through me, but into me and he kisses me again. This time, his lips are relaxed and soft and I try everything I can to do what he's doing, but in such a way so he can't figure out that I really haven't done this before.

I flex my lips when he does. Following his lead, I loosen them after he does. I try to keep a rhythm going on because, let's face it, I'm lost. I have no idea what I'm doing.

I have less of an idea about what I'm doing when Peter grabs my chest and pushes me down so that I'm lying on the bedspread.

He climbs on top of me and straddles my waist with his knees. There's a romantic smile on his face, lowering himself down to kiss me again. And this position, it feels unnatural to me since my head is lying flat. I pull myself up to rest my head on a pillow, anything, to keep it upright and not sinking into the mattress.

In an open drawer of the nightstand to my left is a black and shiny object that I've only seen in video games. "You have a gun?" I say.

"It's my dad's," Peter says to me. He grabs my hands and tries to turn my head to face his.

"Why the hell do you have a gun?" I say.

Peter climbs off of me and rests on his elbow. Staring at me, then the gun, then back to me, he says, "Because I think I needed it." Peter takes a long swallow and says, "I wanted to feel safe."

Peter traces the sides of my face and sees the worry in my eyes. His faked smile turns into a frown and he says, "Don't worry, I wasn't going to keep it. I technically have it illegally since I took it from my dad."

"You said he gave it to you," I say.

Peter says, "No I didn't." And whether he did or didn't, I can't tell anymore. The words "accident" and "injury" and "hospital" flash into my mind's eye and I try to shut them out. I can't accidentally will something to happen.

I can't let someone go to the hospital because I'm afraid.

I take the kind of long, relaxing sigh that makes my entire chest rise up and flatten out again. "I'm sorry," I say. I take long breaths, try to calm down. Trying to think happy thoughts, I kiss him one more time. I grab his ears and kiss him on his cheek, his nose, his chin.

"Wait, so it still bothers you?" he says. "The gun?"

I need to stop thinking about it, because I really, really don't want to talk about this. I don't want to get anyone shot. "No, it's fine," I say. "Really."

Putting my hands back to my side, I say, "I think I should go."

Peter grabs my hands and presses them to the bed. Trying to pin me down, he smiles at me, seductive and slow, and says, "To be continued?"

How can you not smile at such a cute sentence?

"I still need to go," I tell him.

And Peter, he grabs my hands and pulls me up off of the bed. Pulling me in closer to him, he says, "To be continued."

My heart isn't sure just how fast to beat, or if I've died and gone to whatever settles as heaven these days, I say, "Definitely."

. . .

I GO STRAIGHT to my bedroom and my sister pokes her head out of her own bedroom. "Teddy?" she says. "Where did you go?"

"Where's Mom?" I shout back at her through my closed door. I swear to God I need a lock on that thing.

"She's at work. I thought you were making dinner," Vanessa says. She knocks on my door and opens it just a crack.

"Well, at least you knocked this time," I say.

Vanessa says, "Where did you go?"

"Doesn't matter," I tell her.

She says, "Is that so?" Vanessa puts her arms across her chest. She says, "And how was it?"

"It wasn't that!" I say. I throw a pillow at her, which just bounces off of her knees because I throw like a total girl.

"Wasn't like what?" Vanessa says.

"Don't," I tell her. "Don't do that." I fall so hard on the bed that it rejects my body and I bounce slightly. "It was just a date," I say. "Besides, a lady never tells."

In her best drunken and burly guy impression, Vanessa says, "You, madam, ain't no lady."

"Seriously, though," I tell her. "Just order a pizza and I'll pay you back."

"What's going on?" she says. She shifts her stance to her left leg, hands across her chest, then on her hips. "What happened today?"

And I don't know if she's talking today today or tonight today. I don't know that she needs to know either part, so I tell her, "Nothing." I roll over on the bed, half smiling, but my knuckles still sore when I make a fist. "Nothing at all."

"Fine," says my sister. She taps me on the shoulder and says, "So where's the money?"

"In my wallet."

Her fingers dig into my back pants pocket and she pulls out my brown leather wallet. "Careful, it was a gift."

"Ya, ya, ya," she says and drops the wallet on the floor. "I'm keeping the change," she says. "Consider it an I'm hungry tax."

18

Google is a wonderful thing. In the little box, I type in the words "reality" and "powers." What I get back is indecipherable. Nothing I want to actually invest more time with, so I type in the word "God."

Of course, millions of results return onto the screen. The blue headlines tell me that God apparently rules this internet, or at least the half that Porn doesn't officially rule over.

I'll admit, my mom never had the conversation with me about God and religion. From my own research, I can figure out that I'm what most people would call 'agnostic' if they knew what the word was. Yes, I can see that there are forces we don't understand out there. Yes, it's pretty impressive that bad things happen to bad people, good things happen to good people, and it's tragic that bad things happen to good people. Yes, I believe that the world seems to run on a clock that was masterfully put together.

Can we know that this is God Himself? Agnostics such as myself, I guess, would suggest that no, we can't.

My problem is, I over-think way too much. What I do is run so many scenarios into my brain and then pop out the results in a muddled mess onto paper. These are my drawings.

I type in the words "real life superheroes". Sure, I wasn't irradiated or bitten by a radioactive insect. I wasn't treated with some special formulate to make me a better athlete or soldier. None of these things fit. I wasn't born from a different set of parents on a faraway planet that exploded. Unless my mom lied to me all these years, but let's be honest, I look too much like my mother, from the hair to her brown eyes, for me to deny being related to them.

What shows up on Google is the bunch of blue links that lead to YouTube videos. They lead to news reports about people in real life trying to good things.

The top search result: Real Life Superheroes. Even the wiki encyclopedia results lead to some vigilantes running around in tights and costumes trying to save real people and help the homeless.

For serial. Not bullshitting you.

I click on the links and look at people in masks with their pictures being taken in the streets. There are kids who are hugging, one arm around the hero's shoulder, smiling for the camera.

This, this is not me.

There is no way I'm going to get into tights. Let's just say I'm not that gay.

But, if I'm not a superhero, then what am I? What do we do with all of this unknown?

I don't know myself.

What I used to hear is that we needed to pray for forgiveness. When people prayed for money, they prayed to God. When we wanted to wish the United States well, politicians and public speakers ask God to bless us. Hell, even rap stars and country singers always thank God for the awards and prizes they win.

The joke always was at school, not even God listened to whoever was popular at the time. Some cutesy blond country star that dated all the young actors, or the boy band group. The ones who all the girls posted in their lockers and stuffed their pictures in their binders. We bet that one of them was gay more than we thought God wanted them to have a Grammy.

But what happens if you can do what God does? What if you can make wishes come true? What if my dreams can come true? What if I am a walking Walt Disney World? What would you like? I can make it happen. Be my guest!

Okay, I'll stop being cheesy. But, for serial, what does this mean for me?

This website here says that we can wish for things into existence. What is marketed as a big secret, is that if you wish for something and somehow work toward it, you can actually achieve it.

That sounds like the bullshit we get fed at school. Try really hard, really want that A and before you know it, you'll ace that test. Imagine yourself doing well, succeeding in the State High Achievement Measurement Test. What a sham.

But what I do, what I think I can do, it seems to be way beyond that.

In a flick of thought, I can turn my dad's tight-lipped secrets into a series of nouns and verbs and explanations for everything. I've made ten thousand dollars for my mom. I can make or break everything.

Or can I?

Time to experiment. Practice makes perfect, right?

I log into B.S. High's webpage and sign into the online grade report website. The school offers everyone passwords and usernames so we can check our grades online. It's a new school wide initiative that the teacher's haven't completely accepted just yet. Sure, it's the twenty-first century, but some of those old bats, well they're still stuck in the last century.

Looking at my grades, I feel pretty good since I'm passing everything. My English grade, however, is the lowest.

Let's practice.

I look at the grade, the capital C in the rectangle. If I close my eyes and concentrate, maybe I can make it a B. Or a B minus.

You know what, fuck it. Let's go for an A.

Closing my eyes, I put my best imagination into effect. I focus, think about an A and the English class. I get that visual imagery in my head, painting the picture the way I do before I start drawing something. I put lines together and fill in blanks.

This box, will be an A when I open my eyes.

Except, it wasn't an A. Instead, it just stared at me, a big black C in the box.

"Stupid, stupid C," I say. "Now change to an A."

I blink, look again, and it's still a C.

"Come on," I say, like it can really hear me. I guess it can't hurt, really, but I hope and pray no one can hear me sounding like an idiot and talking to my computer. "Please?" I say. I click refresh on the browser and wait for the page to load up.

In the box, a letter C.

I refresh again.

Another C sits comfortably in the box. Mocking me. Mocking my powers.

"Come on, you son of a bitch," I say. I refresh again. And again. And again.

I don't even let the page refresh completely. Just resetting and resetting until, finally, counting to five, I open my eyes and blink to make everything crystal clear.

In the box, a refreshing A. The letter A, seriously, now replaced the C.

On the bottom of the page, small black letters say "Last updated 13 November 2015."

That was yesterday.

"Yes!" I say, slapping my desk and howling into the air.

"What the hell is wrong with you?" says my mom through the door. She naturally doesn't bother to knock before she comes into the room. "Have you lost your damn mind?"

I can't not smile at my accomplishment. "No, I'm just excited," I say. I point to the screen and tell my mom, "Look."

My mom is dressed for bed already, baggy sweat pants hang like curtains from her hips and wave in the breeze caused by my mom taking quick, short steps to my computer desk.

"Good job, bud," she says. My mom puts her hands on my head and rattles my hair. "Maybe we can get all A's this quarter. It used to be so easy," she says.

"I think it'll be easy," I say.

"I hope so," she says. "You aren't going to get scholarships with a C average." And my door clicks closed.

"This is so awesome," I announce to no one in particular.

The big secret that everyone says, the things that you pray for and ask God for, they all say that you need to wait it out. The Lord works in mysterious ways, they say. Life needs time for karma to take effect. You need to be patient. Wait your turn.

What I see on my screen, I don't have to wait. I have the fast track to success. My lane is the expressway to luck and fortune.

If I could just figure out why I didn't win millions of dollars instead of a measly ten thousand. Maybe I need to practice. Maybe I need to train, the way those mutants train in that virtual simulation room in my comics.

I don't have a simulated room. And I'm not good at practice. I tried guitar once. Couldn't keep up with it. I got frustrated because I couldn't figure it out. Then it kept breaking and strings broke all the time. I wouldn't even touch the stupid thing. Just come back to find that the strings were curled up and out, metal spider's web strings ready to rip at someone's skin if they got to close. Oh how many scratches I got because I didn't see that stupid E string when I grabbed for it.

But this? This I can practice.

But on what? What could I do?

And at that thought, my sister knocks on my door and sticks her head in. "Hey, Teddy," she says. "I have an idea I want to run by you." She smiles and says, "Can I come in?"

19

M y television's remote control lies snuggled in my sister's ridiculously small hands. The way some people blink when they have Tourette Syndrome or, you know, something in their eyes? That's as fast as my sister changes channels.

"So I was thinking," Vanessa says.

I don't even realize what I'm saying until the words come out of my mouth. "That's dangerous."

"We need to test this thing out," she says. She changes the channel. A group of barely dressed women high step toward the camera in a flashy music video.

"And how do you propose we do that?" I say. I'm trying not to pay attention to the bullshit music and instead stare at my computer tablet.

"How about we push the limits a little bit?" she says. "We can like, make someone do something, or act strange or something."

What my sister doesn't know is that I think I had already done this with my father. What she doesn't know is that I talked to him. Hell, she doesn't even know that we even met today.

"Naw," I say. "Too easy."

Vanessa changes the channel. A chubby man with a big burly

lumberjack beard shouts at us that he's here for a lemon-flavored cleaner.

Vanessa changes the channel. A flashy, Mexican couple kisses each other in an overly dramatic passionate kiss.

"Easy, huh?" says my sister. She looks at me and says, "Make me famous," she says.

"Famous? Famous for what?" I say.

And Vanessa keeps changing the channel as she talks. Her button still pushing the up button on instinct, she says, "I don't know. I could be a famous singer or famous for nothing, like those three Kardashian sisters."

"Well, gee, that shouldn't be that hard," I say. I made the mistake of looking up from the tablet long enough to witness the flashing epileptic fit on my television.

"I'm serious," Vanessa says. She flings the remote control at me and it flies end over end and bounces off of my skull. "Make me famous."

"Fine," I say. "You're famous."

"Wait," she says. "Really?" Vanessa's hands wander around her body as if there is now something physically different about her.
START HERE

I simply smile and shrug. "I don't know," I tell her. "Maybe."

"Wait, doesn't your nose need to bleed or something?" she says. "How do we know it worked?"

"My nose doesn't have to bleed," I tell her. I probably said too much, but let's be honest, she's not the brightest crayon in the box.

Vanessa pauses, turns to look at me. "Wait, what?"

"I said I don't have to bleed for it to work. I think," I say.

"That's so awesome," she says. "What did you do?"

"I ran into some guy, you know, and I made him talk," I say.

"Cool story. So I was thinking, maybe we can make me popular at school, or like a rock star or like something really cool," she says. As the sentence goes on, she gets more and more excited, her voice raises and her hands clap in anticipation. "Like, I don't have to be the prettiest girl, but I could be, like, popular or interesting or something."

"You could be," I say. "But why do you get to be the popular one?"

"I'm like a lab pig or rat or something," she says. Vanessa dismisses her lack of vocabulary with a wave of her hand. "I would like to go first since it was me who found out you can do that stuff."

"I figured maybe I can start small, you know?" I tell her. "I'm not even one hundred percent sure this is going to work."

False. I'm pretty sure this will work, I just don't want Vanessa to get everything she wants without me getting it first.

"Okay," she says. She's so revved up and excited that she bounces on her ass on the wooden floor. Vanessa closes her eyes and covers her face with her hands. "Do your thing."

I don't know what she's expecting when she closes her eyes. To be perfectly honest, I'm not even sure what I'm expecting or what I'm supposed to do.

I guess since this is a formal experiment, I'll try something more formal. I stand up in front of her and hold my hands against her head.

"What the hell are you doing?" she says. "Get your hands off of me."

I shush her and say, "Hush. I need to focus."

I press my hands against the sides of her head, pulsing my fingers against her skin. Flex and let go, over and over again.

"This feels funny," she says. "Are you almost done?"

I shush her down and slap her on her head. Of course, she giggles and breaks my concentration.

In my head, I try to focus. I think about Vanessa walking down the halls of B.S. High. I picture her strutting, swaggering, down the halls, hip-walking as she puts one foot in front of the other. I imagine something the way a model would look walking down our hallways.

In my mind, I see the other boys all walking up to her, talking to Vanessa and trying to grab her hand. I see them trying to get in front of her. They smile and flirt and give her things. I see the lucky bitch walking down the halls and everyone is just so in love with her. Boys want to be with her, girls want to be her.

I watch as my mind sister walks into the office and the secretaries just give her dozens of passes to wherever she wants. I watch as the principal offers her a soda. No, a coffee, and he smiles and gives her a high five.

All of these things I try to imagine and I look at Vanessa. I stare into her head and I concentrate.

What snaps me out of my trance is my sister's screaming and her hands on my, trying to pull them off.

"You're fucking hurting me!" she screams. "What the hell's wrong with you?" My sister slaps my hands off her head and pushes herself backwards with her feet.

"I'm sorry," I say. "I'm sorry."

"Jesus," she says. "I better be really popular for that shit." Vanessa is rubbing her head on both sides. "Why did you hurt me?" she says.

"I don't know. I just started concentrating on what I wanted to happen," I say. Sitting back on my heels, I say, "I think I got carried away."

"So did you do it?" says my sister. She presses her hands hard against her head, rubbing in circles. "Did it work?" she says.

I shrug. Truth is, I have no idea what I did. To be honest, I don't know if anything works unless I see blood. "To tell you the truth," I tell her, "I don't know what I'm doing."

Vanessa stands up and rests her hands on my shoulder. She looks deep into my eyes, hypnotist style, and says, "Yes, you do." She stares into my eyes again, not blinking, saying, "I believe in you." In a calm and steady voice, she says, "I believe in you."

The problem is, I don't know that I believe in myself.

They—life coaches and public speakers—say that you can become anything you want, all you have to do is believe. They say that you can speak things into existence that all you have to do is believe and want it bad enough, and good things will happen to you.

There is also the belief that worrying about bad things that happen to you will also make bad things happen to you. By worrying and thinking about it, you put energy into its existence. You will it to come to you because you gave it your energy to survive.

This leads to way too many questions. Can I just think of something and make it happen? Do I have to focus, make it be exactly as I see it in my mind in order to achieve it?

Can I make my sister famous?

The research that I've done, they all suggest just a few things.

Did you know that the Bible argues that you can just speak things into existence? Apparently God just said, "Let there be light," and boom! There it was. There are authors that say you can go and do anything you want as long as you think about it first. I remember my mom looking into those "secret" books and hoping to find the way to a million dollars.

Let's just say, I think I actually have the key now. By accident, of course.

Now, I don't know if this is what happened when I was born. I don't know if she saw that I was dead and really, really wanted a living child. I don't know if this need made her wish me to life and make me start crying. I don't know if she decided that she would not have to go through that pain. I don't even know if it was conscious or subconscious.

I could always ask, I guess, but I doubt she'll know the answer.

In this very moment, as my sister stares at me, I'm unsure of what has worked or how it's supposed to work. I listen for the phone to ring, to see if anyone is calling my sister's phone off the hook.

Nothing. Silence.

"Teddy," says my sister, and I put my finger against her lips to shush her down.

"I'm listening," I whisper.

And Vanessa, her eyes go around the room, quiet and slow, looking at the different corners. She puts her hands against her ears, cupping them, and looks off into the corner of the room. "What are we listening for?" she whispers back.

"We're listening for the phone to ring, or people to come knock on the door," I say. "I want to see if it worked."

"Does it really work that simple?" says my sister. And the truth is, I don't know. I am not sure how to answer that question because, just earlier today, I had my dad rambling like an auctioneer, and that was instantaneous.

Is it working now? Couldn't tell ya. When will I know? Couldn't tell ya that, either.

I shrug and my sister stands up on her feet and stares at me. She has to stare at me looking down, now, because she's hit a growth spurt that I haven't yet. Only about a year younger than me, and she can nearly tower over me.

I'm not okay with that.

Not that it's had not had its negative effects either. My sister, well, she's a bit lanky in the knees and arms and wrists. She's the type of skinny that will get either really, really fat or is going to have to introduce herself as "No, I'm not anorexic."

Judging by my mom, I'm going to go with really, really fat.

"So," I tell her. "I think we wait."

Vanessa crosses her arms and stares at me or through me, I can't tell, and she smiles. "Okay," she says. "But tomorrow I better be popular."

It's nothing you can really be prepared for, messing with reality. I mean, when I woke up this morning, I didn't think I'd have to fight through a crowd of seniors to get to my sister. I had no idea that I'd be trying to figure out which one was her in the classroom.

Standing in the hallway right now, at least ten different women at their lockers look just like my sister. No kidding.

How or why some of these girls decided to tease their blonde hair and fix it in the same cut: slightly over the shoulder, parted on the side and just pushed past the ears on both sides. Vanessa's hair is one of the few things I've loved about her.

Now, I can barely tell who my sister is. These bitches, they all want a piece of my sister. I'm tempted to just throw her to the wolves and see if she can make it out alive, but that would be too mean, even for me.

"Vanessa!" I scream into the hallways. Every boy stops in their tracks and the girls slam their lockers, hair and earrings flapping back and forth as like there was a Justin Bieber spotting.

Up shoots a hand from the center of the hallway, closer to where the real Vanessa's locker is.

"Will the real Vanessa Barratt please stand up?" I say when I get to the locker. I'm backed up completely against the locker to make way for the crowd of lemmings, hormones, and assholes.

"Oh. Em. Jee," says my sister. She closes her locker and the smile on her face is the biggest I've ever seen on anyone anywhere. Sort of the way you look when your cheeks get pulled back to your ears.

"I think it worked," I say, looking around. Mentally, I count the different girls that all seem to be wearing Vanessa's trademark "style". If you want to call it that. Different variations strut up and down the hallway. This girl, Caitlyn, is normally a preppy goth type. She could be really pretty if she'd just stop being so independent and against everyone.

The phrase "I want to be an individual, just like everybody else" seems so apropos right now.

Caitlyn struts in her black leather ankle-high boots to Vanessa's locker and says, "Hi." She raises her hand up to her face and waves with her fingers the way a two-year-old waves to his mommy. "So, I've seen you around a lot and I'm wondering if you'd like to sit with us at lunch." Caitlyn looks at me and her face turns sour. The red lipstick on her teeth bears through her grimace and she says, "Excuse me."

"Um, okay," I say but Vanessa grabs my arm. Struggling against her hand that is gripping my elbow tight, Vanessa's looks and raised eyebrows tell me that I'm supposed to stay right here.

"You were saying," Vanessa tells Caitlyn.

"You should sit with us. You know, come hang out." Caitlyn looks happy and optimistic. When I was little, I used to build huge cities and skyscrapers out of plastic building blocks and then destroy them with my feet and military toys. I imagine that kind of destruction is about to befall Caitlyn's pride.

"Sure," says Vanessa. "Why not?"

All this time, I had thought that Vanessa was stupid and retarded. Turns out she's just crazy as hell.

"Vanessa," I say, fake and charming. "I thought we had something we needed to discuss over lunch," I say.

"Like what?" she says.

"Like?" I say and search everything in my head about what I could say or should say. "Like about yesterday and today and what we did today and how it's working out."

And Vanessa grabs my cheeks and pulls me in for a quick kiss on my nose. "It's working out perfectly!" she says. "Thanks for asking."

And I say in my best cute voice I have, "But 'Nessa, I need to talk to you."

And Vanessa echoes back the same tone of voice, "Teddy, I mean, it's not like I won't see you later. We'll talk at home, okay?" And she rubs my head like I'm a dog.

This bitch.

At lunch, I'm left sitting at the table by myself. Around me, people are eating and talking and laughing with their friends. Vanessa, well, the whole school is now her friend. She used to be the psychopathic bitch that protected me whenever I needed it. At her new table with Caitlyn and her new friends, she eats her new food and talks about her new boys and her new everything while I'm left the old Teddy. Mean, stupid, old Teddy.

I eat my ham sandwich with extra mayo and watch as my sister enjoys the spoils of my powers. Everything that is happening now is my fault, and I think to myself, I made you, I can break you.

Tonight, that's what I'll do. It's not fair that she can be whatever she wants and I'm stuck doing the dirty work.

That bitch. That lying, conniving bitch.

Looking around the room from my corner of the cafeteria, the center of the world is all on her. My product test dummy.

There has to be a silver lining here somewhere.

I look over the crowd and envision myself as the center of attention. I can do this, too. Why can't there be a power pair, super siblings?

It'd be perfect, I just know it. She'd get the straight boys, I'd get the gay boys. She'd have lots of female friends, and I'd have the really cool girl friends, but not those friends who only want me as a friend because I'm gay, because that's apparently what's "in" at high school these days.

I can do this. I know I can.

But first, before I experiment on myself, I need another test subject. Grabbing my pencil, I go outside into the flashbulb bright sun. The force of freezing air blowing through the rusty metal vents in the cafeteria finally stops freezer burning my skin. Outside I can finally be warm. My bare forearms feel the way it must feel to be a defrosting turkey on Thanksgiving. The perfect place has lots of hiding places and almost no worries about someone spotting me.

I can't just flaunt my abilities all over the place.

The number two pencil turns from yellow-orange to dark blue, then back to bright school bus yellow, then blood red, then purple. The way Christmas lights flash from one color to the next, that's what this pencil does right now. Without the flash and glowing lights.

Just so you know, just the paint on the outside changes to these colors, not the whole wooden thing. Music—that teeny bopper Top 40 bee-ess—sprays from the loud speaker in the courtyard as the rest of the student monkeys sit down to eat, cuddle with their high school sweethearts, and ignore the little people of their pathetic pitiful planet.

These are the best times of our lives, they say. Being a teenager. Like being thirteen-years-old flips an on switch that magically grants everyone five years of good ol' American fun and carefree living. For what it's worth, they're totally lying to you.

What they meant to say to you was that teenagers are supposed to be rebellious because the rest of the world is full of itself. Go out there, date people. Have fun. Make life-long. Be those fake models in the yearbook poster who smile and hold their friends' shoulders and have perfect white teeth and look better than anyone really should.

Every time my eyes close, this pencil, it turns to a different color of the rainbow. Blue. Purple. Red.

At the table over, a group of nerds sit and talk about the latest video games. Something about moving blocks and destroying the other team's fort. Now, it's not living until it's done on a high definition screen with a controller in your hand.

Orange.

Yellow.

They scream at each other about who has the better team, and one person—Courtney, his name might be—gets up, slamming his hands on the table. Courtney leaves his booing friends, shouting back at them, "Screw you guys!"

The pencil morphs into cyan, then brown.

As he walks past the table, the scent of heavily salted fries and sweet ketchup follows his path. I'm almost a little bit hungry. Words leave the angry nerd's mouth, and none of them are too nice. The difference between high school and the real world? In high school, everyone cusses like a sailor with a paper cut.

Those computer nerds and video game geeks? They'll be best friends again tomorrow because they have to be. No one else will accept them here. The crowds regard them as human calculators and dictionaries and encyclopedias. These smart kids that will do the work as long as you stroke their egos. Give them a little compliment about how smart you are and how cool you really are, then ignore you the next time you say hi when you sit next to them in American history class.

I'm not angry, by the way.

The pencil turns black, then stop sign red.

No one else can see the pencil that sits at my round lunch table because my shoulders hunch over it, hiding it from plain view. My own personal treasure—my precious—and my personal secret.

I life my hand over the pencil and let it hover, the same way Uncle Barney does right before he saws a woman in half in his stage shows.

It adds to the mystique and distracts from the rest of what really creeps behind the scenes.

Take high school, for example. Shielding you from the real world and protecting you from the harshness of reality. In high school, the biggest threats are your teachers and your classmates. In the real world, the biggest threats are your dad leaving you and your mom not having enough money to buy you an Xbox. Again, more smoke and mirrors. More complete and utter crap.

My hand creeps downwards until the palm lies just above the pencil. My eyesight blurs and I pull my hand upwards, slowly and deliberately. I pull up and imagine invisible threads connected to the pencil connected to my hand. As I pull up, the pencil pulls me back down, but I tug harder.

Up, you damn pencil. Up!

The strain on my eyes pulls the lids shut and my hand twitches, radiating heat. My furnace of a hand, I keep it still and wait for the damned pencil to move upwards, but it just mocks me. That damned red piece of crap lies still, right where I put it.

When I open my eyes, the tabletop gets closer and closer until it slams into my nose and forehead. The back of my head turns cold as the hand that pushed me leaves with its owner. And I don't even have to look or listen for his voice to know it was Shane.

"Whoops, sorry, bro!" he says. His buddies, Brian and Andrew, they laugh with him and disappear into the crowds.

I don't know what hurts more, my nose or my pride.

Oh who am I kidding? It's my nose, which feels swollen and numb the way you feel when you just had a hot date with a stove burner. What's left of my pride? It fades with the pencil's color.

It turns from red to a green that reminds me of McDonald's Shamrock Shakes.

I blink and the Shamrock Shake green morphs to charcoal gray morphs to sky blue morphs to the maroon of Peter's vest at work.

And I smile and check my nose for blood. My face, bathwater warm, feels as if it could have been releasing droplets of blood and I wouldn't know. My fingers are still pale white, which means no blood and I'm a ghost-white, tanless freak.

In high school, you can be in nearly any clique, and that's a good thing. You belong somewhere and you can be missed when you don't show up to school for your birthday.

Over there, for instance. The girls sit around the table with empty trays except for a salad that they eat at a snail's pace. None of them want to look fat, so they eat slowly. But none of them want to be thought of as anorexic, so they have some food on their trays.

In college, no one will care. You won't see your best friends all the time, and their opinions will mean less than what they are worth now, right here at B.S. High. More smoke and mirrors. More abracadabra. More alakazam.

Except for this fucking pencil, which still refuses to fucking levitate. I raise my hand over the pencil once again, that mocking, mutinous bastard, and imagine the invisible threads. I play out the situation in my mind: I pull up gradually, and the pencil begins to stand in its tip. I replay it and open my eyes. Still nothing.

I replay it again. This time, my mind pencil twirls on its eraser.

My opened eyes reveal a pencil still on its fucking side, sitting still.

Again. The pencil on its tip.

Opening my eyes, nothing except blood droplets on the green metal tabletop.

I close my eyes again, pull them tight together. The mind pencil lifts up, stands on its side, and twirls around again.

I open my eyes and reality stares me in the face. The pencil ignores me completely.

Dead. Still. Ignoring me completely.

Stupid, stupid, stupid, stupid pencil. Stupid pencil!

I clench my fist in anger, to sight my nails dig into the fleshy edges of my palm and the snapping sound of my pencil breaking into three pieces grabs my attention.

Great. More broken things.

20

F riday seems as good a day as any to be suddenly and magically popular. My mirror-self stares at my real self, deep. Dark. My eyes dilate as I move closer to the mirror.

"You can do this, Teddy. You know you can," I tell him. To my mirror self, I say, "You can be popular. You can be cool. You can be fun and sexy. You can be everything you want to be."

A knock on the door makes me jump up a few inches into the air. "Teddy, who are you talking to?" says my mom through the door.

"No one," I tell her. "Just talking to myself."

"You're such a weird boy," she says and I smile to myself. At least she has a sense of humor about it all.

I close my eyes and play my make believe game, the same one I used with Vanessa. My mind self walks down the hallways of the school, popular and cool. For some reason, I imagine it all in slow motion. People follow, their clothes flapping slowly against their body. Girls' hair waves in the non-existent wind to give the illusion of more motion.

"This is ridiculous," I say to my mind self. "Focus."

I close my eyes again, tightening them so hard I see white and dark red streaks across my eyes. I squeeze tighter and say to the universe or whoever the hell is listening, "I can be popular. I want to be popular. I will be popular. I want to be fun. I want to be sexy. I want to be wanted."

I squeeze harder and focus. My mind's eye goes blank and black and white in waves. My head hurts from the strain and I open my eyes again. Red drips from the nose of Mirror Teddy.

I rip three squares of toilet paper from the rolls and shove it up my nose.

"Ya, that's attractive," I say. The bit of tissue that hangs from my nose over my mouth flutters in my breath like a cartoon mustache. "Dammit," I say.

Why I'm bleeding, I couldn't tell you.

It doesn't happen very often, but my mom always thought it was dry air, or maybe a sinus infection. When I was in elementary school all the time, I practically had a standing appointment with the family doctor. Each time, Dr. Springer told my mom that everything was okay and, if the good doctor felt like entertaining my mom, she would write my mom a prescription for some kind of antibiotics. "Take this and he'll be fine," Dr. Springer would say, adding, "And be sure to finish the whole prescription."

Within a few months, I was right back there.

My parents left it at that when the doctor denied our claim that it was a sinus infection. "It's impossible," the doctor told my mom, "that anyone could possibly get that many sinus infections without something being seriously wrong."

That was then. This is now, and I'm still exhibiting the same patterns. Bleedings and headaches.

Except this time, I think I make myself bleed. I make myself bleed by making something happen.

If I can be rich and famous, I can suffer through a little nosebleed now and then.

I cross my fingers and look at my mirror self. "Teddy, you sexy stud, you're amazing."

When I step outside into the upstairs hallway, I am not sure what to expect. Maybe for the world to be magically at my feet.

Instead, I get my mom shouting to me, "Teddy! Get out of the damn bathroom! You're going to be late."

I go downstairs and notice the significant lack of my sister anywhere. "Where's Vanessa?" I ask.

My mom hands me my blue vinyl and plastic lunch bag and says, "She was already picked up by a few boys." My mom sighs. "Please tell me you know those boys."

I lie. "Sure, they're okay," I say. The car is still in the carport. "Mom, I'm taking the car."

"Sure, honey, whatever," she says. .

"Do you have the day off?" I say.

"Yes, sort of," she says. "I took the day off. I can afford it," she says, meaning the ten thousand dollars that I won us, thank you very much.

"Awesome," I say. "Well, enjoy!" I'm too eager to test all of this out, so I grab the keys and leave. The door slams as my mom tells me that she loves me and to be careful.

I am guided by a force greater than luck. I am luck. Hell, Luck is now my bitch.

At school, there is the perfect parking spot near the back of the parking lot, away from the school and the jams that happen when too many teenagers try to leave all at once. Getting out of the car, I pull my backpack over my shoulder and take a long breath. My backpack is nearly empty, but I'm shaky. I didn't eat at all before I left because I am not convinced that I'd be able to keep it down.

Here goes nothing.

It's only about ten minutes before the bell rings and as I walk through the hallways, nearly everyone gets out of my way.

Instead of being up against the lockers, everyone seems to be moving. For me.

Instead of moving me.

It's already awesome.

For my first couple of classes, I pull my books and shove them in my backpack. I'm not even really paying attention to the books or the bag. I'm putting as many books as I think I might need. Who cares which one.

"I don't think this worked," I say.

And a body thuds against my locker and says, "What didn't work?" Allan's blue eyes stare over my locker door.

"Nothing," I say. "How's the club?"

I close the door and throw my backpack over my shoulder.

"Good," he says. "We missed you coming."

"Did you have more meetings?" I say and I'm not going anywhere in particular.

"We meet every lunch period, but our official meetings are at Tuesdays' lunch," he says. He grabs my backpack and pulls me backwards. "Promise you'll come?" Allan's voice almost lisps when he says "promise". I smile and nod back at him.

"Sure, I'll come," I say.

"Good," he says. "We really think you can add a lot to the club."

"I, uh, gotta go," and turn away and walk down the hall.

"We'll, uh, see you later!" Allan shouts behind me.

And walking down the hallway, it's like I have new sets of eyes. I see the boys and the girls and all of them are smiling at me. I check my nose for blood or boogers. Clean.

I pat my shoulders and check to see if maybe there's dandruff or something.

"Teddy!" shouts a person I don't recognize. I wave because it seems like the right thing to do to a perfect stranger. And this is like the chain reaction that gets the whole day started. Everyone says hi and waves.

And my sister? She's nowhere to be found. Disappeared down the halls and right now, I don't give a shit.

In math class, I'm walking up and down the halls without anyone asking for my passes. The Mr. Proctor let me go without asking a single question. In history class, I don't have to answer a damn question. I didn't do the homework and the teacher let me go to study hall to finish it all up.

I'm untouchable, and it just feels so nice.

At lunch, I can't not be recognized, sitting by myself in the corner tables and alone from everyone else. Watching the crowd, everyone waves back and asks how I'm doing. I wave back, nod, and say, "Hi! Good to see you" like the total cheese ball I am.

It's when the bell rings at the end of lunch that I request a pass to go to the office. "Has my sister shown up to school?" I ask the attendance clerk. Normally a bitch in a dyed red wig, today she's a pussycat and more helpful than ever.

"Yes, she has," she says. "Your sister is in the health office," she says. I don't have to ask for the pass to the nurse before she hands it to me and directs me to walk down the hall. "I'll let your next class know where you are."

I walk to the office and take a step forward to see Vanessa's black and sequined high heels sticking out of the doorway.

"Oh my god, Vanessa!" I shout and bypass all the signage that tells me I'm supposed to stay away. "Vanessa! Are you okay?"

And there she is, crying, her mascara melting down her face in black streams. "Hi, Teddy," she says.

"What happened?" I say and the nurse, she looks at me and tells me to get out.

"It's my brother," Vanessa says and grabs my hand. "I want him to stay."

"Why didn't you come get me?" I ask. "I've been worried sick."

"I thought I could handle it," she says.

"Handle what?" I look up from my conversation to the nurse, who's on the phone with a serious conversation.

The nurse looks at me and sighs, then says, "Yes, I'll hold."

Vanessa grabs my hands and looks at me with her big watery raccoon eyes. She says, "Promise me you won't get mad."

"Why would I get mad?" I ask. "What happened?" I hold my breath, count to three and let it go. "If you just tell me what happened, I won't have anything to be mad about."

Vanessa looks at me and then down at her feet. She blinks a few times, then takes a long pause before she says, "The guys that picked me up, and it was Shane and his friends."

Already my stomach grumbles and I could already finish the sentence before Vanessa does.

"I think they tried to rape me before we got to school," she says. Vanessa cries, hard and deep sobs pour out of her. She cries so hard her shoulders clench up behind her and she grabs my leg and pulls me in. Sitting down, her face buried into my leg where my pants pocket is, she says, "Please don't tell Mom." She sniffs and says, "Please don't say anything."

"I don't know that I can do that," I say and the nurse puts her mouth to her lips to quiet us down.

"Promise," she says.

I take a deep breath before I say, "Mom will never know." I pat her head and say, "You just relax. Are they going to send you home?"

"I think they're calling the cops," Vanessa says, and she looks back at the nurse. "I don't want anyone to know."

I shush my sister and go back to the nurse. "We don't want anyone to really know," I tell her. "I think we should just let her go home," I say. "I'll take her home."

The nurse covers the phone receiver with her hand and says, "We have to call, it's the law."

"I don't think we need to worry about it," I tell her again. My forehead tenses up and something like cold lightning travels down my forehead, into my eyes, and through my fingers. "We are going to go, and no cops will be called."

And the nurse, she puts the phone down and says, "I'll give you a pass and let the attendance clerk know," she says. "You should probably take your sister home."

"Thank you," I say. I look back at my sister and she looks at me, unblinking and mouth opened in shock. "We're leaving," I say.

IT TAKES all of a few sentences for me and Vanessa to leave without anyone stopping us. I wonder, really, how easy it would be to just walk out the front door on any other day, powers or not.

"What did you do?" my sister says. She looks at herself in the mirror in the visor, making tiny circles around her eyes with a wipe from her purse. "Did you do your thing?" she says. She pretends to hold up a watch and swing it in midair in front of me.

I put her hand down and say, "I didn't hypnotize her," At least I don't think so.

"Well, whatever you did, thank you," Vanessa says. For the first time since I saw her in the health office, Vanessa sits back and relaxes and looks somewhat refreshed. "I don't want to go home," she says.

"We don't have to," I tell her. Instead of going home, I take the road that leads to Owl Foods.

"We going to visit your boyfriend?" she says.

Inside, we divide and conquer the area. Coming together at the milk freezers, I look around and notice that Peter isn't here at all.

A tube of ranch-flavored potato chips hangs in the grip of Vanessa's grip. "Where is he?" she says. Taking the potato chips from her grip, I put it back on the shelf.

"We're not really here to shop," I say.

"But I didn't get a chance to eat," she says.

I empty out my pocket and show her my empty pockets. "No money."

"Come on," says Vanessa. "You mean you can do all of this fancy stuff, but you can't even conjure up some money so we can eat?"

And I know she's had a rough day and all, almost being raped, but I want to put my fist in her face so hard right now.

"No, I can't." I look around and grab the chips. "You know, I'm not even sure I like using these powers," I say. "It's like a cheat code for a video game."

Vanessa laughs. "You have a cheat code for life?" she says.

"Sort of."

"Awesome, little bro," she says. "Can I still get the chips?"

Digging into my pocket, I manage to pull out a dollar bill, crumpled up and folded like it was pressed while in the wash. "Huh," I say. "Look at that."

It's easy to see how much you hate a specific flavor of something when it's wrapped up in a pretty little package. In this case, it's a package of bright blue and green onions decorating the box. Looking at the package, I say, "Do you know how many calories are in here?"

Vanessa takes the package. "If you're just going to make me feel bad for eating these, you don't get anymore." Vanessa pops the top of the can and just tips the can into her mouth. Her mouth floods with potato crumbs and pieces that are way too big for her mouth.

"Why did you want to be popular?" I ask. We're sitting in the car in the parking lot. The apartment is less than a mile away, but not one of us really want to go home. "Aren't you popular enough?"

"I don't think I'm popular enough," she says. Staring out into the crowd of people pushing cards and carrying plastic bags, she says, "I don't think I'm popular at all."

"You are known by so many people," I tell her. "You can go down any hallway at school and everyone knows you. Even the teachers say hi to you."

"They only know me because I get in trouble a lot," she says. She turns her head to me. "That's because I'm mostly getting in trouble because of you."

"No you are not, stop lying."

"How am I lying?" says Vanessa. She sits up, a sign that this conversation is getting serious. "Every time you get in trouble, who comes to your rescue?"

"I never ask you to come to my rescue," I say. "I never ask you for shit."

"You don't have to," she says. "That's what we are for. Sisters, big and small, we're for kicking the asses of anyone who messes with our big brothers."

"You have got to be the only girl who has to do that for her big brother," I say and she laughs because it's true and tragic. "I was meaning to ask you," I say. "What's it like being the brother of the little weird kid?"

"What are you talking about?" she says.

"Don't pretend."

"Fine," she says. "It's okay, I guess. I mean, it's not easy knowing that someone might say something. I listen out to everyone. I want you to be okay and safe." She sighs. "If anything happened to you, it would break Mom's heart."

"God, I know," I say. "It sucks."

Vanessa laughs. I laugh. "Pass the damned chips," I say, "and I'll tell you a secret."

Vanessa holds out at me, teases me with the tube and then pulls back, saying, "Tell me the secret and I'll give you the chips."

I grab the chips from her hand and leave the clear plastic lid on my lap. "I made myself popular, too."

Vanessa says, "You what?" After I nod in affirmation, she says, "Shut the front door!"

"I want to be popular, too," I say. "I want to know what it's like."

Vanessa sits back and looks up and out of the car, toward the top of the windshield. "It's pretty cool, isn't it?" she says.

"I wouldn't know," I tell her. "I didn't get to stay at school very long." I grab her leg as soon as I realize how that sounded. "Don't you worry, though," I say. "It's okay. I'll just get to experience it again tomorrow, too."

"Can you imagine the both of us ruling that school?" she says. Vanessa grabs my hand with hers and clenches tightly. "It'd be so fucking cool."

"How awkward would it be for both of us to be Prom King and Queen?" I say.

Vanessa laughs. "You'd make a beautiful queen, your highness."

21

It normally takes a lot to make my mom speechless. Today, all it took was the question: "Vanessa and I were invited to a party by some friends. Can we go?"

I think it felt just as weird to say it as it was to hear it. I went through all of my clothes, trying everything on before I settled on a basic white button down shirt with a blue flower that blooms along the side. It was dressy without being too fancy. The type of look that said, "I know how to dress and yes, I'm gay" without being, "It's Teddy, bitch!"

My sister decided on something a little more seductive. What she was really doing was trying to hide in plain sight. We drove home and waited for Mom to get home that afternoon. No one mentioned anything. Vanessa took a shower and washed her face. She removed all of her makeup, exfoliated and then put on fresh makeup so she could keep up appearances.

Now, she wants to leave the house barely dressed in real clothes. Hiding in plain sight. Maybe if she doesn't talk about it, and does the complete opposite, my sister can avoid talking about almost being raped. She cannot talk about being threatened and able to hold her own by dressing like a common whore.

That's my sister for you.

Against my judgment and advice, she still went to the party dressed in a blue miniskirt and a bright pink, baby doll T. Cute? Yes. Uncalled for? Probably.

At the party, we arrived, and it was like the doors had opened up for the first time. It was us being greeted by everyone, and my sister looking around like a paranoid meerkat. When it came time for the basketball team to do its rounds from one corner of the party to the next, Vanessa's body shut itself down, pulled in. A turtle into its imaginary shell.

"Should we go?" I say, nudging my sister's elbow. "You haven't spoken to anyone since we got here."

"No," she says. She waves her hand up into the air and tries to laugh it off. "No, no, no." She crosses her hands across her chest, then puts them on her hips, then just leaves them to her side. She's over thinking this whole thing. "I'm good. We're having fun!" she says. "Want a drink?" she says and leaves before she can get an answer.

And there I am, Teddy, just standing there alone in a party that I got invited to by proxy.

The house is something you see on the richer side of the neighborhood. All of the houses are recreations of old colonial style houses. This one has a bit of a Southern mansion twist, making the inside of the house look a lot bigger than the outside.

Out back by the pool, groups of teenagers circle around and drink by lamplight. The tiki torches add an island flavor that is completely out of sync with the pine and palm trees just outside of the fence. The afternoon, soon to be nighttime, winds are picking up and I wish I had worn something underneath this shirt.

Where my sister actually went, I couldn't tell you, but I wander around the house, looking at the people in groups and everyone waving and saying, "Hi." As I travel from room to room, I watch the people gather together and laugh. No longer laughing at me. My mom used to tell me this saying when I was younger, "Laugh and the world laughs with you. Cry and you cry alone."

Right now, it feels like the opposite is true.

And as much as I might be popular right now, you wouldn't be able to tell.

When I go to the kitchen to find my sister, I see her leaning against the kitchen's island, two drinks in hand and talking to some random guy that I don't remember. I don't think he goes to our school.

"Can I take that?" I say. I grab a drink from my sister's grip and sip and watch as this moron tries to flirt with my sister.

The tool has big ears that stick out of each side. The way he stands, his shoulders droop the way a gorilla's would if he wasn't dragging is knuckles on the floor. The shirt that barely covers his flat chest has the Nike logo on it and his shorts suggest that he just never wears pants. And while I like my sister, I know for a fact that she can do better than this.

"Come on," I tell my sister. "We should go socialize."

"What do you think I'm doing here," she says. "Todd, this is Teddy. Teddy, Todd." The tool puts his hands out and says something to the extent of "nice to meet you" but all I notice are his lips moving and his body shifting back and forth as he talks.

It's Californian surfer meets would-be jock.

"Oh, hell no," I say. "We need to go."

"We do not need to go anywhere," says my sister. She pulls my hands off of her elbow. "You can go." Vanessa looks at Todd the tool. "I'm having fun right where I am."

"Fine," I say. Storming off in my own little hissy fit, I say, "Whatever."

It's when I'm sitting on the arm of a pretty nice leather armchair that I realize that my powers didn't really work the way I wanted. I mean, I'm not famous. I'm not hated, but I'm not really liked either.

Looking around, the other kids will wave to me if I say "Hi" or try to acknowledge them. But they hardly go out of their way to make me feel special. I did say I wanted to be popular. I wanted to be famous. I wanted to be liked and loved. I wanted to be sexy.

Why can't I just be sexy and cool and fun?

It's here, sitting on the armchair, that I notice that I may not really be necessary. I've failed at this, too.

I can change the color of a pencil. I can make my sister liked by everyone.

I cannot change me.

I can change the world, but I cannot change me.

To my left, a girl flips her hair and smile and laughs at something that probably wasn't funny to begin with because it wasn't me.

"Hi," says a woman's voice beside me. I look over and it's yet another girl who doesn't seem to look familiar. Nearly a thousand different high school students, and I've yet to meet all of them just yet.

"Hi," I say. I take the cup to my lips and pretend to drink. I have no idea what's in it, but it smells sweet and syrupy and spicy. I'm guessing rum or soda or a combination of the two. With the cup at my mouth as a distraction, I measure out the girl. Boots cover her feet, which lead to long skinny jeans that lead to a foresty green shirt that leads to brown hair, loose, hanging over her shoulders.

"You're cute," she says and puts her hands on my wrist.

"Thanks," I say. I lie and tell her, "So are you."

"Where are you from?" she says.

Like she doesn't already know the answer, and I mean, she has to have heard about me, I tell her, "From Japan."

"Where's that?" she says. The girl takes the cup from my hand and drinks from it. There are no trashcans or sinks for me to hang my stuff around. No place for me to dump this out if she gives it back to me. Swallowing what had to have been half of the drink, she says, "I'm Sara. Without an H."

"I'm Aaron, with two A's," I say. If she's going to be stupid, so am I.

Sara offers her drink back to me, but I hold up my hand in protest. "No, really. You can have it."

"Thank you!" she says and finishes the rest of what was probably watered down alcohol. She drops the plastic cup on the floor and takes my hand. "You're really, really cute," she says.

I don't dignify it with a reaction. Looking around the room, it's a pretty predictably party. Sure it's my only party I've been to, at least the only one that was completely populated by teenagers, but looks like everything I've seen in the movies. Maybe even more boring.

"Come on," says Sara. She grabs my hand and pulls me to the glass door that leads outside, then into the garden area and then into the darkened corner of the backyard. As completely obvious as possible, she grabs my hands and rests them on her boobs. "Feel these," she says. Her hands grabbing mine, she squeezes and lets out a moan that just can't be real. "Kiss me," she says.

"I have a boyfriend," I tell her.

It was a gut reaction, serious. I don't know why I said it. Really.

"No I don't," she says. This drunk bitch.

She squeezes my hands, which squeezes her tits and I'm just not enjoying this. No reaction downstairs and absolutely no reaction on my face.

"I need to go," I say. "Look, you're pretty and all, but this isn't where I want to do this."

If you can't beat them, join them? Isn't that the saying?

"I get it," she says. Sara-Without-An-H says, "How about we leave this place?"

"Sure," I tell her. I put my hands on her shoulder and push her back a few steps, up against the wooden fence. "I'll be right back. Just going to the bathroom."

She starts to laugh and says, "I'll be right here!" She puts her finger to her mouth says, "Secret's safe with me."

I'm convinced she doesn't even know what the hell she's talking about.

In the kitchen, Vanessa is still leaning up against the island, holding another full red plastic cup of something else.

"Nessa, we need to go," I tell her. "I'm tired."

Vanessa shrugs me off.

"Vanessa, I'm not kidding," I say.

Todd steps up between me and my sister and says, "Dude, we got a problem?"

"I'm her brother, back the hell off." Grabbing her shirt, I tell

Vanessa, "Let's go."

And Vanessa pulls away from me, and her words slide out of her mouth, slurred. She says, "You can go home." Dropping the keys on the floor, she says, "I'll get a ride home."

"What happened the last time you got a ride from a guy?" I tell her. And suddenly, Vanessa's face goes sour. If looks could kill, I would have died a horrific, bloody death only to be resurrected and killed again. And again. And again. "I'm sorry." I say. I hold my hands up between us because I'm legitimately afraid that she'll hit me. "I'm sorry. That was too far."

"Fuck you," she says and storms out.

"Babe!" shouts Todd the Tool. "You forgot your keys!" he says, and he kicks them to the wall. "Go fetch them, dork," he says to me and laughs.

"I really wish you'd be fucking quiet for one damned second," I tell him and walk away. I try to put all of my thoughts together, thinking about where Vanessa went and just how much time it'll take for me to get out there and find her. The crowd is thicker than normal, everyone coming inside because it's too cool outside. The nighttime wind has picked up and the kids who aren't wearing sweaters or jackets come inside and huddle together, still in their respective groups. Still excluding me. Still trying to get into each other's pants.

"Vanessa!" I call out into the cold, dead air. Out front, you'd never know there was a party going on. Out in the yard, the sky has turned a dark blue, midnight blue, and lonely clouds wander across the sky, lit by the half-moon crescent that stares at me like God's unforgiving eye.

Yes, yes, I know. I pissed off my sister and made her storm out.

"Vanessa!" I shout out into the air. "Where are you?"

"Are you fucking stupid?" she calls back to me. "Over here!"

And of course, she's exactly where I figured she would not be. Because I really thought she'd be irrational and a typical woman, I had least expected her to be next to the car. "Did you get the keys?" she calls back to me?

In the car, we're listening to the radio and saying nothing. I don't know if I could or should apologize to her again. I want to say sorry for everything, but secretly, I know I meant it. I know she needed to hear it because deep down inside, I think I made her get raped.

"Vanessa," I say, looking straight ahead and trying to concentrate on the suburban streets. Apparently, the housing associations or the county doesn't believe in street lights or safety. Vanessa is silent, staring into the sides of the car.

"Am I a slut?" she says.

"I think it's my fault," I reply and realize that we aren't having the same conversation.

"You didn't make me a slut," she says.

"But I think I got you raped," I say. And the words sound ridiculous coming out of my mouth. I close one eye and flinch, expecting to be hit or slapped or punched with something hard and fast.

"No, it's my fault," she says.

"And I'm not popular," I tell her. "Some drunk girl in there tried to do me, and I'm pretty sure no one in there realized that I'm alive."

"Trust me," she says. "It's not that much better being popular." Vanessa holds her head against the cold glass window and says to me, "Can you drive a little bit slower? It looks like you're driving so fast."

"I'm going five miles under the speed limit," I tell her. And just to experiment, I tell think about Vanessa getting undrunk. I imagine her feeling better and not throwing up. I imagine her walking into the house and not being a total mess or laughing at everything.

I imagine her head not hurting and her not feeling sick.

"Hey Vanessa," I say. "I think I can fix this," I say.

"Fix what?" she says.

"How do you feel?" I ask.

"Like I need to vomit," she says. "Fix what?" she says. "Did you make me sick?" she says.

"No, I wanted to make you feel better," I say. "I wanted you to be not drunk." I smile, put my hand on her back and say, keeping an eye on the road, "Do you feel better?"

"No." She starts pulling on the door to open it. "Stop the car. Stop the car." Vanessa is bent over, looking at the car window and then the floor. Staring at her feet to keep her eyes and mind focused on something that isn't moving, she says to me, "Stop."

And on instinct, I pull over to the side of the road. I don't know whose house this is, but I pull over damn near on the green lawn. The post box at the street says 4361, but nothing else. Gorgeous flowers line the stone walkway. "Are you going to barf?" I ask.

I get my answer in the form of gagging and gurgling and then the wet splash of my sister's stomach contents on the grass. She's hacking and coughing and bent over at the waist. Her hands are the only thing holding herself up off of the ground.

I want to get closer, but the smell. You know. I love my sister and all, but that smell? It reminds me of the sweetness of energy drinks and the bitterness of sour apple candies. Even in the dark, it looks pinkish orange and I just have to take a deep step backwards and turn around. "Just let me know when you're done," I say.

My sister hacks and coughs. She's probably trying to cry in the middle of all of this, but her body won't let her catch enough air.

Something feels like it's itching my face and I wipe my nose and cheeks. My hand and wrist just slide off my face and I know that feeling. I've had it I don't know how many times this last week.

"Great!" I say.

"Did I get some of it on your shoe?" says Vanessa. She's on her feet again, walking slowly and blowing into her hands to try to smell her breath. She makes a bitter, sour face and looks at me. "Are you okay?"

I wipe the blood off my thumb and wrist and onto my pants. "Ya, I tell her. I'm good." I look at my shoes. "False alarm," I say with a smile.

"Good," she says. Vanessa's face is pale, even in the moonlight. Her eyes are deep, dark circles and she looks like she hasn't slept for days. "I feel fantastic, though," she says. She looks at me and says, "We should go back."

"I think we've had enough party for now," I tell her.

22

I pretty much spent all of Sunday dodging Peter's calls and messages and emails and making sure that I don't somehow drive or go to Owl Foods. For my drinks and snacks, the gas station will do. I wouldn't say I did anything wrong considering that I don't know what me and Peter are, but right now, I'm feeling pretty guilty.

I grabbed Sara-Without-An-H's breasts and let her flirt with me. I told her I was going to go back to sleep with her and never did. In my defense, I told her that I had a boyfriend.

If that's the right term to use at the moment.

It's not my fault she thought I said she had a boyfriend. Is it? Was that a product of my powers, too?

Not wanting to screw up anything more than I already have, I made the hard decision that I needed to just avoid it all together. That's a good, reasonable response, right?

I mean, what if he finds out? What if he notices that I was with someone else?

Is there a way you can tell? Can you really know if someone is cheating on you? I guess more importantly, I want to know if he can tell if someone is cheating on him. Or if we're in a position that I can cheat on him. If we aren't together, we can't cheat, right?

All of these thoughts make my stomach hurt more, a deep rumbly in the tumbly. My stomach starts to hurt, and I want it to just go away.

That's perfect. Of course, that's what I need to do.

I rest my hands on my stomach while lying down in my room. On my bed, I close my eyes and think about no stomach pains. No worries. No stress.

When everything feels like it's relaxing, I wait for more pains. Opening my eyes, I search every muscle in my body for a sense of pain or a tingle. A sudden push or butterfly to upset my stomach.

I find nothing. Nothing hurts. Everything feels perfectly fine.

I smile and look out the window. What else can I practice on? The dog across the street, a boxer-terrier mix of something that must have been brown and blonde, it wanders back and forth on the streets, barking and following the cars and people on the sidewalks. Every day this dog Jojo stretches the leash tight, pacing back and forth and barking at everyone. He's so huge, my mom calls him Marmaduke, whoever the hell that is.

Looking inward, I look at his leash and listen for his barking. Jojo barks at the cars driving down the aisle. I don't know if he's angry or wants to play, but I think about silence. Closing my eyes, I imagine a world without barking, a world without having to listen to Jojo threaten to run off his leash and eat or play with the boy and girls and cars that cross his path. I pretend that Jojo isn't angry or hungry or playful. Instead, he's calm, cool. Collected. He's Zen.

And when I open my eyes, there's Jojo, barking no more. Instead, he's nestled alongside the pole that his leash is attached to. He's lying down with his head resting patiently on his front paws. His eyes follow the people wandering the street outside, the boys and girls running and screaming and chasing each other. None of this draws Jojo's attention.

I gotta test this further.

"Hey, Mom, I'll be right back," I shout out into the apartment just before the screen door thwaps closed behind me. The air is brisk and almost refreshing. If it wasn't for the chilling wind. That same wind carries the smell of mesquite or hickory burning in fireplaces with it.

This makes me smile. The true sign that colder climates are coming, time to bundle up and think about the holiday season.

I'm barefoot except for my socks, so my steps are close together, slow and careful to not step on rocks or pebbles. The black rocky street of asphalt poses a special problem as I tip toe as quickly as I can across it. My socks are going to have to be bleached to hell when I'm done with this.

Jojo has always been known as a threatening dog by anyone who has been lucky enough to have tried to play with him. The boxer is known as such because it plays with its front paws, usually flailing them back and forth like he's trying to box with you. It's cute and triggers that part of a child's brain that says, "He just wants to give you a hug, Junior. Go give the big old doggy a hug."

This usually precedes the boy or girl crying for his mother for help after Jojo knocks them down and dances on their body with all four clawed feet.

"Here, doggy, doggy, doggy," I say. In the last few months, neighbors near and far have tried to get Jojo put to sleep. Partly because he's left outside to watch all of the subdivision have fun around him, partly because he's a boxer and seen as a threat. All of the complaints and blood and crying present themselves to my mind's eye as I take slow steps to Jojo's leash zone. "Here, doggy. Nice doggy," I say. I hold my hand out and kneel down low to the ground. I heard somewhere that big animals are seen as threats, smaller ones are prey. Maybe if I do something smaller than big, but bigger than small, I can survive and confuse the poor animal.

If this doesn't work, I want as many reasons to not piss off Jojo as I can. Something to defend myself just in case Jojo wants to play or eat or kill me, too.

"I wouldn't do that, mister," says a boy on his little red bicycle. His helmet is too big for his head, but his big cheeks and chubby chin keep it from falling off completely.

"Leave me alone," I say. Turning around to face him, I say, "You're going to piss him off."

"Not as much as you will," he says. "He don't like nobody."

"He doesn't like anybody, you illiterate punk," I say. I probably shouldn't have said that. To a kid, anyway. But he's being a pain in the ass. I need peace and quiet. "Now go," I say. The boy pedals away, but not before giving me the bird.

Kids these days.

I take slow steps toward Jojo. His dark doggy eyes watch me, and the only sign that they are actually following me are his eyebrows, which twitch and shift according to where he's leaving. Just playing with him, I move my hands to my left and to my right. His eyebrows shift the same directions. When I go left, they go left. When I go right, they go right.

"Silly animal," I say. Then I put my hands forward and right up to Jojo's face and says, "Nice boy."

And Jojo, he sniffs my hands and then puts his hands down.

"So far, so good," I say. "Calm doggy."

And then I wonder, just how far can I go with this? If he will let me walk right up to him, did I make him completely complacent? Will he let me do whatever I want to him?

Only one way to find out.

My feet are wet from the dew of the grass. Wet and dark green from the chlorophyll, I rub them on the dog's hindquarters. Jojo's head doesn't move. He doesn't groan or growl or get up. His eyes twitch back to see me, but that's about it. He keeps his dark doggy eyes focused on my feet, but beyond that, no signs of life.

"Wow, Jojo," I say. "Looks like I can tame the wild beasts, too," I say.

"Hey mister!" says the boy again on his red bike. The chubby annoyance says, "You're going to get eatin!" This kid can't be any more than like ten years old, but he's a royal pain.

"Shut up, kid!" I say.

And Jojo, he gets up and walks calmly to me and sniffs my feet and my pants legs. "Nice doggy," I say. For a second, I consider patting his head, but decide that maybe I like having all of my fingers. I've grown attached, you know?

Jojo takes a few more steps out to the sidewalk, which pulls his leash tighter and tighter until it's completely lifted off of the ground in a tight leather line from the pole to Jojo's neck. Jojo pulls his head forward as far as his neck will let it and his nose sniffs the air toward the chubby brat.

"What's he doing?" says the kid, and he puts his feet on the pedals, ready to leave if he needs to.

"I dunno," he says. "What did you do?" I ask.

"I didn't do nothing," he says.

"You didn't do anything," I say to correct him, and that's when Jojo goes berserk. His barks echo across the street and down the street, and I've never seen Jojo get this angry before. Well, maybe that one time when the kid ended up in the hospital and Mr. Jones, Jojo's owner, had to put him away for a few months. For those eight weeks or so, the street sounded quiet. Almost too quiet, really. Creepy quiet. The parents loved it, the kids hated it. I secretly think the boys just loved tormenting the leashed-up fur ball.

And all signs at the moment point to this being a repeat of that last time.

"Jojo, calm down," I say, but the dog, he wants to ignore us. He refuses to actually pay attention to anything except for this chubby little brat. "Jojo, nice doggy," I say. I put my hand out, but pull it back again. Jojo stands between me and the chubby brat.

This boy, though, sits on his bike and just stares the boy down. "Ha ha, you can't come get me," he says. The boy looks at me and says, "What did you tell him? Did you tell him to eat me?"

"I didn't tell him anything," I say. "But you should really get out of here."

"Ya," the boy says, and he picks up a small rock from the ground. "Get out of here." He holds the rock above his shoulder, ready to launch it at the dog.

"Have you lost your fucking mind, kid? Get out of here!" I tell the fat fuck. "Get out!" And as I shout out at him, Jojo shouts louder. The angrier I get, the angrier Jojo gets.

"Stop that!" I say. "Just go!" I say. I wave both of my hands away from the area and out into the street. "Leave!" I say.

And Jojo, his barking gets louder and louder. His barking is so intense, it feels hot against my skin. The anger he has moves every muscle in his body. Every time he barks, his shoulders flex and let go. His front paws drop his body down and his tail, or what used to be there before it got cut off and turned into a little nub, isn't wagging or moving.

"He's pissed off," I say. "Just go."

And the lithe shit, of course he throws the rock. It flies into the air, flipping around, and like slow motion, I can see it turning and spinning, turning and spinning until it hits Jojo right in the ribcage.

And this is it. This is the last thing I remember before all hell broke loose. I don't know when or how it happened, but when I opened my eyes and looked down the street, Jojo was busy chewing and tearing apart the back tire of the chubby boy's bike. The boy? He cries and rolls on the dirty asphalt of the street. Holding his knee, he's screaming into the air for anyone to help him. "He's eating my bike," the boy cries in syllables between sobs.

And all I can think is, Did I do this?

When I look back at how angry I got and how angry Jojo got, did I make him attack the boy?

I have to fix this, I say. This has to be fixed.

I don't even care that the dew from the grass has completely soaked through my white socks. My calloused feet are probably waterlogged. They feel slick and heavy. But that's not the important part right now. I need to save this poor boy's life.

"Come here, Jojo," I say. I pat my lap and try to summon him to me. "Come on." I try everything I can think of. I've never had a dog, so I have no idea how to actually call a dog over to see you, but this always seems to work on television.

"Come on," I say. The boy, he tries to crawl across the street in military moves, using his shoulders and elbows to pull himself off the street and onto sidewalk. Pointing at the boy, I say, "Don't move!" I take a few more steps over to him and shout out, "Let me see if you're hurt."

And the little shit, he shouts back, "Fuck you!" and he keeps crawling.

Fine then. Get eaten.

"Come here, boy," I say. I pat my lap and whistle through my teeth. I can only whistle by sucking in, not blowing out. I'm sure there's a joke somewhere, but I'm too stressed out to find it.

"Come here," I shout out and across the street, my mom watches from the edge of the sidewalk.

"What the hell are you doing?" she says. My mom walks nonchalantly across the street with her bare feet, making me feel like a little pussy when I had to tip toe carefully across. "What are you doing with Jojo?" she says.

"I had to help the boy," I say. She doesn't need to know the whole story.

"And you're going to do this how?" she says. My mom grabs my shirt and pulls hard toward her. "Get your ass in the house." My eyes don't leave the boy, who is sitting on the side of the street and watching Jojo go to town on the bike. The back tire is flat completely, but that doesn't keep the reddish-brown boxer from chewing on the metal spokes and sinking his teeth into the rubber. "How did he get off his leash?" I say.

There are no signs of stress on the pole, I note. "I don't know," I say, completely lying, I think. "It must have been old leather." My mom says nothing to this and pulls on my shirt sleeve and says, "Get in the house."

I follow her orders. To get across the street, I try to walk across like my mom did, painlessly and quick and confident, but I fail halfway. A sharp rock digs into the fleshy part of the ball of my foot and gets stuck there. With every step, it gets pushed in further and further. I don't think it's broken the skin by the time I get to the other sidewalk and I scrape it off.

I figure this is a good place to watch and see what happens.

The boy, he's crying and worried about his bike.

My mom, she's walking over to the Mr. Jones's house and knocking on the door. The conversation isn't loud enough for me to hear it, but I notice that he's not happy. Mr. Jones pushes my mom aside and takes long stomps to the sidewalk and looks down the street. He bends over at the waist, snaps his fingers and Jojo's head pops up and twists around, listening and looking for the source of the snapping.

"Come here," Mr. Jones says. "Here boy."

And Jojo hauls ass back to his owner. His tongue hangs like a flag in the wind and this weird beast looks nice and friendly and harmless. The complete opposite of what just happened no less than ten seconds ago.

"You've got to be kidding me," I say and my mom grabs my shirt.

"Get in the house," she says.

I follow my mom in the house and watch as the dog goes back into the house with Mr. Jones. My mom goes outside and checks on the boy, again a conversation I can't hear. The boy's face is red with streaks of gray and brown down his face, trails of tears tracing the contours of his face. The poor boy got caught up in this, but I can't just say anything.

It was his fault, right? He should have just left like I asked.

When my mom comes back in through the door, she says nothing and grabs the phone. I know where this is going. I know who she's calling and I go upstairs. My stomach feels sick again. My intestines feel like they are on fire and I run to the bathroom and stare at myself in the mirror. It takes a shitload of running to make me sweat normally, but right now, my face looks like it's wet and shiny from perspiration. Not heavy beads of sweat or lines dripping from my forehead. Instead, my face looks plastic and shiny, the way a Halloween mask or Hollywood special effects looks shiny.

My mom knocks on the bathroom door. "You okay?" she says.

Out of habit, I shout back, "Ya."

"Jojo is getting put down," she says. "That monster should have been put down a long time ago. He's too dangerous."

And my stomach feels like it's about to drop everything right now. My intestines feel like they've been on fire and feel heavy. "I'm sorry,"

I say, not realizing that my mom is still there. Her shadow of her standing just outside the door shifts its weight.

"What are you sorry for?" she says. "You were trying to help," she says.

"Ya, I know," I say.

"Don't worry," she says. "He was too dangerous and Mr. Jones never took care of him." My mom is trying to make me feel better, but for all the wrong reasons. "That's no way for a dog to live."

When I'm silent enough, my mom's shadow leaves and I breathe a sigh of relief. Looking into the mirror, I say, "I can fix this." My mirror self reflects my words back at me, but he doesn't look convinced. His eyes look tired and sad, every muscle drooping downward from the burdens of being responsible for the world.

"I can fix this," the mirror says back to me and as I close my mouth, he closes his. "We can do this."

23

Monday morning, the person in the mirror echoes back everything I say and do. Talking back to me, he says, "I'm serious, dammit. You need to be more popular. You need to be liked and awesome." I close my eyes and wish, deep down as deep as I can push my visions, I say out loud, "No fucking around."

I open my eyes and stare into my reflection's eyes. "Can you do it," I ask Mirror Me. Blinking and taking a long breath, I see my mirror-self do the same. "We can do this," I say. Then I say, "Correction, let's do this."

Vanessa and I run out the door and into the car. Vanessa drives us to the school and parks our car, putting up the parking permit and we exit the car. Immediately Vanessa leaves me at the car and doesn't even bother to wave back to me. "Bye!" I shout out to her, and she shows me the back of her right hand and waves it back and forth.

"Bye to you, too," I mutter back to her and walk to my locker. The hallways are crowded with the usual groups of people blocking everyone else. The groups of freshmen trying to get to everywhere they can as fast as possible. The way they move and scurry about like lizards in the desert sands.

At my locker the usual couple, Kerry and Carrie, the make-out king and queen, aren't against my locker, playing tonsil hockey as usual. Instead, the coast is clear and free of obstructions. A nice change, I'd say.

Going to my first class, I notice that everyone is extremely nice and friendly and I smile and swagger down the hallway.

It's going to work, I can just feel it.

And then it's when all of this happens that I realize just how well it's working.

"Hi, Teddy," says Bryan in my English class. He sits directly in front of me and talks about how much sex he and his girlfriend had in and around his restaurant job at the Chicken Joint. The stories this boy tells are the type that can't and shouldn't be repeated anywhere. A few of them, I didn't think were possible.

"Hi, Bryan," I say. As I sit down, he turns around and says, "So I can't wait to tell you something," he says. I'm putting my notebook on my desk and reading the journal prompt on the Smart Board when he drops the bombshell, "I think I want to break up with Erica."

"Really?" I whisper back. "What prompted that?"

"I don't know," he says. "I just don't feel like I like her that way anymore."

By "that way" I don't know what he means. The relationship was based on sex and how many times he can possibly brag about it. At one point I didn't believe a damn thing that came out of his straight mouth. That was, until last quarter in September, when I ran into Erica and Bryan just outside by the dumpsters.

I never went back even though they didn't notice. Scarred for life, let me tell you.

"Got tired of her?" I ask.

"I don't know," he says. Bryan locks eye contact with me and says, "I guess I just wanted to try new things."

Oh, dear God. I don't ask questions because I don't want to know.

"So, uh, did you do the homework?" I ask. That should buy me a few more minutes until the teacher gets here. Especially since there was no homework.

"Dude, there was homework?" Bryan says and digs through his

backpack, tearing out papers and tossing them on the floor with sudden violent thrusts and movements. "Don't go anywhere, okay? I think we should hang out sometime."

"Can I borrow your homework?" I ask. Keep the boy on topic and no one gets hurt, or embarrassed. Or uncomfortable.

"Of course, man," he says. He winks at me and says, "We're friends."

You see, the trick to flirting is eye contact. Eye contact and you have to mean it. The feelings, I mean. You have to mean the "I want you so bad it hurts" or the "You're so damn hot". You have to want what you say with your eyes.

It works like this: You take a long, hard look at the person's face and smile with your eyes. Make sure you mean it and you'll be fine. For whatever reason, though, you can't stare at their mouth or their nose or their ass. It's the eyes that let the them know you mean business. I guess it's because everyone notices eye-on-eye action. Making out with the other boy—or girl, I guess if you're into that— with only your eyes across the counter at restaurants or the store.

It's this kind of eye contact that nearly gets me in trouble a second time. And for the record, it's not me trying to lock the eye contact. I'm serious.

In P.E., that hellish class that kicks my eyes every day, we run what we call the Panther Course. It's just a mile long circle of land that we run on. We get timed and graded on how fast we run. Like this is something we can study for, our grades for the semester are based on how fast I can run a mile.

Or maybe it's in comparison to the other boys. All I know is, I can't do a damn pull up, and I can't run a mile in five minutes. What I can do is attract the attention of an unlikely victim of my charms.

Or magic. Or powers. Whatever you want to call them right now. I'm still trying to figure it out myself.

So it's in the P.E. lockers at the end of the period that Shane walks up to me while I'm changing my shirt. He looks at me as I pull the sweaty T-shirt off of my arms and over my head and says, "You're kinda fat."

I said nothing, afraid that he'd kick my ass and throw me in the showers yet again. On closer observation, though, he's smiling and standing there shirtless. Did I mention that he didn't have any pants on? Because he definitely had no pants on.

Shane puts his arms up against the lockers and looks me over.

"Um, thanks?" I say. "You're looking, um, good."

And Shane, playfully, I hope, kisses his biceps and flexes them for me. "Thanks," he says with a smile. "I work out."

"Looks like it," I say. Can't quite keep my eyes only on the locker and on my clothes. Keeping my head directly in front of me is all I can do to not stare at the jocks.

"I heard we're playing basketball today," says Shane. When he begins to speak, I flinch at every syllable because I'm just waiting for that awkward moment when he starts trying to kill me with his gigantic fists wrapped around my neck. The way he looks right now, though, is like those underwear models you see on the internet. Posing, almost sweaty, glistening while they smile at you inviting your imaginations to take over.

I consider myself lucky, however, since he shows no signs of wanting to pull my face through his ass. So far so good. "Nothing much, how about you?" Keep changing, keep my focus. Don't let my eyes wander.

"You played a good game today," says Shane. He sits down on the bench right next to me. His legs are spread apart, and as much as I try, I can't keep from following the contours of his thighs, his legs, and his shoulders.

"Thanks," I say, "but I sat on the bleachers the whole time."

Shane laughs and smiles again. "What are you doing later today?" he says. Shane takes one last look at my stomach before my shirt covers it and I close the locker door shut.

"I'm a little busy," I say. "Homework, I think."

"You think?" he says. He stands up and gets his face as close to me as he can. His breath is sweet and minty from the gum he was chewing earlier. From this up close, his pores look perfect, his moles are flawless.

"Ya, I think," I say. "Bryan wanted to work on it together."

And around me, everyone is just walking out, hauling their backpacks over their shoulders and leaving us alone in the lockers.

"I think we need to get going," I say and try to walk around him. "The bell is going to ring soon."

And predictably, Shane stands up and puts his chest just right there in front of my face. "Listen," he says.

And this has to be a joke. The other boys left so they can distract Ms. Lalane. Keep her busy so Shane can destroy me and hide the body.

"You got me all wrong," he says and I flinch again at his every syllable. I try to go to my happy place. Think about flowers and happy bunnies. Think about being at home and playing online. Happy thoughts, Teddy.

Shane's nearly naked body stands before me and looks sexy as hell.

Not now, Shane.

"What are you doing?" I manage to stammer out until Shane grabs my ears and pulls me toward his face and kisses me. Like his lips on my lips. I'm scared stiff so I stand there and wait for his next move.

When he pulls away from me, I tell him, "You're kidding me, right?" I look around and no one is around. The entire locker room looks clear, no one hiding behind lockers waiting to kick my ass. No one sneaking around to grab me and toss me in the showers again.

"What do you mean?" he says. Shane blinks and looks confused, but his smile slowly drifting downwards into a confuzzled frown.

"Nothing," I say. "Listen, that was sweet, but I'm sort of busy later and, wow you're a good kisser, but seriously, I can't do this. I can't really do that again and I want to just leave so if you'll excuse me, I'll be on my way."

I forgot that there were two ways out of the locker rooms, so I back up, take gradual steps as I explain my problem and walk around the line of lockers and out the front door. Sitting on the bleachers, waiting for the bell to ring, I look around and no one looks at me weird. No one smiling and giggling and waiting to say something about what just happened. Like they didn't know.

Wait, they didn't know, did they?

I just got hit on by Shane--my archenemy--and no one knew about it? This just seems way too impossible.

The bell rings and I exit the gym with the rest of the other boys and girls. As we leave out, we are forced out the door bottleneck style, squeezed through the little entry of the double doors.

I wave my fingers at Shane and smile over my shoulders. I take careful effort to make sure that my eyes lock in with his brown eyes. "Bye, Shane," I say and he waves back.

"Bye, dude."

On the way to my locker to grab my homework, every teacher surveys the halls, saying goodbye to the students. Teachers I've never had, they call me out by name. These same teachers that might have heard about my sister, they are giving me high fives in the hallway and asking me how my day is. How's it hanging. How I'm doing.

The students in the hallway, well, everyone knows me.

"Hey, Barratt!" says one of the basketball boys. "You going to the party tonight?" he says.

"I wasn't invited to anything," I say. I shrug and smile and play it off. Of course, these random people should be talking to me. It makes perfect sense that these people who don't know me are now talking to me.

And Shane, well, I can't explain that.

When I close my locker and fling the backpack over my shoulder, the obvious finally slaps me in the face.

This morning, I asked to be sexy and popular. I wanted to be famous.

What I got instead was Shane's body and teachers wanting to give me a high five. What I got was invited to a party that I would have never heard about.

I CAN GET USED to this, having a cute boy waiting to see me.

Shane leans against the glass case of debate and sports awards for the school, his arms crossed, presumably waiting for me.

"Teddy!" he says and waves me down. "Come here!"

I move my feet slowly, cautious, looking around for traps or someone to bum rush me from the side. Instead, I approach Shane unopposed.

"What's up?" I say.

"Listen, about earlier," he says. "I just wanted to apologize." His voice wavers, shaky as a nervous schoolgirl. "About earlier."

"Listen, it's fine," I say. "I just, um, I'm sort of seeing someone so it was a bad time, you know?" I try to let him down easy, not even sure what the hell is happening.

"No, it's not okay," he says. "I don't know what came over me." Shane's body shifts its weight to the other leg, and he leans over. "I can't explain why I feel this way. I mean, at first I hated you, but now I kinda like you." Shane's eyes scream "Help me" while his body sounds puppy doggy and whiny. I don't know which Shane I believe.

"It's okay," I joke. "I have that effect on people."

"Maybe you do," he says. "But I can't help this. I just had to talk to you."

Shane takes his hands from his pockets and puts them on my shoulders. Then, in plain view of virtually everyone, he looks into my eyes like he's ready to make some kind of move. And while this is completely awkward, and he's like twice my size, all I see is his naked chest in my mind, the way his toned body reflected the light in the locker rooms just perfectly.

"I can't do this, Shane. I'm sorry."

"You can't just leave me like this," he says. "I don't know what to do."

Shane tries to grab my shirt as I walk away, but slips his fingers into my backpack instead. He pulls me backwards, and I fall flat on my ass. "Please, just stay and talk to me," he says. "I want to talk to you."

"Shane, I need to go," I say. "Let go of me." I pull on my backpack to keep as much distance between us as possible. "You need to let go," I say.

My mind begins to burn and I just need Shane to leave me alone, for something to happen so that he can finally stop all of this.

This, this is not what I wanted. Or was it?

Shane refuses to pull his hand out of my backpack, so I pull and walk away anyhow, down the stairs and to the glass doors. At the top of the stairs, Shane's feet stop, and me along with him.

"I'm not messing around, Shane, stop it."

"Can't you just wait a second?" he says. "Just to talk?"

"There is nothing to talk about," I say. "Leave me alone!"

Shane's hand must have grabbed hold of something in my backpack, a textbook or a binder, because now his entire meaty fist is in there. He pulls back fast and pulling me off balance and to the bottom steps.

And of course, the bigger they are, the harder they fall. When I fall, my backpack comes off my shoulder and Shane's hand--stuck like the meathead that he is--takes the rest of Shane to the floor.

I look over to the backpack and I stare at Shane's wrist and with every fiber of my being, I say, "Let the fuck go."

"Dude, how did you do that?" he says and pulls his hand out of my backpack. He pulls it back and rubs red and raw fingers. "Thanks, man."

"Jump," I say. My eyes lead a trail from his chest to the railings by the stairs. "Jump now."

Shane looks at me and shrugs. "Alright, dude." His raw, meaty hand grabs the railing and his feet push his body off the ground. Like an action movie, he jumps the railing and quickly disappears over the wall and into the ground below. What breaks his fall is the railing down below, which bends his body in half at the stomach and he slaps to the ground. He groans and rubs his stomach and side.

"Thank you," I say and go downstairs. Shane doesn't move, except for the rolling around and groaning. As I open up the big blue metal door to the outside student parking lot, I look back at Shane. He's looking at me with his face twisted in what must be a hell of a lot of pain. A metal pole in the kidney can't be pleasant.

The door closes behind me and Shane's voice says my name. And as I look back around my shoulder, Shane's fist slams into the ground and he roars into the empty hallway.

24

One of the biggest loads of shit I have ever heard is that being gay is a choice. It's the type of argument that makes me want to punch someone--anyone--that is in arm's reach. These are the things I think about when my sister drives me home today. Her questions hit me like a barrage of punches, "So what happened today?"

My sister asks me, "Did anyone mess with you today?" She asks, "Did you do anything cool with your powers and stuff?"

"Drop me off at Owl Foods," I say.

And Vanessa, she puts her stinky face on--the one where she scrunches up her face like it's been wrapped with a rubber band--and pouts. "Why?" she says.

"I need to talk to Peter about something," I say. "None of your business about what." If anything, she is predictable.

"Do you guys have another date?" she asks.

"No," I say without even thinking. It is a combination of reaction and pure instinct that makes me tight-lipped and not wanting to say anything about what been happening. "I just need to talk, that's it."

The car pauses and squeals from Vanessa hitting the breaks for half a second. "You're not breaking up with him, are you? I swear to

God, I'll kill you if you do." Vanessa lets off the brake and starts driving like a normal human being. "I mean, he's a great guy, you shouldn't break up with him."

Eyeing her to make sure that Capt. Crazy persona is gone, I say, "I am not breaking up with him. I don't even know if we can break up. It's not like we're dating or anything." I pause and think. All we did was make out, right? Does that mean we're officially together?

"We aren't officially together."

"You should be," she says. It's times like this I wish I was the one driving. The only reason why my younger sister of one year is driving is that she hides the car keys. Yes, I said it: she hides the car keys because she wants to be the one to drive. Sixteen years old and probably illegally driving since she only has a graduated learner's permit. Technically, she needs someone over the age of eighteen in the passenger seat for her to drive. Let's just say that Vanessa has never been a girl to pay attention to laws.

Laws? Pfft. More like suggestions.

"I just need to talk to him, that's all."

"Fine, but you're buying me something to drink," she says.

"Deal," I say and thankfully, she shuts the hell up for the rest of the drive.

I have to ask around for Peter to show up finally. I wait by the doorway to the back warehouse, just a huge concrete entryway with white plastic noodles that look like the insides of a carwash separating us from them. Peter is probably back there since neither Vanessa nor I could find him stocking anything anywhere.

When Peter does come around the corner, pulling a pallet of something wrapped in a translucent plastic wrap. "Watch out," he says without looking to see who is actually behind him.

"Will do, sexy," I say and Peter stops and turns around.

"Excuse me?" says Peter. When he turns around, I seize the moment, grab his cheeks, and pull them toward my face with a big wet kiss. "Whoa, there, tiger," he says after he pulls his face away from mine and wipes his mouth. "Dude," he says, "I work here."

"I know, how do you think I found you?" I say.

"You can't just come in and do that," he says. "My boss will fire me."

"Sorry," I say and put my head down. If I try to look cute, the next few things I request from him won't seem so bad. "When is your break?" I ask.

Peter searches his wrist for his watch but can't find it under the gloves and long sleeves of his thick midnight blue jacket.

"It's three-thirty," I say. "Give or take."

"My break should be in about a half hour," he says. "I get off at eight."

"Maybe," I say with a smile, but he clearly didn't get it. "Get off at eight," I say. "Got it." I look around the aisles to make sure that Vanessa isn't snooping around. She's not around. I take few steps closer to Peter so I can whisper. "How about you and me, we meet out front at your break? I want to talk to you," I say.

Peter looks at me and smiles. His big, gloved hand pats the side of my face and he says, "Sure, big boy."

"Vanessa," I say. "I'm going to hang out here and wait for Peter. You can leave." Vanessa sets her hand out and pokes her fingertips into my chest. I don't even ask, just dig through my pockets until I can fork out a couple of dollars for her. "There?" I ask, but Vanessa shakes her head.

"I want a snack," she says.

"But you know we're going to eat soon," I tell her. "You'll ruin your appetite," I say.

"No I won't," she says. "And we won't eat until you get home, and who knows when that's going to be."

I can't argue with that. Honestly, I can't argue with a lot of things she tells me. She knows me better than I know myself sometimes. "Fine," I say and I hand over everything in my pockets. "Just take it."

Vanessa smiles and turns around to walk down the aisles. "What should I tell Mom?" she shouts at me.

"Tell her not to wait up for me," I shout back and go check out the frozen food aisle to stare at myself in the mirror. You'd never think it, but it's nearly impossible to waste time in a grocery store if you don't have anything to buy. For serial. For the next twenty minutes I wandered every aisle until the same clerk had asked me if I needed help like five times. Then she radioed in to someone, whom I'm guessing was in Loss Prevention or something. Loss Prevention is the department to keep people from stealing from the stores. I've been in stores where the Loss Prevention people are dressed in regular clothes and pretend to shop to catch other shoplifters. I've also seen them just follow someone and request the stolen items and their quick removal from the store.

I tell the nice little lady that I'll just wait outside and I let the sun warm me up. I guess if you're going to be storing massive amounts of produce and prepackaged foods, you need to keep the area as cool as humanly possible. People walk in and out of the stores in pairs and in singles. Parents with kids and adults by themselves. What's interesting is I find myself imagining me in their places.

What if I was walking into the store with kids? Do I want kids? Can I even get kids?

What if I was walking with my significant other? Do I use the word husband? Partner? Why is everything so complicated?

Peter comes out of the store wearing just his work shirt and pants. No jacket or vest means he must be off of lunch.

"Nice shirt," I say, and Peter smiles and sits down next to me.

"What was that all about in there?" he asks. "The kiss?"

I put my hands on my lap and smile back at him with, I hope, the same cutesy intensity. "I was happy to see you?" I say.

Peter isn't buying it and looks everywhere except at me.

"Pete," I say. I grip his right hand and pull it toward my lap. "Pete, look at me," I tell him. "I think we should be together," I say. Immediately I wish I could take those words back in my mouth and edit. "I mean, will you be my boyfriend?" I say. I smile and wait for Peter to look back at me and smile.

"Why now?" he says.

"Because I was thinking that I like you, and I think you like me, and I thought that's what you wanted?" I say.

Peter turns his head at me and radiates with happiness. His

cheeks turn a bright red blush and his hand squeezes mine. "Okay," he says.

"That's it?" I say. "I don't just ask out anyone, you know."

And Peter grabs my hand and kisses the knuckles. "You couldn't wait to come here and ask me out?" he says. "That's so totally adorable." He kisses my knuckles again with his cold, wet lips. It tickles and feels sensual at the same time.

"You'll make me shiver," I say. "Try this," I say and I pull his face over to me and kiss his nose. "That's just as good."

And in reply, Peter grabs the back of my head and kisses my mouth again, licking my lips and gradually pushing my lips apart with his tongue.

When he lets go of my head, he looks at me and his hazel eyes glisten for a second in the sunlight. "Are you okay?" he says.

I take a breath and hold up my finger to him. "Hold," I say. I take another breath and exaggerate the moment as long as I can. "On."

I fan my face with my hands. "You might just be giving me the vapors," I say with my worst Southern accent available.

"I gotta get back in there," Peter says. "I'll call you tonight?" he says. "When I get off work?"

"You better!" I say and he gives me a big hug before getting inside. His body smells the way a rugged working man should, sweaty, dirty pheromones of hard labor. My boyfriend waves at me as I walk past the door and wave back.

And it's a strange concept, really, that I have a boyfriend.

I say the words to myself as I walk home. Only a few blocks, I'm sure I almost got hit by a car back a couple of times without even knowing it.

"Boyfriend." The words feel slick like oil coming out of my mouth.

"Boyfriend," I say again. It doesn't feel much better this time either.

"I have a boyfriend." It's cute in a way.

Teddy Barratt has a boyfriend.

25

It didn't take a lot of convincing to let me go to the party tonight. It was Peter's idea that we go to this party. He said he heard about it from work and lots of his coworkers were going to go. It was supposed to be "awesome". Those were his words.

My mom's response when I asked was, "Why don't you invite your friend over so I can meet him?"

I declined, saying, "Mom, we're going to be late. He doesn't get off work until eight, then he has to change for the party and then we'll maybe get something to eat before we go." I look at the clock, "That'll take a few hours, and we don't want to be out too late."

My mom kisses my forehead. "Good," she says.

Peter was right on time. Not in terms of being here at the designated time. On time in terms of being here right before I felt the need to kill my mother.

"Are you going to wear that," she asks.

"Why can't I?" I ask. My button-down shirt had pink and black stripes that were flashy and dark at the same time. "It's perfect," I say.

And my mom says, "I don't know, it's just so dark."

Peter honks just outside. "That's Peter, Mom, I gotta go." I lean over and kiss her on the forehead. "Don't wait up."

I don't know that she actually will. She'll most likely fall asleep on the couch while she's watching her favorite whodunit television shows and the late night reruns of sitcoms where the people laugh at their own jokes. Those are her favorites.

"Lookin' good, Barratt," says Peter when I get into his cherry red two door coupe. The car has to be made two decades ago, but the interior is perfectly vacuumed and clean and smells like fake cherries, that overly sweet smell of cherry air freshener.

"What's that smell?" I ask and Peter puts his wrists right under my nose.

"You likey?" he asks.

"It's awesome," I say. His wrists give off a faint orangey smell, but darker and heavy, like musk and chocolate. "Smells good."

"My mom got it for me," he says. With a smile he adds, "I thought you'd like it."

I kiss him on the cheek put my hand on his hand, which is resting on the gear shifter.

The orange yellow streetlights blink past us on the way to the party. The lights, they remind me of the landing lights on the tarmac in airports. Or the floor lighting in movie theaters. The way they lead us to the destination of party with my boyfriend.

My first public outing with my boyfriend.

"So is this like our coming out party?" I say.

"I came out a long time ago," he says.

"No, I meant like coming out as a couple?" I say. "Wait, just how long ago did you come out to your parents?" I ask.

"I came out to my parents when I was about fourteen. To my friends, about thirteen," he says with his eyes focused on the road. The orange streetlights illuminate his face in a steady Morse code.

"Wow," I say. "That's way early."

"When did you come out?" he says. His raised eyebrows make me think Peter believes I still haven't come out to my mom, or it was just yesterday.

"Um, about a year ago, I guess," I tell him. "It was sort of by accident."

"This sounds juicy," he says and pinches my hand gripping his leg.

"You could say that. My mom found me abusing myself to gay porn."

Pete bursts out into explosive laughter that makes me worry about our safety.

"It's not that funny," I say, but he's laughing so hard that I start to laugh, too. "Okay, maybe it is," I say.

"That's a painful way to tell your mom," he says. "How awkward," he says. "I'm sorry." Peter grips my hand gripping his leg, and he squeezes again. "That was insensitive."

I'm still laughing from both the embarrassment and because Peter's laughter triggered some giggle fits of my own. "It's okay," I say, wiping my eyes of the tears from laughing so hard.

DESPITE LOSING THE DIRECTIONS, we knew this is the place because the door is wide open and more colorful teenagers flood into the front yard with plastic cups in their hand. The music? Techno remixes of songs I think I've heard on the radio pounds out into the street.

"Teddy!" a woman's voice says as a hand grabs me at the sleeve. The girl's voice had managed to sound out over the pounding techno music. That could only mean one thing: Vanessa. "You made it!" she says and gives me a hug. I could barely nod to her before she forces a cup into my hands. "Here hold this! Have fun. Mingle. There's a couple of cute boys outside if you want to go mingle."

"Uh, you remember, Peter, don't you?" I say and push Vanessa in front of Peter. "I came here with him." Then, clearing my throat, I say loud enough to drop the hint without actually saying the word boyfriend, "I am with him, you drunk."

"Oh my God!" she squeals. "Hi Peter!" she says and gives him a gigantic hug. It's amazing, but she doesn't drop a single drop from her cup.

"How's it going, Vanessa?" Peter says. Somehow, this must have given Vanessa permission to steal my boyfriend, because she tugs on his hand, leading him forcefully through the crowd. I take a sip from the drink and realize whoever mixed this was already drunk.

I am careful not to drop the drink anywhere, but I'm sure I can follow both Vanessa and Peter through the mass.

"Guys, I'd like you to meet a friend of mine," Vanessa says to three guys who were lounging out back. "This is Peter and Teddy. Teddy is my brother," my drunken whore of a sister says. "Isn't he the cutest?" She points to the other boy and I immediately recognize him from school. "I'll leave you all to get acquainted," says my sister, and she forces her way back into the crowded living room without a sound.

"Hi, Bryan," I say. Those awkward moments when you don't want to talk to someone, but you have to anyway because you don't have a good reason to leave. "Bryan, this is Peter, my boyfriend." Peter extends his hands, but Bryan doesn't do anything but stare at Peter.

"Hi, Bryan," says Peter. He tucks his hand back into his jeans pocket and looks at me. "I'm going to get a drink." He kisses me on the cheek and asks, "Did you want something else?" Peter points at the red plastic cup and makes a sour face.

"No, this will do," I say. "Come back soon!" I mean it.

Peter disappears into the crowd and Bryan looks back at him and says, "Boyfriend, huh?" Bryan looks around and says, "Well desperate times, I guess."

"I'm sorry," I say. "What was that?"

"I said Peter's cute," says Bryan.

"Ya, he's adorable," I say. Looking over to the crowd, I search for the top of his head bobbing up and down through the crowd, hopefully drink in hand and ready to go wander somewhere else away from this creep.

"I guess," he says. He isn't moving anywhere and looks around the room with what could best be described as disdain for the party. "This party sucks," he says.

"I just got here," I say and look up again. Please, Peter, be on your way soon.

Bryan takes a step closer to me and speaks slowly and carefully to me, "What are you doing later?"

"My boyfriend," I say, putting more emphasis on boyfriend. "Creep." I take another drink of my cup and look forward. Peter is trying to come in through the crowd of people just standing in the kitchen, blocking the way. "Move, you fuckers," I say. Even though I'm nearly ten feet away from the crowd, and the music is blaring something that sounds like a remix version of a Wynonna song, the crowd disperses and out emerges Peter, victorious. A bright red cup in his hand and a smile graces his lips. Peter looks the way the heroes always look at the end of a disaster movie. To say that I'm getting the hang of this is probably an understatement.

I feel the warmth of my face turning red. This needs to be done. Like now.

"Teddy!" says Peter when he's finally close enough to be heard. "It's a little loud in here," he says. "Want to go look around?"

"Teddy!" says another boy coming up to our group. "Hey, man, how's it going?" Mystery boy number one's red hair glows in the patio light directly above him. The red freckles over his face give him the look of a subtle tan and his green tried to penetrate into me but the heavy drinks make that damn near impossible. "I've seen you around," he says. With the same hand that holds his drink, he extends his index finger and points it at his chest. "I'm Damon."

"You have?" I say and grab Peter's left hand in mine.

"Mr. Taylor's history class, right?"

I nod in reply and take a sip from my cup. To make sure that Peter doesn't feel too out of place, I grip his hand and squeeze as hard as I can. His fingers tighten around mine and my lips form a smile hidden by the plastic cup.

"I've seen you going to that room before. I didn't think you were gay at first," he says.

I nearly cough into my drink. I want to ask, but can't get the words out.

Peter pats my back and rubs in small circles. "Are you okay?" he asks and I nod because I can't force the words out of my throat.

I grind my teeth together and let go of Peter's hand. Taking a long breath, I say, "Um, thank you?"

"Ya, you don't normally give off the gay vibe, but now that I see you in that shirt, you look way hot," says Damon.

Damon's drink almost falls out of his hands when Peter extends his hand to introduce himself. "Hi, I'm Peter," he says. "Nice to meet you."

I look at Peter and realize I'm still quote-unquote popular. Great, this will be a fun night. "Damon, this is my boyfriend, Peter."

Damon says, "What the hell is wrong with you, bitch?" Damon secures the grip on his cup and shoots a glare at Peter and his hand. "Party foul," he says.

A coy smile slips from Damon's lips as he looks at me directly in my eyes. Oh, God. Not you, too.

This is too much. "Uh, I'll be right back," I say and grab Peter's hand and pull him out front.

"What the hell is going on here?" says Peter. He drinks from the cup and says, "Is everyone at your school gay?"

"No," I say. "I swear to God. I have no idea what's going on." Only half true, really, but he doesn't need to know this. Not now. Maybe not ever.

"You're getting hit on a lot," says Peter. He takes yet another drink and I hope to God that I can drive his car back home. "It's a little fucking weird."

"It's uncomfortable for me, too," I say.

"You look like you're enjoying it," says Peter. It's too early for the alcohol to be affecting him so soon. He means it.

"Listen," I say, "I swear I'm not flirting back. I'm just talking." I empty the rest of my cup into the grass by the rose bushes. "I'm not used to having people know me and talk to me. That part is nice," I tell him. I grab Peter's hips and pull them toward me. "Don't be mad, okay?" I say. I kiss his cheek and then his lips and smile my puppy dog smile.

"Not mad," says Peter, and he kisses me back. "But seriously, it's making me jealous."

"I'm going home with you," I tell him. "Don't be jealous." I kiss him again, but this time, I'm not so certain that he's kissing me back. His lips are dull and still. Not like he's into it. Another drink? How do I fix this? "We need another drink," I say. "I'm empty."

"You poured yours out," says Peter, and he points at my upside down cup in my hand. "You can't say you drank all that."

I never did, alkie. I say, "You're so adorable" and kiss him on the cheek. Grabbing his hands and wrapping them around my waist from behind, I walk us into the house. "Excuse me," I say and push a straight couple up against the wall inside. We wander back inside to the blaring speakers and guys drinking beer and playing beer pong. The table was definitely not there before, and guessing from the cups still standing, they just started a few minutes ago. Something from Nine Inch Nails or Chemical Brothers plays on the speaker. The bass is turned down quite a bit. I only know this because I know the song. A bass speaker must have gone out.

When we get into the kitchen, Peter lifts up each of the bottles and eyes the labels, then nods his head and looks at the rest of them. "You're not a drinker, are you?" he says. I guess this was rhetorical because he starts pouring something into another plastic cup and tops it off with red syrup.

"What's this?" I ask.

"Just something I came up with. Try it. It's good."

I take a sip and smack my lips at the sweetness. "Mmm," I say. My lips feel coated with a thin film of syrup. "So where are your coworkers?" I say. "And why does he know a lot of high schoolers?"

"I have no fucking idea," Peter says with a laugh. "It's a little weird."

"I know," I say. "More people know me and it's your coworker's party."

Peter takes a sip of his drink and looks around for anybody he might know. "I think I might want to leave soon," he says.

"We just got here," I say.

"Ya, but I'm bored," he says. Peter notices my frown, lets out a loud, overly dramatic sigh, and rolls his eyes. "Fine," he says and kisses me on the nose. "Let's take a look around."

"So how long have you been here in Saraday?" Peter asks me as we're walking around the perimeter of the party.

"Been here all my life," I shout back at him.

"Oh, I don't remember seeing you around before up until a few years ago," he says.

"We moved back and forth between houses," I say.

"Wow, how many houses does your family own?" he asks, a hint of being impressed in his voice.

"None," I say. "My mom had a hard time finding a job, so we had to move because we couldn't pay rent."

Peter stops in mid-step and, putting his hand to his heart, he says, "I'm so sorry." He gives me a hug and the first thing I smell is something cinnamon-like spicy and bitter. Rum, I think.

"It's okay," I tell him. I hug him back and say, "It's not like you had anything to do with it."

"But still," he says. "That was rude."

"And I'm over it." I point over Peter's shoulder. "Let's find your friend."

Peter takes me by the hand and leads me to the living room. The occupied brown leather furniture was set into a half-circle around the large fifty-eight inch high-definition television. From what I could see in the little bit of lighting made available by expensive track lighting along the tops of the six-foot tall wooden cabinets, the rug was a light cottony red that matched the décor fairly well. Clearly straight people could coordinate, too.

"Teddy?" a high-pitched squeal of a voice said just over Teddy's shoulder.

"Yes?"

"I'm Bridgette. I know you from somewhere." She moves in closer, clearly trying to get into my direct line of sight. "History? Chem class?" Her hand starts to wander over my waist.

"Um, I don't think so," I reply as I take small steps backwards. I really don't need this shit right now.

From somewhere in the living room, there is stifled laughter, the type of laughter that means someone thinks this is a joke, and a funny one at that.

"Oh come on," she says and her hands wander further, this time rubbing across my stomach and chest.

"Excuse us, bitch," says Peter, who takes her hand off me and throws it back. "You are in our way."

"Don't need to be rude, faggot. I was talking to Teddy," Bridgette blurts out in her slurred, twisted tongue. Her gold hoop earrings toss back and forth with her head movements.

"Leave us alone," Peter says. He steps up, right into her face and stares into her eyes. "Now."

"We don't need to fight," I say, again taking a few steps backward to avoid the commotion.

"I was just trying to say hi. Damn," Bridgette says. This bitch tosses her hair back. Her actions are too dramatic, wide arcs her hands make, the way her hair flips over like we're shooting a shampoo commercial. She pushes herself back into the crowd behind her. Her eyes get suddenly sweeter and she smiles at me. "Later, cutie."

"You're going to give me a fucking complex," says Peter. He chugs the rest of his drink in an impressive gulp and puts it on a wooden coaster on a cupboard near the stairs. "You know that, right?" I don't know what to say.

"There were people laughing," I say. "Someone is just messing with us. Don't let it bother you." I put my hand on Peter's, but it doesn't seem to do any good. He looks right over my head, then right through me.

"Whatever, they're drunk. Let's go," Peter says and grabs my hand again, pulls me to the front door. We pause for must have been half a second as Peter surveys the area and tugged me to my left. "This way. No one should bother us here."

I simply follow, dragging my feet, a little boy being sent to bed without supper. But this time, my nose feels warm and tingly, the way it feels whenever I have a nosebleed.

What the hell am I wishing?

I have to make it stop. Think of puppies. Think of darkness.

Wait, no. No darkness. Maybe light?

Think happy. Think good. Think being close to Peter. Think about making this all go away.

My head now bursts with pain. The pressure around my eyes makes me think of grapes being squeezed to pieces. I close my eyes even further, tighter. It makes me think vices around my head. My head packed with dry sand.

"What's the matter?" Pete says.

I say, "My head. It's fine."

"I hope you aren't drunk already," Pete says. He takes a breath and holds it into his chest, then lets it out in a long, exasperated sigh. "You know what, let's just go. This party is bullshit."

"No, no. I'll be fine. Sinuses, you know." Of course I'm lying.

"Are you ready to go?" Peter says. His voice sounds upset, eager, and deeper than usual. I'm pretty sure he's pissed off, and I do not want to be in the confined space of his car, him all pissed off at me.

"Ya, maybe," I say. If you can't beat 'em, join 'em, as they say. "Let's go say bye to Vanessa and your friend."

The group sitting on the couch had apparently been exchanged for a group of girls who didn't look very entertained by their presumed boyfriends' jokes and bathroom humor.

"Peter!" shouts a woman's voice from up above us. Tracing the line of the stairs going up, I finally find a strange girl with long brunette ponytails held up with red ribbons tightly wrapped to her head. "Up here!" she shouts.

Peter lets out another sigh and looks upwards. "Finally," he tries to say under his breath, but I still hear it.

"Is that your friend?" I point upstairs to the girl trying to wave us upstairs to see her.

"Allie," he says. "My coworker. Let's just say bye and get out of here."

Peter trudges along upstairs, pushing people out of the way. As much as I'm learning to love aggressive traits in men, I'm confused about why he's just so pissed off at me. Was it something I did?

I follow Peter upstairs and apologize to everyone we push past or shove to the side. The people on the stairs, they barely pay any attention to us. We get a few bad looks from the flaming homos, but that's about it.

"I didn't know you were going to be here," says Allie. She gives Peter a great big hug and then stops to look me over. With her index finger, she makes a circle in the air. "Turn around," she says.

"Hi," I say. "I'm Teddy, Peter's boyfriend." I extend my hand to shake hers, but she leans over to Pete and whispers something into his ears, something I can't pick up over the music in the background. Peter laughs politely.

"Allie, Teddy. Teddy, Allie," says Peter.

"Pleased to meet you," she says and finally shakes my hand.

"We're gonna go," says Peter. He looks at his bare wrist and realizes that he's not wearing a watch. "It's late."

"Where are you going?"

"Home," says Peter. She doesn't really need to know or probably even care.

"It's true," I say. "It's past my bedtime."

"Well thank you for coming!" says Allie, and she gives us both big hugs.

"Where's your bathroom?" I ask and look around upstairs.

"Use the one downstairs, next to the kitchen. That's the guest bathroom," says Allie.

I kiss Peter on the cheek and point downstairs. Peter nods and resumes his private conversation with Allie. I wish I could be a fly on the wall, but right now, my bladder calls for relief.

"Hey, buddy!" Bridgette says. This time stumbling into the side of the stairs at the foot, she waves at me. Her face looks happy and relaxed and more drunk than I've seen anyone at this party.

"Go home, Bridgette. You're drunk," I tell her when I get down to the bottom.

Bridgette's walk changes and her body twists. Her drunken stumbles make me think she's going to fall down any minute now. She's at least blacked out. Probably beyond that. In her drunken mind, she's probably the sexiest thing here, with her stomach was forced forward to accentuate her nonexistent ass.

"That is not cute," I say.

Allie said the bathroom was right around the corner, but from the bottom of the stairs, I can't see anything. The crowd looks to be slowly thinning out and going out back, which is good. I can get in and out and not worry about any more weird distractions. When I get home, I need to do something about this ridiculous magnetic attraction.

I'm pissing off Pete. If I keep this up, I don't know how to explain it all. I'll lose him. Maybe I can tell him about everything and what I can do. Maybe it's for the best?

Not tonight. I am not even sure what I would do or say if I were to confront this.

Damn bladder. Where is the bathroom?

"Can't find your boyfriend?" asks a familiar voice that I really didn't want to hear. I follow the voice to the leather couch in the living room. Shane sits there with a few of his jock basketball friends. All of them lanky and athletic and laughing at something that probably wasn't funny. I couldn't tell you their names if you pressed me, but they weren't exactly the type to introduce themselves to the outsiders. "What a faggot."

"Now is not the time, Shane," I warn. I don't know where that tone of voice came from.

"Excuse me?"

"I need to find the bathroom. Just leave me alone," I say. Just ride the wave, Teddy. Stand up to the asshole and find the damn bathroom before you wet your pants.

"Oh, faggot. I thought you could use a friend," Shane says. "So I told someone about you, and turns out she likes you."

"Friend?" I ask. And right on cue, Bridgette holds herself up in the doorway. Her legs wobble like a foal's first steps, trying to make it to where I'm standing.

"A few drinks in and she was ready to fuck, Teddy," says Shane. He looks at Bridgette's ass and approves. "You're a lucky guy."

"I don't have time for this shit," I say. "Shane, seriously, this is getting old. Leave me alone." And my head starts to pound again. I sniffle from something tickling my nose. The iron taste of pennies covers my mouth. Warm blood trickles out of my nostrils. If I keep sniffing, I can keep the blood from spattering across the floor.

"What? Are you going to cry now? Jesus Christ, take a joke, fag," Shane says.

I wipe my nose and inspect the back of my hand. Blood, bright red.

Not now. Not here. I don't know what I'm wishing, or what's going to happen, and for the first time, I think I might just not be able to do this.

Bridgette grabs my shoulders and jumps onto my hips. "Come on, baby," she says. Her legs wrap around me and squeeze so she doesn't fall off. Her arms hold tight around my neck.

"What the hell?" I say and push on her as hard as I can. The blood trickles in thicker gobs down my nose and spreads to my shirt. To her shirt. To the floor. To everywhere and everything is just so wrong right now.

Bridgette, however, doesn't seem to notice. Her sour vodka breath presses further and further into my nose. She leans over to kiss me with her big, red sloppy lips that make me think Twizzlers.

I can't kiss this. I can't let myself be seen kissing her, especially with Pete around, so I wrap my hands around her neck. My fingers are barely touching at first at the base of her spine. And I feel angry and rage. My eyes only see her neck and my teeth clench as tight as the clutches of death. "Fuck off."

Bridgette gasps for air, her lungs making some kind of gurgling noise but her body just tightens up around me. This must be what the bulls at Pamplona feel.

What else was happening around me, I couldn't tell you. What Peter was thinking or saying or doing at that moment completely escaped my mind. What I could tell you is I barely was able to stand up. I wanted nothing more than to just run away and get this bitch off of me. I wanted her to leave me alone and die.

I was tired and bloody. My shirt stuck to my chest from blood and sweat and probably even tears. And all I thought was, I need this bitch off me.

Bridgette's face starts to turn from pink to red and some shade of violet from struggling to stay up on me. "Come on," she says in an airy, wispy voice.

"Go to hell," I say. The pressure in my eyes, the clenching of my teeth, all of this physical power travels into my fingers until finally I feel her grip loosen around me. Finally, my fingertips do not just touch each other, but the back of my hands as well. Bridgette's throat has folded like paper-mache in my grip.

When I realize this and blink to catch my focus, Bridgette falls to the floor motionless.

Someone in the crowd shouts the obvious over the banging thumpa-thumpa of the Chemical Brothers' background music. "Teddy killed that girl!"

My headache fades from my eyes the way the tide leaves the beach. My nose, however, still dripped crimson blood all over my used-to-be fabulous shirt, now saturated in the thick red liquid.

My heart shakes my chest and beats like a rabbit's. My blood-soaked shirt shows no signs of drying. I need to keep calm. No more killing.

"Oh god, oh god," I say. "I didn't mean to. I swear to God," I say. Everyone backs up away from me, slow and steady. Fear paralyzes their faces, which are all turned to the corpse on the floor.

"I can fix this," I whisper to everyone and no one in the world. I rest my nervous hands against her chest and wait for her to breathe.

Oh god. Her chest doesn't move. I slap my hands around in the air and put them back on her chest. Maybe I'm shaking too much, can't tell if she's breathing.

Her lungs don't move, not even a little bit. Her chest doesn't move up or down. I press hard on her chest, something like CPR.

True confession: I have no idea what I'm doing, but the rest of these vegetables in the room aren't going to do anything.

"Call 911!" someone shouts and I put my hand up to stop them.

"No!" I say. "I got this."

The back patio door rolls open and then closes in a dull thud. Someone has slipped about back.

Great. Witnesses.

I press on her sternum in steady pattern, pressing harder and harder each time. "Come on, dammit," I say. Every blink pushes tears out of my eyes. "Please, please, please. Don't be dead," I say in syllables, each one in time with the pounding on her chest.

I stop and look at her mouth, her lips. Examine the details for any sign of breath. Maybe I pushed her back to life.

Nothing.

I sit back on the heels of my feet. I straddle Bridgette's lifeless legs with mine.

I'm screwed. I'm screwed and I'm going to jail.

I'm crying and sniffling back all of the tears. Hands grab the back of my shirt and pull me away from the corpse. "We're leaving," says Vanessa with Peter grabbing my shirt.

"No we're not."

"Yes, we are," says Vanessa. "I'll drive."

Peter screams into the quieted house party. "You're drunk," he says. "You're not going anywhere."

Someone somewhere shuts off the pounding background music.

"Call the fucking cops!" says Shane. "Call them now. He killed her."

"Don't you do a goddamn thing," says Vanessa. She points a drunken, dizzying finger at Shane's face and says, "Shut the fuck up." Vanessa rests her hand on my shoulder. "Can't you fix this?" she says.

"What the hell is he supposed to do?" says Peter.

The back glass door opens and shuts repeatedly. Escaped teenagers run out into the suburban night air, scared as shit that I might kill them, too.

"I don't know," says Vanessa. She stumbles over her own words. "He can, like, fix stuff. You know. Do things."

Allie opens the door to the outside and looks around. "No one fucking leaves," she says.

Someone from the party tries to say something over the music, but Allie screams to the party, "Shut up!"

"I already called the cops," says one of Shane's friends. "You're fucked."

There is a collective slapping of foreheads and profanities shouted into the air.

I can't go to jail. Not for murder.

I grab her chest, pushing her breasts to each side of her chest and press down in short, firm strikes. Maybe a last-ditch effort can wake her up and we can pretend this never happened? I count to three on her chest, pressing every time, until Peter pulls me off. I prepare a story in my head. She just fell over. She was fine and then she just fell over.

That seems believable.

Oh, fuck. "I didn't mean to, honest." I can't control the sobs and heaving in my chest. My hands go limp. There's no point. No use. "Take me to jail," I say.

"Get up," Vanessa says. She slaps me on the back of my head, which really just feels like a scrape from her long fingernails. "Fix this," she says.

Shane clears his throat. "Dude, you are so fucked."

My throat was paralyzed, all of the words I want to say, the different ways of apologizing, they're all caught in my throat. Flies in spider's webs. My chest pounds from the words and my breath trying to pry their way out.

All I hear is my own sobbing. Seventeen years old and crying like a little bitch.

"Wake up! Please! Wake up!" I shout with what little breath I can force out of my windpipe. My eyes blur from the tears, so that everyone looks like a faded, yet colorful ghosts of themselves. What forces me to blink and try to focus is the warm drop on the back of my left hand. The dot isn't clear and watery. It's red and thick and for a moment, I think I might actually be out of the clear.

"Oh my god," says Allie.

A cough and a gasp echo into the still house.

Out front, no reds and blues flashing around and around, nothing to announce that I was going to go to jail to get raped.

"What the hell?" Peter says above me.

More coughs and wheezes.

Vanessa pats me on the back of my head and says, "Teddy, you did it!"

Bridgette twitches and coughs. Her hands run over her body like she's trying to rip and grab at something on her.

"Hoooleee fuck," Shane says. "She's alive."

"She's alive?" I say. I'm not sure how much of this I all believe, but I wipe my eyes anyhow and try to focus long enough to see the proof for myself.

Bridgette's eyelids flash open and her eyes dilate wide and black. Her breath wheezes in and out of her chest. She sounds like she's drowning.

"Dude, your CPR shit worked on a dead person?" says Shane.

Bridgette's body twitches more and gasps for oxygen. Her black and blue throat flaps in and out, making a gurgling sound that reminds me of a garbage disposal.

"Help me," she says. The words barely escape from her lips. Her hands claw and grab a weak hold of my leg. I kick off her hand in a terrified gut reaction. No matter what you know, if you feel attacked it's funny how fast you'll kick and push to stay safe.

"You didn't kill her," says Vanessa with a smile.

"Call an ambulance!" says Allie into the crowd. "Someone have a phone?"

And without hesitation, at least a dozen teenagers reach into the pockets and produce cell phones and start dialing.

Some teenagers actually are calling 911. Others take pictures and send them to friends. The real assholes record all this.

Bridgette's moans for help subside, and her head twitches in spasm. She flips over onto her side and then onto her stomach and tries to do what looks like a pushup. Her legs wobble and can barely remain still. Her steps become smaller and smaller until she's climbing on me to stand up and find some balance. Her neck just pulses and flaps in and out the way a fish tries to breathe underwater. In the ceiling lights, my handprint bruises come out of the shadows and surround her neck.

"Dude, like a zombie," mutters Shane. "Fuck this," he says and runs for the door.

Allie walks over to Bridgette and puts her hands up, but tries everything to keep from actually touching her. "Just stay there," the responsible host of the party says. "We're going to get you help."

The new zombie Bridgette doesn't seem to listen, and she lets out whimpers and stifled sobs. Her hands grab onto Allie's blouse and pull herself to Allie.

"Help me," says Allie. No one moves.

What sounds like "Help me," come out in a guttural moan from the zombie's mouth.

With Bridgette turned away from me, I had a better view of her neck better now. I had nearly crushed her esophagus where I grabbed her neck. My handprints, which had helped to outline her trachea, were still on her neck. My evidence was all over this girl.

"I'm gonna be sick," I say and bend over, resting my hands on my knees.

"We're trying to help you out," says Peter, "but you need to stay still." Peter grabs her hand off of Allie and pushes her off to the side, safe from the zombie's grasp.

"Herrp," the zombie gurgles. Zombie Bridgette body paces ever so slowly toward me and puts her hands up in front of her.

"Stay right there," says Peter. "We're trying to get you help." He looks into the crowd, "Are any of you assholes actually calling 911?"

"Ya, they're coming," says someone tall from the crowd. Probably one of Shane's basketball teammates.

My back feels itchy and cold and wet, and that's when I turn away.

"Let's go," says Vanessa. She grabs my shirt at the neck. "We need to go, now!" Vanessa grabs at my arm and pulls me up and to the front door. "They are coming and we need to leave," she says.

"We can't just leave her," says Peter. As helpful as he is trying to be to Bridgette, even he keeps his distance from her.

"Do you want Teddy to go to jail?" says Vanessa. Peter shakes his head. "Then get your asses into the car now!" Vanessa approaches the front door with such authority that Allie gets out of the way. My sister opens the door and the breeze of the cool air rushes in and soothes the itch from the sweat on my chest and back.

"Bridgette! No!" Allie screams at the top of her lungs as Bridgette's body drops back to the floor and grabs at its own throat. Its legs kick at everyone. Bridgette's corpse was choking from not having any air. But I still made her still alive. Caught up in an eternal hell of being forced alive but not able to breathe.

What the hell did I do? Am I that kind of person?

"I can fix this," I say. I look over to Vanessa, but her hands tell me that we're leaving.

"Peter! Come on!" says Vanessa and she grabs me and pushes me out the door. Bridgette's body and the entire crowd are in the house, just out of my sight. I take careful steps to get to the front door, back inside, and Peter's body appears to block my view.

"I can fix this," I say.

"What did you do?" Peter says. His eyes are so glassy they reflect my eyes. The way he looks right now, I just want to give him a hug. But I can't. Blood and sweat everywhere.

"I can't stay here," I say. I pull the front of my shirt up. "I look like I killed her," I say.

"You," says Peter, but he can't finish the sentence. He doesn't want to say what he's thinking. He can't bring himself to say the truth. I don't blame him.

Bridgette's spasms make wet slap sounds against the floor inside.

"Oh my god. I didn't want this to happen, please," I say to Peter.

Peter pushes me aside and walks to the driver's side of his car. Vanessa comes following after and I'm motionless. I can't take any steps.

How do you explain this?

How do you tell the one you love that you just brought someone back to life after you killed them?

I'm not that person.

26

Once the bottom of the casket has filled with dirt, I can finally start to sit up. This whole that I'm digging, it's the opposite of what those kids dig to get to China. Instead of going down, I'm going up.

My shirt is starting to feel heavy and damp against my head. It's difficult to breathe down here, and the more I strain to sit up and dig, the more I breathe. The more I breathe, the more I realize that I am using up my air supply.

Gotta work fast, Teddy.

The ground in this part of the country is really wet usually. South Carolina is in what we call the humid subtropical range. What this means is we get a lot of rain, we get a lot of humidity, and it's really hot.

None of this is conducive to working this hard. What I can tell you is, the more you relax, the easier it is on your muscles.

I'm guessing that Peter is still above ground, hopefully gone home and living his life. I want him to be unsuspecting. I want him to be busy watching television, playing on his Gamestation 3, or jerking off. As long as he's distracted when I come into the same room as him so I can kill him.

Stab him, beat him.

It's true, you know. You do only hurt the ones you love. The rest I could care less about.

When I said I'm not a murderer, I meant it.

What happened with Bridgette, that wasn't important. That was what happens in life. Sometimes we lose people. And sometimes they come back.

These are the things I ask myself with every dig and push. With my hands and fingernails filled with dirt and moist soil, I think about what I could have done better. What could I have done more? Or less?

Was I really that heartless? Do I deserve to die down here?

The old question used to be, if you could go back and kill Hitler, could you? If you could prevent it all from happening, would you?

If I could do all of this over again, would I?

No. People need to know. They need to suffer and they need to learn from their mistakes.

If life has taught me anything, it's that you cannot avoid suffering.

But I believe in short suffering. Learn your damned lesson and move on.

Believe me, Peter, I've learned my lesson. And now, you're going to learn yours.

27

What Vanessa had called "a necessary evil," I called "crossing the line." We had to agree to disagree considering the circumstances.

The ride home was filled with the kinds of silence that make you want to dig out your own eyeballs for pleasure. Not one of us felt like we needed to say a single word, but it's funny the things that go on in your head when there is no one else talking.

It was natural to want to fill that silence with something.

Me? I choose sobs.

"You're not going to jail, Teddy," says my sister. "I won't let them take you."

On the way to back to the house there was a sense that everyone was trying to make sense of it all. If I were pressed, it would be easy to say that Vanessa is taking it the best out of all of us.

"What?" says Peter. He takes a long breath and says again, "What the hell happened back there?"

Butterflies rule my stomach. Their wings flitter about my insides and since I didn't lose it at the party, I might have to lose it here.

"Nothing," I say.

"You're not going to tell him?" says Vanessa from the backseat. "Really? After all of that?"

"Shut up," I say. "There is nothing to talk about."

Outside, the stars twinkle at us. The planets hover over our heads and the Cheshire cat moon smiles at my fortune of not going to prison.

"So you killed this girl, and she just woke up because of your CPR?" says Peter. His eyes want to leave the road and look at me, but we had a lot of things going against us right now. With it being nighttime, no street lights in this part of town, and the fact that we'd all been drinking, it wasn't the best idea to leave our lives in the hands of fate.

But again, maybe we can fix this.

"I can fix this," I say.

"You keep saying that, Teddy, but I have no idea what you mean." Peter's eyes look at Vanessa in the rearview mirror. "Do you know what he's rambling about?"

Vanessa looks outside, then back up front to us to avoid Peter's line of sight. "Maybe you have to do it to him, too," she whispers.

"I am not killing Peter!" I say.

The car's brakes nearly stop the car to a complete halt. Tires squeal and the burnt smell of rubber comes into the car from outside.

"What?" he says.

"Peter, no one said anything," I say.

Peter's face glows red. I can nearly feel the heat of his rage and frustration from over here on the other side of the car. "What. The. Hell. Is. Going. On. Here?" he screams. His screaming rattles the insides of my eardrums, the sound you get from crumpling and uncrumpling tin foil.

"Nothing!" I scream back.

"You have to fix him, too," says Vanessa.

And I close my eyes. "I wish you didn't have to know these things," I say. "No one saw anything," I say.

"I know what I saw, Teddy," says Peter.

My eyes go to the rearview mirror to the side view mirrors to the rearview mirror again. I pray that another car does not ram into us at this time of night. I can't take all of this life and death in one night.

"Peter, you have to trust me," I say. I look right into his eyes. I've never tried to intentionally apply my abilities to someone, I have no idea what I'm doing. The closest approximation I can make is try to be a hypnotist. "Nothing happened tonight." I look at Vanessa and she nods.

"The party was boring, so we went home. You had a lot to drink and everything was fine." My forehead muscles strain and feel like gauze wrapping my head tight from the concentration. "We're going home and everything was fine. You saw nothing weird tonight." Peter's face goes from tense to relaxed, his mouth slipping back into a relaxed smile from the menacing growl of before.

"And Vanessa looked absolutely fabulous and Teddy was as cute as ever," says Vanessa.

"You're not helping," I tell her. "Just shut up." I take Peter's hand in mind and rub the back of it. "Do you understand?" I say to Peter.

Peter nods, silent and mouth slightly open. He looks like he's been asleep and just woke up. "So that was a fun party, eh, guys?" says Peter. His hand clenches mine in our "I love you" manner.

Vanessa taps me on the shoulder, nods, and smiles. "Of course it was!" she says.

"It was kind of boring, though," says Peter.

"Totally," I say. "It's a good thing we left early."

Vanessa takes off her shoes in the car and puts her feet up on the plastic armrest between the two of us. "We should try to do it again sometime," she says.

WHEN WE GET BACK to the apartment, Vanessa gets out of the car first. She takes quick, high-footed steps to avoid the sharp gravel rocks in our parking lot. "I'll leave you two alone," she says.

"Thanks for taking me to the party," I say.

Peter grabs my head and leans in to kiss me. "Thank you for coming." His hazel eyes smile back at me. You can't not smile at how cute he looks right now.

"Do you remember anything weird tonight?" I ask.

Peter keeps his smile but his eyes narrow. "No, nothing weird tonight. Why do you ask?"

I shake my head and kiss him on his cheek. "No reason," I say. "Just wanted to make sure you were okay."

Peter grabs my hand and kisses my middle finger's knuckle. "I'm always okay when I'm with you."

The warmth rushing to my cheeks tells me that I'm blushing at his Prince Charming dialogue. It's all perfect.

"I'll see you tomorrow," I say. I open my door and set my foot outside on the ground. "Good night," I say.

Peter looks at me with an intensity I haven't seen in his eyes before. "I," he starts to say, then shrugs it off and looks back at me. "Good night, Teddy."

I watch Peter drive away and go directly to my bedroom inside.

"You fucking pulled it off!" says Vanessa. She tosses her shoes across my bedroom and the land next to my pile of dirty clothes. Okay, okay. Next to one of the piles of dirty clothes I have in my room.

"I don't want to talk about it," I say.

"You brought her back to life," she says. "With your powers!" she says. "You're like a superhero."

"I am not a superhero," I say back to her. I bury my head under my pillows. In my mind's eye, I see Bridgette's neck flail in and out like watching someone breathe into a paper bag.

"Well, you're something," she says. Vanessa rests her ass on my bed and touches my leg. "What's your problem?" she says.

"I'm a fucking murderer," I say through the pillow. It's a little too hard to breathe through all the down and fabric so I pull it away from my face. "I wasn't in control and I nearly hurt someone," I say. "This can't happen." I take a deep breath and try to fight off the tears, which are already building up in my tear ducts. "I used my ability on Peter and made him forget and all of these people wanted to be around me and were saying hi to me but I didn't want to talk to them. I just wanted Peter, but he was so pissed off tonight because everyone was hitting on me. Even the straight ones were hitting on me." All of this comes out in a sobs and sniffles.

"This is how popular people feel," she says. "I read in the magazines all the time that they are always being approached by people and how fake everyone is," she says. "But the truth is, this is how it is to be popular. It's the natural order to things. When you're popular, people need to be near you, they want you. As a friend or as a boyfriend. It's how things have to go. You can't be upset about it."

"I can be if it costs me Peter," I say.

Vanessa's face looks serious and stern. With a motherly serious voice, she says, "Actors and singers, you think they just become famous and everything is perfect for them?" Vanessa shakes her head. "Of course not."

It's clear that Vanessa is on autopilot. I begin to wonder just how long she's had this speech ready for me, or how long she has been telling herself this in anticipation of becoming famous herself.

"We can't just be whiny and complain because people want to be around us." Vanessa rubs my calf muscle with her hands in a somewhat odd attempt to be soothing. "We can't wait for someone to condolence with us. We need strong people in our lives who can tolerate what we are and who we are. If they can't deal with your entire life, then they don' deserve you."

If I had the strength, I'd punch my sister right now. "But this isn't my real life. In my real life, everyone hates me. I'm a freak and people talk about me behind my back. In the real world, our entire school isn't somehow gay for me. In the real world, people can't die and come back to life as a zombie," I say.

"Keep it down or you'll wake up Mom," says Vanessa.

I ignore her and keep my tone of voice. "No, you won't listen to me." I swallow my spit to buy me time to figure out just how to say this, "I made myself popular, and this is how it turned out. And I bled.

I was bleeding when this all happened, and I think maybe if I bleed when I use my powers, then something goes wrong. I told Bridgette to go to Hell, and she died." I sob. "I didn't mean to use my power then. It's starting on its own."

"What if you really wanted her to die? What if you said exactly what you meant?" she says. Ya, now's a great time to start being smart, Sis.

"What if I didn't, and it was just a figure of speech?" I say. "I can't control this," I say. "What if I do worse next time?"

My sister looks at me, looks at my floor, and then stands up. "I don't know what to tell you," she says.

"See?" I say. "I'm fucked."

"Maybe not," Vanessa says. My sister grabs her shoes from my floor and takes small steps to my bedroom door. "You also saved her from dying." My sister opens the door and walks through it, saying, "Good night."

With the door closed and the light on, I'm finally alone to process my thoughts all by myself. I try my hardest to stare at the walls and not blink. Every time I close my eyes, Bridgette's bruises come back to haunt me. In those moments in the darkness of my eyelids, the sounds of her throat gasping for air thunders through my eardrums.

I can't blink. To avoid being in complete silence, I turn on my radio alarm clock and just let it play. It's an alternative rock station, playing something with a whiny Canadian punk sound.

Vanessa was wrong. This isn't the way things are supposed to be. I can change it.

I can change anything, if I focus hard enough, the world can change and be a better place. It's my job and my right.

Why else would I have these powers?

The possibilities are endless. I can make people nicer. I can make them all love each other. I can make them happy. I can love openly and not worry about whether someone is going to call me a faggot or fairy.

These are all things I can do. These are all things I will do. I command it because I can make it happen. I just have to want it, to bend reality to my will.

The trick, I've been told, is that you have to change everyone else's mind.

My will be done.

28

So, I guess when you bring people back to life, the general consensus is that you're a hero. What I didn't predict when I did all of this was that Bridgette's family would be thankful for me, poor old me, for saving their daughter.

At least that's what I tell them when they come knocking at my door.

It's good to be king of your own little world. I am my own genie, screw ever needing a lamp.

When the police come to the front door, Mom's hands could not keep a steady hold on anything. Her fear that I was going to be imprisoned or put in rape prison kept her from being able to offer anyone something to drink without dropping.

"Please, ma'am," says one of the policemen, "we're looking for your son Theodore?" The policemen refuse to sit down, turning down every offer of my mother's to actually come in and sit down. "Please, if we could just talk to Teddy."

I listen from upstairs and it's not a hyperbole to say that my heart nearly burst through my chest. "Mom!" I call downstairs from my bedroom. "Mom? Is everything okay?"

From downstairs, my mom shouts up, "Teddy, these men would like to talk to you."

I trudge downstairs, every step a new reasoning I can use to push into their heads. I was saving her from choking. I tried to massage her neck. I was pretending to choke her and someone bumped into me.

In a perfect world, let me tell you.

The cops are talking to my mom by the front door. The porcelain rattling of my mom's uneasiness shakes the coffee cup and saucer she holds underneath it. From the bottom step, where I hide behind the white plaster corner, I can hear my mom's banter about the weather and her pleads about what I did wrong and please, could I just get a slap on the wrist.

The cops are saying, I don't know what.

"Mom, what's up?" I say. My feet bounce on the floor. I'm in my socks only, so I glide across the hardwood floors.

"Teddy," says Mom. "What did you do?"

"I didn't do anything," I say. Looking at both of the cops directly in the eyes. Rule number one of Teddy's Rules for Flirting. I say, "What can I do you for?"

"We have questions for you," says the tallest cop, a cute, chiseled, square jaw type with blond hair that curls around his ears. "Do you mind if we come in?" he says. His hands motion to the living room where I think he wants me to take a seat.

I nod and follow his hand motions and sit down and cross my legs. "Is this about last night?" I ask.

My mom gasps and the cops look at each other with a look that they didn't think I'd admit to anything.

Newsflash, morons. I still won't.

The blonde cop says, "We need to get some information about what happened." He flips through a notepad of paper. "A girl" he says, flipping through his paper.

"Bridgette," I say. "Ya, she fell to the ground, and I used CPR and woke her up." I smile and look at both of them. Be honest, Teddy. Tell them the truth. Your new truth.

The front of my head tingles and feels tense, my muscles turning to tight wires across my head.

"So that is your story of what happened?" he asks.

"Yes," I say. Focus on what I want. Stare into his eyes and tell him this is the truth. "She started to choke, and I saved her." The more I tell, the more I can prove, right? "I know it looks like she was choking, but I swear that she was just choking on something," I shrug, look like I'm looking for an answer. "I don't know, ice or something?"

That sounds believable.

"Well, she was talking to me and she started to grab onto me, then grabbed at her neck and I dropped down and saved her."

"But reports say that you ran," says the other cop. "Why?"

"We ran because my sister was scared. Listen, they dragged me out of the house because I wanted to make sure that everyone was safe and okay," I say. The way I see this, the more I mix truth with lies, the more I can get away with later. Focus on your thoughts, Teddy.

Focus on his thoughts. Make a new reality.

"That seems reasonable," says the blonde cop. His puppy dog green eyes glance back and forth between my left eye and my right eye; he wants me to lock his eyes with him, too.

Is my other wish still working? Does he want me, too?

"I thought so," I say.

"What was that?" says the other cop. He takes a step closer to me, but carefully. In his mind, I might be leading them on, lying to them, or going to attack them. Who knows with cops?

"Thank you, Teddy," says the blonde cop. He nods to my mom and then offers his hand for me to shake it. "We'll let you know if we have any other questions," he says.

"So is everything okay?" says my mom. "Will he be okay?" she says. My mom rests the cup of coffee on the side table and clasps her hands together. "Will my Teddy be going to jail?" she says.

"No, I don't think he's going to jail," the blond one says. "Like I said, we'll let you know if we have any other questions. Just make sure that you don't go anywhere. It tends to look more suspicious," the cute one says.

"Mom," I say. I put my hand on my mom's back as a reminder that yes, I am still in the room. "Mom, I'm okay. Everything will be fine."

The blonde cop smiles at me.

I say, "I'm sure of it."

My mom thanks both of the cops and the front door clicks shut behind them.

"What the hell did you do?" Mom says. Her hands move to her hips and her face flushes bright, warm red. "Did you kill someone?"

"What?" I say. Shrug it off, don't let her believe it. "Of course not. That's stupid, Mom."

"So I'm stupid now?" My mom takes a step closer to me and I take a step back to avoid her wrath. "Because it clearly sounded like someone said you killed Bridgette."

"I didn't kill anyone, I save her," I say. "You weren't listening."

"I was listening plenty," Mom says. She reaches for the coffee cup and saucer from the side table, but drops it from the nerves and shakes. "Damn it to hell. Go get the broom."

"I swear, Mom, I didn't do anything." Mom's eyes narrow and I think I hear her foot tapping, but I'm too afraid to break eye contact to find out.

"So just what else do you do when you're not home at night?" she says.

"Just hanging out, Mom, I swear."

Mom takes her dishes into the kitchen and drops them into the kitchen sink with an eardrum-piercing clink. Then, a dull thud follows, the sound of her hands holding herself up on the edge of the sink. She lets out a thick sigh, then calls me into the kitchen.

"You're not going out for a while," she says. "You're grounded."

"I'm seventeen. You can't ground me," I say. "Remember?"

"Oh, I remember all right. Don't tell me what I can and cannot do, Theodore." My mom crosses her arms across her chest to show that she means business. "You're still my son, living under this roof, and I say that you're grounded."

"And what are you going to do about it when I'm at home and you're at work?" I say.

And to up the ante, my mom says, "You will not leave this house, end of story." My mom literally puts her foot down and I'm supposed to somehow follow her will.

"Fuck that, and fuck you," I yell back at her. From the kitchen I grab my jacket from the door handle of the closet. I rage open the door and slam it shut so hard it shakes the carport. The world seems so big when you stand against your oppressors. From here I can go anywhere. I can go across the street, to the left or to the right.

Where I decide to go, you can probably already guess.

"Theodore! You get back here," my mom shouts behind me. Her voice echoes into the cold empty air of the subdivision. "Teddy!" she screams.

I just walk, quickly at first, to get my distance away from the house. I figure once I get a certain distance--and no, I don't know how long that will take--I can stop and determine my real destination.

But right now? I need to mean business, and you can only mean business when you walk with a purpose. You mean business by meaning what you say and do. And right now, I really mean to piss off my mother.

A small four-door sedan peels around the corner, announcing its presence in a screech. This can only mean one thing and one person. I love her to death, but my sister can't drive worth shit. Vanessa, my dear speed demon sister, pulls up onto the side of the street when she sees me walking by.

"Where are you going?" she says.

"To Owl," I say. "I want to talk to Peter."

"Did you hear what happened?" Vanessa says. "To Bridgette?"

"Ya, the police came by," I say. "They wanted my side of the story. The kids are telling everyone that I killed her." I look back at the house and then to my sister. "I wouldn't just go home yet," I say. "Mom's pretty pissed off at me."

Vanessa sighs. A click from the inside car cracks the door open. My sister gives it one great push, and she shoves it wide open. "Get in."

Almost to the parking lot of Owl Foods, she finally asks, "So what did you do?" She smiles and looks at me and flicks the blinker with her middle finger. "I mean, what did the favorite child do to start all of this?"

"The police came by and I think Mom got scared that I was accused of killing someone."

"That would do it," she says. Vanessa decides to take a parking spot near the end of the lot. This was a habit she did frequently, possibly driven by the fear of some vehicularly transmitted diseases.

"Then, she told me that I can't leave the house and she was going to ground me, so I left."

"You've never been grounded," Vanessa says. "You must have really fucked up."

"Her baby has grown up and she thinks I'm getting into trouble," I say. "I just wish she'd realize that I can't be controlled all the time."

"She knows it," my sister says. "She just doesn't like it."

"I'll get a ride home," I tell her. "You don't have to wait for me or anything." I get out and close the door and poke my head in by the opened window. "If she asks, you didn't see me," I tell her.

"You got it, boss," she says and waves her pink fingernails at me. "Don't do anything I wouldn't do," she says with a coy smile. She thinks she's being clever, like I've never heard that one before.

"That's a short list," I say and laugh. Vanessa's rear lights disappear as she turns right past the traffic lights and drives home.

PETER IS STOCKING eggs in the refrigerator freezer section near the back of the store. "Pete," I say and tap on the glass door to get his attention. "Pete? Do you have a minute?"

"For you, anything," he says. His hazel eyes blink at me, talk directly to me. I follow them to the break room, which is really just off to the side of the warehouse near the refrigeration units. "You can't come back here," he says and kisses me on the nose. "Just wait a second."

Ten seconds pass and I'm caught up in the layers and layers of colorful boxes and pictures of food everywhere. Clear plastic wrap--

giant versions of what you wrap food in at a normal kitchen--covered what Peter called pallets all over the back area. Near the corner, a red monster of a metal box sat, hungry, ready to eat the next thing that any innocent person threw in there. Boxes, tape, hands.

"I convinced my bosses to have a lunch break now," says Pete, reappearing from behind the break room door. "Want to go get something to eat?"

I follow Pete to the front of the store and out into the bright and humid outside. God's flashlight, that little sun, follows us as we walk to the Taco Hell in the same shopping complex. It seems God knows what we're up to today.

"Pete," I say. "I was wondering if you knew anything that happened last night."

"You already asked that," he says. He grabs my hand and squeezes. "Why do you ask?"

"Just making sure." My lungs let go of their air and freeze while the words run around in my head. Just how do you tell someone that you're virtually a god? "I was visited by the cops today, Pete. They think that I killed Bridgette."

"But you saved her life with CPR. That doesn't make any sense."

"I know," I say. "But it's like they don't believe me." I shrug, pretend that I don't really know what happened. "I guess they aren't sure just why Bridgette passed out to begin with."

"Is she going to be okay?" he says.

"Listen," I tell him. I step in front of Peter and look over into his hazel eyes. If eyes are the window to your soul, then I guess Peter's soul must be warm and cozy. "I need to tell you something."

Just for reassurance--and to make sure that he can't run away--my hands grab both of his and they pull him directly in front of me.

"Look at me," I say.

"What's wrong?" he says and kisses me on the cheek with a quick peck.

"I don't know how to say this," I say. My eyes glance to the ground, stare at his feet to get away from the pressure of admitting all of this.

Peter glances back into my eyes and says, "Teddy, you can tell me anything."

"Okay then," I say, "here it is."

"Faggots!" says a man's voice from a white truck that drives past us on the parking lot.

"Morons," I say. My hands clench Peter's, claw-like, as the truck comes around the cement blocks and drives up our section of the parking lot.

"What are you pansies doing?" says the boy, not man. The voice, the only person in the truck, was Shane, still upset that I turned him down, I see.

"Going to get food, want to join us?" I say.

"Fuck no, I don't want to join you," he says. The truck keeps running, but the white door opens and reflects the sunlight into our eyes. I cover my face and stand back. When I uncover them again, Shane is standing right in front of Peter and me. "This your boyfriend?" he says.

"Yes," I say.

"Is this the guy from last night?" says Peter.

"I wouldn't worry about him," I say. To Shane I say, "Get back in the truck and go home, Shane."

"I just wanna talk with you, that's all."

"We don't want to talk to you," I say. "Peter doesn't have a lot of time on his lunch break."

"Aww, a lunch with your fag boyfriend?" he says.

And as much as the taunts are supposed to piss us off, all that runs through my head is the consideration that no, Pete does not really look like he is gay. A little emo, maybe, but not gay. His dark choice of clothing and hair draped over his eyes adds more of a mysterious quality than a gay one. Maybe that's what I like most about him. He doesn't look like that stereotypes of skinny, short hair, and effeminate motions. If I wanted to date a man who wanted to be a woman, I'd just be straight and date women.

"He's not faggy at all," I say. Am I surprised that I was able to speak up? Yes. Do I think, in retrospect, that this is going to be beneficial? No.

Shane responds by grabbing my shirt and slamming me up against the truck's door. He hits me so hard, my body slams the once opened door shut and he smiles in my face with a toothy grin that could pass off as a grimace, too.

"Shut the fuck up," he says.

Peter stands there, paralyzed as before. The way he couldn't do anything when the store was held up, too.

"Peter," I say.

Nothing. No response.

"Peter's not here right now," says Shane, like three centimeters from my face. His nose barely touches mine. "Please leave a message after the beep."

And Shane's legs, it goes up into my crotch. Fire shoots up my groin, my chest, and my head. My head fills with the words "pain" and "revenge."

"Shane," I say between wincing. "Stop." Peter needs to snap out of this. "Pete!" I shout. "Run for help!"

Peter stands there, looking at the both of Shane's hands shoving me up against the truck's door.

"Peter!" I shout at him again. Peter's feet steps backwards, one after the other, until finally he's starting to run but trips and lands on his back.

"This is ridiculous," I say. "Shane, leave me alone, I don't want to hurt you."

"You're not in a position to hurt me," he says.

"Then why are you so upset after I turned you down?" I say. "In the lockers?"

"Fuck you, I'm not gay," he says.

"You were gay enough to hit on me completely naked," I say. "Are you?" I say. "Gay?"

Shane's grip on my shirt tightens under his knuckles and he slams me up against the truck again. And again.

"I'm."

Slam.

"Not."

Slam.

"Gay!"

Slam.

"Fag!"

"Stop," I shout and Shane's hands and body tighten up like he's carved out of rock. "Back off!" I shout at him. Shane's eyes open wide at my screams. My blood flows hot under my skin. My palms sweaty, I grab Shane's head and push him backwards.

Shane barely stands up and stares at me, frozen.

"Fuck, man. Leave me alone!" I say. Tears stream down my face. I know it's coming, and I know what has to be done. My tears tickle as they drip down to my chin and drop to the asphalt below. "Please, just leave me alone!"

"What the hell?" Shane says. His hands pull themselves forward, then freeze, suspended in thin air.

Teddy's head, the muscles underneath my skin, they all feel on fire, a pearly fire that circles around my line of vision. His nose begins to drip. An iron metal taste fills the back of my throat when I sniffle back a few drops of blood. "Don't make me do this," I say, finally standing up away from the truck.

The terror in Shane's eyes speaks for itself. But it's too late.

My will be done.

It's a shame that there's nothing we can do about it now.

Was the same look of terror in everyone's eyes when I made Bridgette drop to the ground? When I sent her to Hell?

I can barely keep from screaming, so I clench my jaws tight and speak through the sides of my mouth. Shane's frozen figure looks like a mannequin with lifelike eyes. So lifelike. So real. Almost like he really does feel pain and remorse.

"Don't make me do this," I say underneath my clenched teeth and burning eyes.

"Do what, faggot?" says Shane.

"Shut up," I say.

"How the fuck did you do that?" Shane's muscles flex but his arms, his legs, his body doesn't move anywhere. They don't go anywhere because I don't want him to.

Shane's eyes follow me when I walk around, staring down the figure of my would-be assassin. "I can't fucking move!" Shane cries. But his chest, it doesn't move. It, too, frozen in time.

Whatever I wanted for Shane, looks like I forgot to let him breathe.

"Why can't you just leave me alone? All you do is terrorize me." I have no fear in my voice. It's refreshing to speak this clearly and so demandingly to my attacker. I am possessed of the words of God, my will be done. "I wanted to believe that you can change, that you can be a normal, decent human being. But you don't change. Things never. Freaking. Change."

"I'm sorry! I'm sorry!" Shane tries to cry through his closed mouth. His voice cracks from little or no air. His chest can't move and he doesn't have the lung capacity to shout.

"I'm going to change it, again. I really need for all of this to stop, Shane."

"What the fuck are you doing, Teddy?" says Peter from behind us. His voice shakes from the terror of knowing that my hands control what happens to Shane. "How the hell did you do this?"

"Shut up, Peter! I know what I'm doing." I close my eyes and Shane's lower jaw is forced upwards like being hit from an invisible uppercut. A sound of pop and Shane's teeth shattering sounds like a beautiful tune in my ears.

Shane cries as much as he can through his locked lips. "Help!" he screeches. "Help!" His lips smack when he speaks, and he cannot quite make the 'ha' sound.

Nice ventriloquist act, Shane.

"Why can't you just die and leave me alone?" I say. I stare down Shane, looking for humanity or fear in his eyes. What I find instead are tears streaming down Shane's face and fall onto the rocky black asphalt below. "No more crying, no more mercy, no more anything. I'm fucking tired of the bullshit."

Cars pass by on the street, and Peter lays stuck, frozen as Shane, but that's not my doing, I swear, on the ground. Why doesn't he try to stop me? Why doesn't he run for help?

"I'm tired of it all. Don't you realize I can tear you apart? Right here, as painfully as I want." I continue to circle my whimpering victim, checking him up and down. "You don't seem to realize that you picked on the wrong boy, Shane." I close my eyes and freeze. I concentrate on his fists. The pearly fire that burns the inside of my head appears closer and closer around my eyes.

The cries and muted screams of Shane get progressively fainter and fainter.

Shane's fingers look lighter and fainter, almost transparent. The way things look when you look through colored saran wrap? That's how the world looks like through Shane's hands.

Shane remains frozen in the middle of the parking lot, holding nothing but air.

"Here's an idea!" I say to Shane. Nothing like announcing your plan in that good ol' fashioned bad guy kind of way.

"I wanna fuckin' tear you apart" I sing. My nose drips blood at first, then it streams down my nose, my front lip, and finally falling off my chin.

Shane whimpers and shrieks, somehow, despite not being able to move is chest. This must be incredibly painful, poor boy.

Shane's shoes turn transparent, then disappear like mist into the afternoon sky. I can only imagine what that feels like. His socks, too, disappear.

I feel Shane's body wanting to shiver from the fear. That terror of his body shakes him uncontrollably. That's how in command of his body I am right now.

"Bye, Shane," I say. "I'm tired of your shit, and it's time you go away."

Shane's pants and shirt rip off his body, each thread disappearing and evaporating into the air. What sounds like muffled screaming pushes out of Shane's mouth. That same naked body that tried to tempt me now stands before me, terrified.

I'll admit, the way he waved it around at me, you'd think he was bigger downstairs.

Shane's feet, and toenails and the hair on his legs, all of it shreds off his body like mist. They break down into smaller pieces and flutter into the air into nothingness.

I am completely enraptured by the miracle I am creating.

Shane's eyes search some kind of remorse from Peter, but Peter is practically comatose right now. No signs of support or wanting to help. Deep down inside, Peter must want this to happen. He understands that this needs to happen if we're going to be better.

That saying that the world would be better if you weren't born? Shane is about to find out if that's true.

I want to say something that this would be over soon, but I can't. It's not easy just wiping someone from the world like a stray mark on a sketch.

Flakes from Shane's back disappear and evaporate. Shane's entire hairless body is bare before me. His flesh becomes exposed as more and more of his skin just flakes off and dissipates into the ether. Blood and mucus and hair and bones, all of it evaporates like water.

I turn around and start to gag. There is a reason why I could never be a doctor. Sorry, Mom.

Now that I'm turned around from the decomposing corpse, I become aware that the world is not watching this. Out here, halfway between the store and Taco Hell, no one is watching. Peter is frozen to the ground and watches in a blank horror.

My greatest masterpiece, and no one is here to share it.

My stomach gurgles and my throat wants to close up. I cough to loosen everything up and keep breathing.

In my head, the visions of Shane's blood and muscles exposed and praying for my mercy won't go away.

I turn back around to my victim. Shane's facial muscles are made bare against the warm afternoon and the setting sun.

I don't know how much I can actually watch of this. The feelings of cold sweat and butterflies turn his stomach and he coughs up a white, thick foamy fluid.

"Jesus Christ, what are you doing?" shouts Peter.

"Now you decide to say something?" I say between spits and coughs. A pile of white mucus covers the toes of my shoes. My vomit and tears mix together underneath me. I kneel down to keep from feeling woozy.

"Dude, are you ok?" says Peter.

"No!" I scream back. I don't want Peter to get hurt. "Stay back!"

Peter holds out his hand and lifts me up. He rubs my back with his giant calloused hands and squints around me. "What happened to Shane?"

"I killed him," I say. My head feels like something is trying to dig itself out of my skull. "I killed him," I whisper again to myself. It's a question as much as a confession.

"Where's the body? What happened here? How did you do this?" Pete fires these questions rapid, machine gun style. He probably isn't even sure if he wants to hear the answers. He most likely can't handle the answers.

"I just tore him apart." My calm at being able to say all of this surprises even myself. "He's all gone."

"Teddy, can you tell me what happened? What's going on here?" Peter says.

"I don't know how to say this. I don't know what happened. I just wanted him gone. I had to. I had to save us. You understand," I say. I grab Peter's arm at the elbow and pull myself toward him. I need for him to believe in me. He needs to believe that this is the right thing.

Pete drops his grip on me and I cry at I don't know what.

"What's happening?" Peter says. He points at the truck, then points at where Shane used to be standing. "Where is he?" Peter's eyes fill with tears that fall down his face when he blinks and looks to me for an answer. "I know I just saw him here, Teddy. He couldn't have just disappeared." Peter's eyes search the truck for traces of Shane's existence. "I'm not crazy, Teddy. I know he was here!" Peter sits on the ground and starts talking words, incomplete sentences, things I don't understand from the mumbling.

Pete stops the mumbles and stares up at me, searching my eyes. "Did you do this?"

My eyelids feel heavy and my muscles want to stop moving. My head has the same feeling as being underwater. All I want to do is sleep. Curl up into a baby ball and sleep.

"Teddy!" Peter shouts. "What happened?"

"No!" I say and close my eyes.

"I'm sorry, Peter."

"I have to do this."

"You have to do what," Peter says. Peter takes a few steps backwards, kicking rocks and backing up against Shane's white truck. "What do you have to do?"

"Peter, nothing happened," I say. "You don't have anything to worry about because you saw nothing."

29

It's easy to take complete advantage of someone's confusion. When Peter realizes where he is after I wipe his memory of the event, he offers to take me home. I don't think he is supposed to leave just yet, but I am too shaken to just wander home alone.

I hope he doesn't get fired for taking an extended lunch break.

Peter does not say much when we get back to the apartments.

"Are you sure you're okay?" he asks me. Peter grabs my hand and caresses my palm with his thumb. "You've been quiet this whole time."

"Ya," I say. Lying, of course. "I'm perfectly fine."

Peter searches my eyes, squinting. "No, you're not," he says.

"No, I'm not," I say. "If I told you what was going on, you'd probably run away and never talk to me again."

"You think that little of me?" he says in that sweet little voice of his.

It's tempting to be honest, but instead I tell him, "I can't. Maybe tomorrow?"

Peter raises his hand, his pinky extended out. "Pinky promise?"

How I not smile? I hold out my pinky and wrap it around his. "Pinky promise."

Peter kisses me good-bye and I go inside and to the bathroom.

"Teddy! Mom is almost home!" says Vanessa. "Where the hell were you?"

"Where is Mom?" I say through the closed bathroom door. My shirt is already in the ground and I don't feel like putting anything back on to talk to her face to face.

"She left looking for you." There is a pause and I consider running the shower if the conversation isn't going to go anywhere. Vanessa says, "She left like a half hour ago, just after I got home." There's another pause and Vanessa knocks on the door. "Can I come in?"

I don't say anything because Vanessa will open the door anyway, even if I said no. Her knocking was only a considerate warning first.

When the door opens, Vanessa's mouth opens in shock and she stops in mid swing of the door. "What the hell happened to you?"

"I did it again," I say. My hands sweat and shake. I shove them into my pants pockets to keep from being too obvious. "I think I did it again."

"Did what?" says Vanessa. She comes closer and gives me a hug, but stopping once her bare arms touch the skin of my shoulders. "You're sticky sweaty. What happened?"

"I killed someone, I think." I sit down on the toilet and sniff to keep back the tears. "I killed Shane."

"You killed him?" she says aloud, then looks around as her question echoes in the perfect acoustics of the bathroom. "You killed him?" she whispers.

"He started to beat up on Peter and me and I just wanted him to go away and so he disappeared." I sniff to keep more tears from escaping my eyes. With the back of my hand I check my nose to look for signs of blood. "The blood," I say, "from my nose, it only comes out when I am going to do something bad," I say and this time, I just can't keep from crying.

My chest heaves up and down, barely able to take in enough air to talk. My sobbing comes over my chest and my shoulders. Vanessa kneels down and grabs me in a tight hug.

"It's okay," she says. "You did what you had to do."

"I don't know if I had to," I say. "I could have just made him stop, but I was so mad."

Vanessa's body freezes and she stops hugging me. "Peter saw all of this?" she says.

I nod. "I made him forget again."

"Good," she says. "That's good for now." Vanessa hugs me again and squeezes tight around my shoulder.

"I can't control this, Nessa. I can't do this anymore."

"You can control it," she says to me. Her hands run over my sticky back, dried up sweat from watching my arch nemesis unravel before my eyes. "You can do it," she says. "You can do anything."

"I can fix this," I say. I sniffle back some of my tears. "I can bring him back, maybe?"

"Why bother?" says Vanessa. "You saw what happened with Bridgette. Let the poor bastard stay dead, or whatever happened to him."

"I'm a monster," I say. "I can't be a monster. I'm a murderer and a monster." The more I say these words, the harder the reality begins to hit me. Can I really be trusted? Can I control all of this?

"You're not a monster," says Vanessa. "You did exactly what you needed to do. The world is a better place without people like him. He was a bully and a jealous asshole."

There is a comfort in her words, but the sight of him unraveling, his skin peeling off his chest and disappearing like vapor in the air.

"I'm not sure he deserved that," I say. "I tortured him."

"Didn't he torture you?" says Vanessa. She stands up and gives me the hands on her hips look, the same one she gives me before she reads me the riot act. "You are gifted, Shane. You needed to do exactly what you needed to do. What we all wish we could do. Do you know what I would do if I had your abilities?" Vanessa kneels down and grabs my hand. She stares directly into my eyes, looking sad and comforting at the same time. "You did the right thing, Teddy. Trust me. Ask anyone. They will all tell you the same thing." There is a pause when we both hear the front door slam shut.

"Mom's home?" I say.

"If you ask me, you should have done that to him a long time ago."

A knock on the door and it opens to reveal Mom's head sticking in. "Where were you, Teddy?" she asks. She, too, comes into the tiny bathroom and gives me a hug. "I'm so sorry," she says. "I thought you were hurt or worse."

"Mom, I found him," says Vanessa.

"I just got home, Mom, it's okay."

Mom pulls away from me and looks at my face. "You look like Hell. Where were you? What did you do?"

"Why do you always assume that I'm doing something wrong when I leave the house?" I say.

"I was with Pete, Mom. I went for a walk and to talk to Pete and clear my head. Is that okay?"

"Don't you dare talk to me like that," says Mom. "I'm still your mother," she says.

"But I'm not a baby anymore!" I shout back at her.

Vanessa's eyes open as big as her hoop earrings and she backs up into the wall. "I'll go get dinner started," she says and slides out of the bathroom. Her shadow, though, doesn't leave the hallway, which means that she is standing in the hallway listening to everything.

"But you are my son, and you live under my roof."

"What the fuck ever," I say. "You never let me do what I wanted since I was born. You're just pissed off because I can do whatever I want," I say.

And my mom, she stands there, mouth open and a pain in her eyes. "I can't help that I want to protect you," she says. "I almost lost you once."

"Oh for crying out loud, Mother, that was nearly seventeen years ago. Get over it! I know I have."

Vanessa's gasp comes in from the hallway outside.

My mom's eyes, they begin to tear, turning a dark red. The whites of her eyes turn pink from frustration. "Fine, if that's how you want to see it," she says. "Do whatever the Hell you want. I don't care."

My mom leaves in a huff, slamming the front door closed behind her and leaving me alone in the stale white bathroom walls. The walls are completely bare and I know that feeling all too well right now.

It takes nearly thirty seconds for the water to warm up enough for me to get inside. Thirty seconds too long. When I get in the shower, I just let the water beat up on me wherever it wants. I am hardly in a position to tell anyone what to do right now. My legs shake and tire from all of this standing up for myself.

I sit down in the bath, my legs stretched out as far as the tiny tub will let me. I stretch each one out, reaching as far as I can go to work out all of the strain and anxiety.

Just a few minutes ago, I basically told my mom to fuck off.

In a perfect world, your mom would know when to leave you the hell alone. In the world that everyone should live in, I should be treated like an adult. If I'm old enough to have sex, I can be an adult.

I turn my face downward so I can look at the tub beneath my ass. I let the water beat on the top of my head and think massage. I close my eyes and think soothing and relax.

To feel better, I focus on the soap in the built-in soap dish ledge that comes out of the shower wall. I think green. Think blue. Think purple.

The side of the wall, it turns different colors to the images in my head. The way the pencil changes, so does this wall. Changing, gradually morphing to a different color to whatever I think.

I change my thoughts and think faster, more colors. I practice and move the colors up and down the rainbow. First one way, then the other. The wall changes colors, keeping in time.

The more I practice, the more perfect I get at this whole thing.

What people really want when they aren't happy is control. What people really want is to do whatever they want when they want it. What is so easy for rich people is hard for the rest of us because we can't control anything.

Money gives control gives security gives happiness gives perfection.

I close my eyes and visualize the blue bar of soap. The blue and white streaks that run down it make it look like it has layers of colors spread through it, a colorful wind in the form of soap.

I close my eyes and control the color, then the shape. I think purple dinosaur. Opening my eyes, the colorful new soap stares at me, jaws open like a tyrannosaurus rex.

I think yellow circle and the soap morphs to a round tennis-ball yellow sphere.

For fun, I think red ball, and the color changes yellow, then orange, then the perfect red.

What people don't want in life is decisions made for them. What they don't want is the unknown. The unknown scares us. We go searching into the unknown to answer our questions.

We invent religions to tell us how to live and to answer the age-old question of "What is the meaning of life?" We go to people in white robes and in red robes to tell us what we should do to go to wherever they think we go after we die.

We are too afraid to take control, to believe what we see in front of ourselves. Most of us, we are afraid to make our own reality.

The ball turns into a red flower and it makes me think about Peter. The soapy flower melts into a puddle of a red, translucent liquid and drips off into the tub like candle wax.

Mom's going to need to get more soap.

I gather what I can into my hands and rub the red liquid over my body and soap up. Still sitting down, I just sit and let the water roll down my back and shoulders and arms. The massage beats on my muscles and tears the tension right out of them.

I think up and to the left and the water stream washes down my shoulder and my left arm. I think right, and the water stream moves and washes over my right shoulder.

For fun, I think the words "purple" and "rain" and showerhead spits out a lilac-colored stream over my body. Purple water droplets drip down the sides of the shower.

I think "clear" and the water goes back to normal, washing the last of the purple down the drain between my feet.

Standing up, I think "off" and the water faucet follows my every whim. I drop off with just a couple wipes of my towel and get dressed in my bedroom. No one bothers me when I leave the bathroom. No one comes knocking in my door to tell me that I'm missing dinner.

Not a single person comes to see how I'm doing.

And secret confession: even though I told them not to, I wish they would.

30

My chemistry partners and I were rocking the exam until Thomas couldn't find the pink dye that we needed.

"I swear it's right there," he says. His hands are picking up all of the little plastic tubes and squinting at them to read the labels.

"It's right in your hands," I say. "That's pink."

Thomas looks at the label and then at the bottle. "I thought you guys were just messing with me," he says. "This isn't pink," he says.

Jon and Marilyn try to stifle their laughter. Thomas pays no attention to the two of them and he gives me the tube of pink dye. "You guys do know I'm colorblind, right?"

"You are?" says Jon. "I thought you were just being stupid." Marilyn stomps on his foot and Jon says, "Sorry."

"You didn't know I was colorblind?" he says. "Wow, you really do not pay attention." Thomas was the tall goofy guy that everyone loved because of his puppy dog stupidity. He did things in such an oafish kind of way that you just wanted to hug him, rub that bump on his head, and send him off to play with the rest of the other kiddies.

You really wouldn't have known if Thomas was colorblind or not. His clothes always matched, and he was good at figuring out when to drive and when to stop in driver's ed last year.

"Some things you just learn to deal with, you know?" says Thomas. He puts his goggles back on and picks up his pencil and scribbles something on is notes. What he's scribbling is beyond me.

"You've never wanted to be able to see color?" I ask. "Don't you feel like you're missing out?"

Thomas looks at me and blinks, blankly. "I don't know any different," he says. "So I guess no, I don't wish I could see color. I don't know what that would be like."

I lean in over the table so no one else can hear us over the table. "Do you want to be able to find out?" I ask.

"No, I don't think there's no kind of surgery that does that," my partner says.

"Lab write ups should be completed in the next fifteen minutes," warns our teacher. She puts the timer on the SMART board and then goes back to grading her work.

"I'm not taking surgery, Thomas. I think I can fix it," I whisper.

"Dude, you guys got the answer to number three?" asks Alex. He shoves his nose directly between the two of us and holds out his paper. "Can I borrow it?"

"Ya, sure, whatever. Get lost," I tell Alex and hand him the paper. "No seriously, Thomas," I whisper again. "Right here, right now. What do you say?"

"You're full of shit," he says. Thomas pushes his glasses back up on his eyes. "You can't do anything like that."

I look into his eyes and Thomas keeps blinking and trying to look away. "Look at me," I tell him. "Or it won't work."

"Are you doing some kind of magic?" he says. "I don't believe in magic."

"Shut. Up," I say. The iris of his eyes dilates as he stares into my eyes.

"This is weird," he says.

"I said shut up," I warn him again. "I need to concentrate."

Thomas's eyes dilate even further the more they stare into mine. In our psychology class, the teacher told us that that usually means that someone is looking at a person or an object that makes them happy or comfortable. That way it lets in more light to see the object better.

Same reason a cat's eyes will dilate before it pounces. To let in more light to see it better, not because it likes what it's going to pounce on.

My mind floods with images of color and bright lights. I try to push into his eyes what I see, the ability to see in color and not be colorblind.

"Tell me if you can see differently," I tell him. "Just tell me when."

I continue to concentrate and Thomas blinks his eyes a few times and says, "I don't think it's working." He blinks at me repeatedly. "My eyes are drying up."

"Ten more minutes," shouts our teacher.

"We need to get our assignment done," says Thomas. "And this is kinda weird."

"It's not weird," I tell him. "Let me concentrate."

My head muscles tense up, and my eyes feel like they are on fire again. "I think I'm almost there," I say.

And Thomas, he grabs his eyes and screams in pain, dropping to the ground. "What is this?" he screams.

"Can you see better?" I ask.

Thomas kicks around on the floor at everything that around his feet. Alex, our other partner, gets kicked in the ankles like three times before he finally moves out of the way.

"Get up, man, this thing's almost due," Alex says, stepping out of the way of Thomas's legs.

"Class, everyone sit down," says our teacher. She picks up the phone and tells the nurse that we're going to need assistance up here. "Everyone, sit down immediately. We need to give him room."

When she puts the phone down, she waddles to Thomas's screaming body and kneels down next to him. "Let me see," she says. "What happened?"

"He was just talking to me and then he dropped to the ground and started screaming," I say. I need to build an alibi as quickly as possible so this doesn't go wrong. "He said something about his eyes and then screamed."

"Thank you, Teddy," she says and points in the general vicinity of the desks. "Now sit down and move out of the way. The nurse will be coming soon."

Thomas's screaming quiets down, but he continues to cry. His hands remain over his eyes, which he rubs with the base of his palms.

The nurse, her only exclamation when she sees Thomas is "Good God." With the teacher's help, she picks up Thomas by the shoulders and helps him sit into the wheel chair. When Thomas's hands are moved from his eyes, they look white and the skin around them is swollen red and pink.

"Dude, what the hell exploded on him?" says Alex.

"Did you see anything explode?" I say.

"Well, no," he replies.

"Then nothing exploded," I say. "Stop trying to get us in trouble."

"Dude, I didn't say nothing," says Alex. "Here's your damn paper back."

When the teacher gets back into the classroom, she tells us to not worry and that we need to finish our assignment in the next few minutes. Our group, since Thomas wasn't there to help us out, was given an extra day after Thomas gets back. "Which," she adds, "I hope is tomorrow since grades are due soon."

The bell rings and we exit out of the hallways, eager to spread the rumors that Thomas's eyes have exploded, or a paperclip flew across the room and hit him in the eyes. By lunchtime, these are the rumors that drifted like ghosts from table to table.

"Okay, what did you do?" says my sister, who is only really trying to sit with me at lunch because she wants to know the truth. "I know you have chemistry with Thomas. What did you do to his eyes?"

"Screw you, I didn't do anything," I say.

"Liar," she says. Her smile and laughter when she accused me lead me to believe that she already knew the story before I can even tell it to her.

"Then why did you ask if you knew I did something?" I say. I bite into the ham sandwich I whipped up together earlier this morning.

"I want to know what you did," she says. "And to ask a favor, por favor."

"No, I am not your personal wizard, here at your beck and call," I say. I take more sandwich into my mouth before I say something that will really get me in trouble. "Everything is fine, Nessa. Go away," I say.

"You shouldn't talk with your mouth full of food, Teddy," she says. "So I was thinking that there is this boy I want you to hook me up with. I saw what you did at the party. You can do that for me, right?" she says.

"Are you deaf or just stupid?" I say. Swallowing the sandwich and licking the mushy bread out from between my teeth, I say, "I am not doing anything for you. What happened at the party was an accident. I don't know why those people came on to me."

"Because you wanted them to," she says. "And I want you to want me to be with John Cardenas." She points her pink fingernail all the way over across the cafeteria. "That guy, right there."

"Ya, I know him," I tell her. "Not going to happen. He's an ass and already dating someone."

"And you can break them up," she says. "Just for me? Please? You're already in a relationship, so don't get all greedy on me now."

"Are you listening to yourself?" I ask. "Now leave before I make you," I say. I look directly into forehead and squint my eyes and wave my hands in front of her the way cartoon wizards do in the movies.

"You're so fucking creepy," she says and gets off the seat next to me.

I eat the rest of my food in silence before the bell rings, telling all of us student-lemmings that our next class will begin in four minutes.

When I toss the bag and go into the three hundred wing of the main building, someone grabs my backpack and pulls me backwards. My ass bounces on the ground and I look up to see and hear the laughter of little feeble minds. "Hi, Thomas, how are you?"

"What did you do to me?" says Thomas. The skin around his eyes look the way a face made out of pork would look. Raw and red and dry, he blinks in stagnant, slow movements.

"I was just trying to help," I say. "Seriously. Why so pissed off?"

"You did something to me," he says. He lifts his foot and hovers it over my face. "What did you do to me?"

I push his foot out of the way and stand up, dropping my backpack at my feet. If this is going to come to a fight, I want to be able to move without restrictions. "I just tried to make you see colors," I say. "But you look," I try to choose my words wisely here, "good." I smile and say, "You look really good."

Thomas rushes toward me and forces me back against the lockers, holding me there with his forearm braced against my neck. "You're going to fix it," he says. "I hurt. My eyes hurt. It's unbearable," I say.

"But there was no blood," I mutter to myself.

"No, there isn't any blood, but it doesn't mean that it doesn't hurt," says Thomas. His forearm goes deeper and deeper into my neck. I get flashbacks of Bridgette's neck, flapping and gasping for air.

"Get. Off. Me," I sputter through my quickly closing esophagus. "I can't breathe."

"And I can't see," says Thomas. "Now we're even."

Of course, if he couldn't see, he wouldn't have such a tremendous grip on my throat, but I see where he's coming from.

"You need to stop," I say. "I can fix this."

"Like you tried to fix my sight?" Thomas says. My attacker pushes on my throat even more and I can't concentrate to do anything. I can't force him to stop, I can't change anything because I can barely breathe.

"You're going to kill him," says someone behind the crowd. The entire hallway, even classrooms empty completely to watch this fight in the hallways.

Someone in the crowd--probably a freshman--begins the chant, "Fight! Fight! Fight!" True to their lemming nature, the rest of the crowd chants the same thing.

If I could rip this kid apart right now, I'd have done it in a heartbeat.

"Stop!" shouts Vanessa. Her head emerges from the crowd, then giving birth to the rest of her body. She pulls Thomas off of me and slaps him across the face.

Seriously, though, she should have punched him or kicked hard in the nuts.

I fall back to the floor, coughing and wheezing to let enough air into my lungs again.

"Can't you do anything?" says Vanessa.

"What am I supposed to do?" says Thomas. "You interrupted."

"I'm trying to catch my breath, sorry," I say.

"Can't you change this?" she says.

"I'll change your mom," says Thomas, and he grips my sister and pushes her to the floor. His shiny, pork meat eyes stare at me. The way a bull charges at a red cape, Thomas charges at me and I move out of the way just in time to hear his head and chest bounce off of the lockers.

"This is getting ridiculous," I say. "I really wish everyone who hated me would just disappear," I say out loud. Immediately, I wish I could grab those words by their tails and drag them back into my mouth, swallow them whole and rephrase the entire sentence. "Shit," I say. I turn to Vanessa, who is picking herself up from the floor and I say, "Vanessa, do you hate me?"

Vanessa looks at me and shakes her head, "Why do you ask?"

I close my eyes and brace for what I know must be coming. "I fucked up, Vanessa." When I open my eyes, Thomas takes steps toward me and pulls back his fist. Helpless doesn't even begin to explain how trapped I feel, until Thomas and the rest of the crowd turns to ghosts in the hallways.

"What did you do?" says Vanessa.

The students in the hallways, most of them go to solid to fading to white to gone completely in an instant. The heat from their bodies, it disappears and a wave of cold air rushes to where the students once stood.

The halls, they're empty except for about twenty kids or so. Most of them freshmen and sophomores.

Great.

"We need to go," I say. I grab Vanessa's hand and run. I snatch my backpack up from the ground and toss it over my shoulder. It nearly knocks me down into the lockers beside me, but my momentum keeps me moving forward. "Come on!" I scream.

"Where?" says Vanessa. She tries to run, but her heels slow her down. "Wait!" she says and I turn my head to watch her take her high heels off. She grips them by the thin leather strap that goes over her foot and she follows me down the carpeted hallway. The teachers, they stare at the empty hallway and watch us both run past them. Vanessa waves at them and says, "Sorry."

She has nothing to be sorry about.

I echo her words in my head. Sorry.

Am I really? Sorry?

If this is really what I wanted, what I wished for, do I deserve to be sorry?

We run out of the building and into the playground next door. I stop just short of the sand-filled pit that is the playground out back to catch my breath. The playground is where the preschool meets for teachers and students who have little kids. The program is run by students at the high school for some technical education credit. It doesn't really matter because they, too, all seem to be gone.

"What happened?" says Vanessa. She looks around. "This is like a ghost city."

"Ghost town," I say.

"Why, what'd I say?" she says and sits down on the logs that serve as steps to the giant wooden castle in the center. "Did you kill them?" she says.

"You sound happy about it," I tell her. "I told you this was unpredictable."

"You're not unpredictable," she says. "They deserved it."

"Did they?" I say. I stand so close to Vanessa that I shadow over her. "Did they really?" I sniffle back a few tears.

"Apparently they did," she says. "You just got your revenge. No longer a problem," says Vanessa. She stands up in front of me and stares me directly in the eyes. "You know you wanted this to happen. Why feel bad about it now?"

"You're such an evil bitch," I say. The wired fence gate looks inviting, so I decide to leave and go somewhere else.

"I'm the evil bitch?" says Vanessa behind me. She shouts louder as I walk away, "You're the one who just killed like half the fucking school!"

With the gate closing behind me, I know Vanessa is right. Police sirens scream into the air down the street. Someone called them, probably to report a murder or a disappearance. With so few survivors and witnesses, it will be a few days before they can put everything together. Even then, they won't be able to indict me, but it never hurts to hide anyway.

I decide to skip the street path and go the scenic route through everyone's backyard. My first destination will be the Owl Foods parking lot to see if Peter is there.

He always makes me feel better even though I hurt him so much.

As of now, he hasn't noticed. Not yet, anyway.

I have to walk past the apartment complex to get to the parking lot, so I ditch the backpack at home to make it look less likely that I ditched school. No doubt the police will be raiding the area, looking for disappearances and missing persons. The least I can do right now is try to not look like a high school student.

It's a straight walk to the parking lot from there. To keep from crying and screaming at everything, I focus on the pencil in my pocket.

I think smooth. I think rough. I think hot. I think cold.

With each thought, the pencil changes textures and temperatures. This sense of control, this is what I need right now.

With each step, I think about distractions. I think light, I think dense.

I think feather and it feels soft. I think fur and the texture of the pencil reminds me of my cat Puzzles.

The parking lot is almost empty except for just a few cars. Peter parked his car at the end of the parking lot, same as Vanessa.

Inside I look around from aisle to aisle, checking the back refrigerated part and hanging out around the bacon for Peter to come out from the back.

For every dark blue jacket that appears, I want to shout out Peter's name, but each time it's just a person, no one in particular.

I could just make him appear. I could.

I can just close my eyes and focus on Peter coming around the corner. Boom! He'd be right there.

But no, not again. I can't use this on Peter. That would be unfair.

I've already done it twice. Three strikes and I'm out.

"Teddy, what are you doing here?" says Peter's voice from down the cookie aisle.

"I was looking for you," I say. I smile and try to give him a hug, but he backs off.

"Dude, I'm at work," says Peter. His eyes peek around aisles and he gives me a one-armed hug by grabbing my shoulders and squeezing tight. "Out of school early?" he says.

"I sort of ran away," I say. "Needed a mental health day."

"Don't we all," he says.

"Listen, Peter, I needed to talk to you about something," I say. I hold onto Peter's jacket and pull him closer to me so I don't have to shout this aloud. "We really need to talk."

"What happened at school today?" he says. Peter's gloved finger points at my throat and his face turns from happy to disappointment. "Who was beating up on you?"

"No one," I lie. "I was just rubbing it earlier since my head and neck hurt."

Peter's left eye narrows because he doesn't believe me. His right eye searches my face for a glimpse of lying, but finding nothing, he tries to smile. "You mark up pretty easy," he says.

"Some kids at school disappeared today, and I think I am the reason why," I say. The words waterfall cascade out of my mouth so quickly I'm not sure either Peter or I had time to process them.

"Slow down," he says.

"They just disappeared?" he says, skeptical. "Like just ran off somewhere? All went to a party? Didn't show up to school?"

"They were at school, and then they weren't at school. Like magic," I say. If only magic were really the word for it. And for my next trick, I'm going to make my boyfriend believe that I'm not really a monster.

Peter reaches into his pants pocket and pulls out his phone and answers it. "Ya, he's right here. Do you want to talk to him?"

Peter's eyes look at me and he mouths the words "It's Vanessa."

"Ya, I can keep him right here," he says into the phone. "No, he looks okay. Rubbing his neck a lot, though." Peter's eyes widen, then turn dark and close shut. His face goes cold and still, then hangs up the phone.

"Why are the police looking for you?" he says.

"They are?" I say. "Shit."

Peter points to the back warehouse of the store and says, "Get in there."

I follow his command and look to the break room. It's empty so I go in and sit down, pulling up a seat. The break room is bright and pale with only a single table and gray metal folding chairs as seats. "This is where you guys eat lunch?" I ask. "Looks, um, cozy."

"The police," says Peter. "What happened?"

"I don't know what happened," I say. "Look, there is something I need to tell you, but I'm not sure you're going to be happy to hear it." Peter's face already looks unhappy. His hands run through his perfectly mouse brown hair and his hazel eyes close, then scrunch together.

He opens them and says to me, "Try me."

"You should know that a lot of weird shit happens around me, and I don't usually mean for it to happen, but sometimes, people get hurt."

"You don't usually mean for it to happen?" says Peter. "What do you mean usually?"

My heart wants to beat out of my chest, shatter my ribcage and destroy me whole. "Aw, man, I don't really want to say this."

"Talk, Theodore," he says. His voice echoes off the walls and screeches its fire alarm screech into my ears. "What happened?"

"I didn't mean for it to happen, I promise," I say.

"Didn't mean for what to happen?"

"I think I just got a little scared when I was attacked and then," I sputter.

"And then what?" screams Peter. Every syllable of his words reaches into my soul and sets it on fire. My nerves carry electric impulses that tell me to run, flee for my life.

"And then they all disappeared," I say. "I killed them."

"How can you just make them all disappear?" says Peter. His words crack with frustration and fear. His eyes, his face, his everything turns red and blotchy. True confession, I think he wants to hit me.

"I just think stuff and it all happens!" I say in one quick breath of air.

The silence silently becomes a scream in my mind. I don't believe what I just said.

Peter, he seems to be processing what I just said. Tears come from his eyes and fall down his cheeks. My first reaction is to kiss them away, but I hold back.

"You did this, didn't you?" he says.

"Did what?"

"To me?" he says. His gloved hand clenches up into a tight, gray Kevlar fist and pounds against his chest. "I remember now."

"There is nothing to remember," I say. "Honest."

"You're lying," he says. Peter hits the white plaster wall and plaster dust bounces off and dances in the air around his fist. "Don't lie to me," he says.

"I only did it to protect you," I say. My words fall to the ground, they are so heavy with sorry and regret. This must be what Superman feels like around Lois Lane. "I just wanted to make sure you were happy and not afraid of me."

Peter cries, too, wiping the back of his hand with the Kevlar fist. "You need to leave," he says. "I can't do this, not right now. Not at work."

"But Peter, let me explain," I say. I stand up and try to give him a hug. Not for him, but to make me feel better.

Peter holds his hands up and pushes me away. "Don't!" he says, then says in quiet, deliberate syllables, "don't touch me."

"I'm sorry," I say, but Peter turns his head and wipes his face again.

I leave the store in a blur. I don't know if I am running or walking or if I'm just daydreaming this whole thing, but life right now doesn't feel like it's running at normal speed. Slowed down or sped up, I can't quite tell you.

At the apartment, I bury my head into the pillows and finally let it all out. My cries, my sobs, and my screams, my pillows block them all and take in everything I dish out. In my mind, the words "why" and "me" circle around.

"Teddy?" says a woman's voice from outside the bedroom. "Teddy!" I recognize my mom's voice. The door opens and my mom rushes in and gives me a hug, then slaps the back of my head. "You had me worried," she says.

"Mom?" I say. "What are you doing here?"

"I came home early when I heard about what happened at school. I thought something happened to you," she says. She slaps the back of my head, then kisses it.

"I'm fine, Mom," I say. "I swear."

"What happened?" she says. "It's all over the news. I called the school, and you weren't there and I got worried." My mom smacks the back of my head, then kisses the red spot on my head. "Don't you ever do that to me again."

"Mom, I'm fine," I say.

"You've been crying," she says. "What's wrong?"

I'm a complete screw up and everything is falling apart. What I really say is, "Nothing, Mom. Promise."

"How is nothing wrong?" she says. "You're supposed to be at school. Why are you home?"

"I left when everything happened. They let us out early."

My mom takes a long, cold look at me, that look that tries to pry the truth out of my skull. "Your school said that you didn't make it to your next class," she says. "What happened?"

"I skipped," I say. Say as little as possible so she leaves.

My mom sighs and gives in. "It's fine if you want to stay home today," she says. Mom grabs my chin and looks me in the eyes, first my left then the right. "You're crying."

"Mom, I think I messed up," I say.

"Oh, sweetheart," she says. She gives me a one-armed hug, grabbing my shoulder and squeezing. "You can't have messed up that bad," she says.

"I messed up big," I said.

"You're my perfect little gift, Teddy. You couldn't have messed up."

"Are you serious?" I say. "All of this time, you've tried to tell me I'm your little gift, this miracle that somehow made it. All this time you refuse to believe that I can make mistakes." Standing up, I try to put some space between me and my mom. "Have you ever wondered if I wasn't supposed to be born?" I say.

"Teddy, don't talk like that," she says. "You had an accident when you were born, and you recovered," she says. Her eyes get bloodshot red, her cheeks flush. "Why is that such a bad thing?" she asks.

"What if I wasn't supposed to be alive?" I say. "What if I wasn't supposed to make it?"

"Teddy! Stop talking like this!" she says.

"I'm sorry, did I say something true?" I ask.

"There is nothing wrong with you." My mom steps up and grabs my hands and holds them to her chest. "You're perfect, honey. You're my little angel, my gift."

"Yes, I know, your perfect little Teddy who can do no wrong and can hurt no one," I say. "But guess what, Mom? I fucked up, and big time."

"You keep saying you messed up. What did you do?" she says. My mom's need to be nurturing is the only thing holding back her tears at the moment. I can feel it.

"You know those weird things that always happen when I'm around?" I say.

"What are you talking about?" she says. My mom crosses her arms and turns to the side, looking out my bedroom window.

"The time Puzzles came back from the dead? Or the time the birds all ran into the glass door where Dad was standing because I wanted ice cream before dinner?" I say.

"Those were weird coincidences," she says. "You are thinking too hard about this."

"Maybe you're not thinking enough about them," I say. "Look at this," I say and grab her arm. Holding her left hand in front of her eyes, I shake it as I shout in her face, "Look! Look at this!"

I let go and her hand drops to her side. Mom pulls it behind her, hiding it in her back.

"What about that, huh? I fucking hit you with lightning, Mom."

"So you're saying you can control the weather, too?" says my mom. Her smile on her face is a mixture of frustration and arrogance. She thinks she's caught me in my argument.

"No!" I clench my fists and slap them tightly to my side to keep them to myself and not be violent. "I control everything!" I say.

"Teddy, you're being ridiculous," she says. "What happened to you?"

"I don't know what happened to me!" I say. A burst of laughter escapes my lungs. The irony hasn't escaped me. For everything I can do, I can't explain something so simple and stupid. "But I've changed. I can't go back to being this secret little kid who can do no wrong, because that's not me, Mom. I can't go back to hiding and pretending that everything is okay."

My mom steps closer to me to give me a hug, her arms extended in front of her in a welcoming Jesus kind of look. I step backwards, pulling away from her grip. "Teddy?"

"Everything is not okay," I whisper. "You're not okay and nothing is okay. These kids are gone, I hurt everyone I love, and I'll be alone for the rest of my life."

"Alone? Gone? Teddy, you need to start making sense," my mom says. Tears finally win the struggle against Mom's willpower. Streaming down her face, they trace the soft lines of her cheek and fall without apology to the area rug below.

"Mom, I've been seeing someone for about a week now, and I think I made him break up with me. He hates me and I don't know what else to do. I'm afraid to do anything," I say.

"Who have you been dating?" she says. "I mean, I guess I suspected something." My mom's shoulders relax, and she's finally giving in to the emotions. This is a nice surprise, but if she's going to start letting go, then so am I.

My tear ducts itch, so I rub them. When I do, the tears are released and I'm back to where I was when my mom came into my room.

"You know Pete from the grocery store?" I say. "Well, we're more than just friends."

The corners of Mom's mouth turn upwards, but just barely. Her eyes glisten with the rays of sun from the window bouncing off of her tears. "He's a nice boy," she says.

"He's perfect." I sniffle back some tears. The back of my throat feels the mucus collecting in tiny globs that refuse to be swallowed. "But he's gone."

"There will be others," she says.

"No!" I say. "There won't be," I say. "Do you realize that I turned seventeen and started dating at the same time?" I say. "I'm a freak of nature and everyone, even life, seems to hate me."

My mom stares at the ground in silence. I imagine the words running around in her head, trying to find the right words to make me feel all right.

But there are no words. There isn't anything anyone can say that can fix this.

Except me. I'm the only one who can fix everything.

"Mom," I say. "I just want to be left alone for a while," I say.

True to how this damn family works, Vanessa walks into my bedroom with her backpack still strung over her shoulder. "There you are!" she says. Midway into the bedroom, she stops and stares at me, and then Mom. Her concern shows on her face. In her right hand is our white cordless phone. She holds it out to my mom and tries to say something, but can't.

"Who is it, honey?" Mom says.

My sister gives the phone to Mom and says, "Did you know that Dad lives in town?"

My mom grabs the phone and walks out into the hallway. She sniffs back her tears and runny nose from crying so hard and says into the phone, "Hello?" before closing the door behind her.

"Did you know that?" Vanessa says.

"Yes, I knew that," I say. I wipe my nose with the back of my hand and wipe my eyes with the other hand.

"What the hell happened?" she says.

"Which time?" I ask.

"With Mom?" she says. "Did you tell her?"

"About?" I ask. I let my body collapse backwards and bounce my head on my down pillow. "You have to be specific. My whole life seems like a big secret lately."

"About you," says my sister. She punches my knee. "Your powers?"

"Will you stop calling them that? And no, I haven't told her. Sort of."

"Sort of?" she says. "You need to tell Mom." Vanessa pulls both of her feet off the floor and sits, cross-legged Indian style on my bed.

"I tried to, but she refuses to believe anything. She thinks I'm the perfect little angel God delivered to her," I say. I throw the pillow over my head and scream into it.

"Maybe you should show her," she says.

The idea runs through my head and I laugh into the pillow. Lifting it off of my face, I say, "Are you retarded? You saw what happened at school. Why would I do that? Maybe I'll make her head explode or something."

"No you won't," says Vanessa. "Don't be retarded."

"Did you not just see all of these people just disappear?" I say. "All I wanted was these people that didn't like me to disappear."

Vanessa stops to think, looks down at herself, and then says to me, "But isn't that what you wanted? Didn't you just want everyone to disappear?"

"Not like this!" I say. "Now what?" I ask. "How do I bring them back?"

"Maybe you don't," she says. "Maybe they deserve to be gone."

"You just do not," I say, but my mom knocks on the door and then comes in. Her round face looks puffy from even more tears. She holds the phone in her hand by just a few fingers. The energy to hold on to anything has completely escaped her.

"Kids," she says. Her voice is something just above a whisper. My sister and I, we look at each other and then to Mom and wait for her to finish the sentence. Mom takes a deep breath, and she says, "Your father just had," she says. "He's gone."

"He's dead?" says my sister, master of the obvious.

My mother nods and looks at the both of us. "I'm so sorry," she says.

"Why?" asks Vanessa. "Not like we knew him. We haven't even seen him in like, what? Forever?"

"I just saw him at the mall the other week," I say.

"Why didn't you tell me?" Mom says.

"Because I almost nearly killed his kid," I say.

"Jesus, you're destructive," says my sister.

My mom cries again. "Why did you almost kill Elias?" my mother says.

"You knew his name?" I say. "You knew about all of this all along?" I stand up, away from the both of my sister and my mother. "You never told us anything?"

My mom begins to cry again, this time, my sister grabs my mom's shoulder and hugs her. "Teddy, you need to calm down a little."

"This woman has been lying to us, hiding our family from us all of this time," I say. "What else aren't you telling us, Mom? Huh? What else is going on?"

Vanessa stands up and walks over to me, pushing me in the chest. "You better get your shit together, Theodore, or I'll kick your ass. You will not talk to Mom that way. You hear me?" she says. With each sentence, my sister shoves her pointed pink fingernail into my chest.

"I really don't want to hurt you," I say.

"Just like you hurt dad?" says Vanessa. "Or was that an accident, too?"

"You little bitch," I say.

"What did you do to your father?" asks my mom.

"Nothing, Mom," I say. Looking at my sister with a look that dares her to speak more and suffer the consequences. "Nothing happened."

"You really did do something to him, didn't you?" she says.

"I didn't mean to," I say.

"What did you do to your father?" says Mom.

I stare right into my sister's eyes, those brown eyes that challenge me to be everything that she knows I fear. My sister, who wants me to make everyone pay for what they did to me, to her, to everyone. "I didn't do anything."

The words "Go to hell" race in and out of my brain.

"I don't believe you," she says. "How could you do that to Dad?" she says.

"So now he's Dad?" I say. "Just a few seconds ago, you didn't give a rat's ass that he died. We haven't seen him in like, forever. Remember that shit?" I say.

My sister shoves her hands against my chest and pushes me back into my television. "You had better undo everything," she says. "Make it all better. I know you can."

"No I can't," I say. My blood boils underneath my skin, my face feels so hot it can melt off my skull. "You have no idea what will happen."

"Do it!" she says and shoves me.

"No!" I scream back at her. My throat is raw and painful. The mucus in the back of my throat even gargles. "Shut up!" I scream. "Leave me alone!"

My sister's hands slap her mouth, and she tries to speak, but only muffled ventriloquist noises come out. Her hands pull on her mouth and her lips, trying to separate them. With her jaw pulled shut and lips tight, she tries to scream.

My mother, she's pulling herself along the wall against my bed. Her eyes are wide, bloodshot. Full of fear, the fear of knowing that your beautiful baby boy is a horrible monster from Hell.

My sister collapses to the ground, clawing at her mouth with her fingers. Blood creeps out through fingernail-sized scrapes along her mouth. The flesh of cheeks and chin are red meat raw with dry white claw marks across her face.

"I won't hurt anyone else," I say. "I'm so sorry," I say as I run out the door. My sister's screams echo down the hallway and through the downstairs and out the front door, where I am. I run into the parking lot and keep my mind clear.

In my mind, my sister screams for air. My mom claws into the white plaster wall against my bed and I think red. I think fast. I think faster.

My feet carry me across the parking lot in only a few seconds. I blink and I'm across the street, then down the block, then at the mall. I don't know how long I've been running or where I'm going. I just focus on my feet, focus on faster. Focus on away. Focus on escape.

My blood flows hot through my body. My heart pumps battery fluid through my body, a flesh and blood Energizer bunny. Going and going and going.

I want to undo everything and wipe away my mistakes. Start all over.

But I can't. I don't know how. I have become a god of destruction, my will be done. I am no longer the little innocent baby boy my mother gave birth stillborn. I can fix anything. I can destroy everything.

In my mind's eye takes a tour of Peter's bedroom, and I think faster. I think Peter's apartment. I think the answer.

My feet carry me at superhuman speeds to the apartment complex where Peter lives. His car isn't in the parking lot. As I try to stop, I realize I don't know how. My feet refuse to stop moving, and so my hip nearly shatters along the bumper of a Ford SUV. My hands fly up to protect my face from the glass window of the back door. My cheekbones crack against the impact.

I learn firsthand about what we studied in physics about Newton's laws of motion and bounce away from the truck and hit the asphalt parking lot below. The rocks dig into the flesh of my bare hands and digs and tears at my shirt. None of this matters right now.

There is no time to dust myself off. No time to make everything better. I just have to escape.

Peter's apartment is only a few feet away from where I land, so I don't bother to run. With my hands on the doorknob, I think "open" and turn the handle.

I see Peter hasn't been keeping up with the usual upkeep. A pot of Spaghetti O's or some other canned pasta still sits on the yellowing stovetop. It looks fake and plastic, it's been sitting out so long. The apartment smells like cologne and mint, all coming from Peter's bathroom.

He just took a shower and went somewhere.

Did he really find a new boyfriend already. That bastard.

I search his nightstand and there is nothing there but his alarm clock, a small table lamp with a black lampshade, and a glass of half-empty water. I pull out the single drawer and find nothing but paper. Bank statements and notepads mostly. Nothing important.

Thinking about all the action movies I've seen, I run my hands underneath the cool underside of the pillow. Nothing.

If I were a gun, where would I be?

Teddy, you're doing this all wrong.

I think "gun" and the words "under the bed". In my mind, I imagine a dark metal object lying underneath in the darkness.

I kneel down, reach my hand underneath and pull out the gun. It's heavier than you would imagine it to be. My index finger traces the trigger. It feels smooth as water under my fingertips. All of my concentration is needed to keep from pulling it now.

I'll save that for later.

"This is necessary," I say to, well, really no one in particular.

Directly in front of me is a blank white wall, the creases and bumps of the uneven plaster make me feel suddenly larger, each little crack, a cavern. Every bump turns into a mountain range.

When you take time to look at things, I guess, it's easier to see the big picture. My big picture twists my stomach into rollercoaster spirals. It sends my insides into a three-hundred mile an hour turn against the cascading stomach acid and up the intestinal tunnels to a deep drop.

At home, my sister suffocates from not being able to breathe. My mom lies on my bed, powerless, trying to keep my sister alive and wondering what went wrong. Why was she being punished for all of this?

Being this big above the picture, I start to see the lines between the crags and the mountains. From up here, I can see connections, about how I wasn't supposed to be here. My death wasn't the accident. Me breathing when I was supposed to be dead, that was.

My existence is an attack on nature. You know that feeling when life is against you? How about having that happen to you every time you go outside. Imagine feeling like Mother Nature herself, in all of her fury, wants to kick you in the ass and wipe you out completely. Imagine having the power to keep that from happening.

My life, my accidents, the disappearances of the students, Shane's disintegration. My dad's death. All of these things are what happens when you fuck with Mother Nature's plan.

This is me getting the memo.

I'm sorry, Life. I'm sorry, Fate. Sorry, Mom. I'm sorry for everything.

I hold the gun up to my head. Still staring at the white wall, a flat basin-like crater catches my eye. It seizes my attention, pulling me further and further into it. When I look deeper, I see the shadows of movement outside.

I can't see the front because of the bed's placement against the wall. What I don't see is someone coming in from outside. What I hear is the closing door.

"Hello?" says a male voice.

"Peter?" I say. The words "I'm sorry" and "I shouldn't have hurt you" come to mind, but I say nothing.

Quickly, before he comes into the room.

Peter's hands touch the blanket that drapes over the gap between the living area and the bedroom. His hands grip the sheet slowly and he begins to pull back.

And I have to do it, so I pull the trigger.

31

When people say they had a near death experience, I don't think this is what they meant.

The first thing I feel is Peter's hand gripping the back of my head. His tears drip off of his cheeks and onto mine. The salty splash filters down the cracks of my face and into my mouth.

If I didn't still love him, this would be really, really gross.

My chest expands upwards, pulling in fresh air. Coughing pushes out the stale, stagnant air that remained when I stopped breathing for, I don't know how long.

"What the hell?" says Peter. His hands move from under my head at a lightning speed. The fleshy part of his thigh catches my fall and I look up at the beautiful weeping boy above me.

I want to speak, but all I can do is cough and hack.

"You're alive?" he says. I nod and try to sit up. Peter's hands push my head down, and he examines my temples. With his big strong knuckles, he nudges my head left, then right. My hair feels wet and warm and the makes the same sound as spaghetti in pasta sauce when he searches around on both sides. "How are you alive?"

"I'm alive?" I ask.

"You shot yourself," he says. He wipes tears away from his eyes and cheeks. Red-orange blood smears his face like war paint, his red eyes and skin giving the impression that he's full of rage and ready to kill.

"But I'm alive?" My hands search my body and tap every part.

Peter grabs my head again, turns it from side to side. "How?"

"I'm sorry," I say. The rush of emotions hit me like a burst of fresh air. My lungs heave air in and out. My hands claw at his shirt and I bury my face as deep as it will go between his body and his arms.

"Why didn't you die?" he says. He searches my head, pushing it back and forth. It makes me dizzy.

"I guess I didn't really want to die," I say. "So my ability didn't let me die."

"Why?" Peter looks into my eyes, searches them for an answer. "Why do this? Why now?"

"I couldn't live with this," I say.

I look up into the Peter's eyes. He blinks and more tears fall from his eyes, dripping down one raindrop at a time onto my chest and neck. His tears itch my neck as they dry, but I'm too weak to move my arms and scratch.

"Is this because I broke up with you?" he says.

"No," I say.

What I mean is yes.

"I did some bad things, Peter. I am a very, very bad person. I don't deserve to live."

Peter pulls his hands off my body and slides his legs gently from underneath from me. When he thought I was dead, he gripped my body the way a mother mourns a lost child. Now that I'm alive, he doesn't want to touch me.

My blood makes dark Rorschach prints on the lower half of his jacket and sleeves. My ex-boyfriend's war-painted face turns away from me, toward the light coming in from the living room window, and he says, "You need serious help." He takes a deep breath, pulls the blanket between the two rooms to let in light, and he says, "Look at yourself."

My hands reach around on the ground. Everything feels soggy

and wet. I don't dare look down. I never did handle blood very well. Especially mine.

"Peter, I'm sorry," I say. "I'm so, so sorry."

"You tried to kill yourself in my apartment, Teddy!" His words shake my walls and my chest equally.

"I didn't know where to go," I say. "You had the gun." I look around the floor and search for the evidence of the shooting. "And I thought."

"You thought?" he says. "Really? Because that sure as hell surprises me." Peter unzips his jacket and tosses it across the room. His jacket leaves a broad stroke of red blood painted on the walls.

"I wasn't thinking," I say.

"That!" he says, pointing at me. "That is more like it."

"I'm sorry," I say.

"Why? Why me? Why here?" he says.

I search my thoughts for everything I might have been feeling. As much as I will it, I can't come up with a decent answer to his question.

"It just felt right," I say. Wrong thing to say, but the awkward silence felt like it needed some kind of filler.

"Get out," he says.

"But," I say and Peter slams his hand against the wall.

"Teddy! Get out!" he shouts at me. The bloody smears nearly blend in with his face, his skin is so red.

"I can't leave. I have nowhere to go," I say.

"How about go home," he says. Peter takes his shirt off and tosses it in a hamper. Peter's body disappears into the closet and I hear metal clothes hangers scraping along the bar as he searches for another shirt to wear.

"I have nowhere to go," I tell him. "I can't go back there."

"You know," Peter says. His hands hold a red T-shirt, bundled up in his fist. "You've been on this grand power trip since we started dating, and now you're this suicidal mess that can't even handle going home to his family." Peter arms lift up. The T-shirt covers his cute, dark brown armpits, then is pulled down around the button-fly of his pants. "What the hell happened? Why are you like this?"

I take a few steps toward me and forget that I must look like a total reject from a gory zombie flick. I grab Peter's belt loops and pull him closer.

I think "love me." I look at his lips and think "kiss me".

Peter's eyes relax as he looks at me and his eyes dilate again. I smile.

"Don't you fucking dare!" Peter says. I trip on clothes on the floor as Peter shoves me backwards and I land on the bed.

I think "love me" and "I'm sorry."

"I'm sorry," says Peter. There is a long pause of Peter blinking his eyes and shaking his head. "But I can't do this."

"What can't you do?" I say. Sitting up from the bed, my muscles hurt and brain must be spinning, I feel so dizzy and disoriented.

"Don't you use your thingy on me," he says. His hands go up to his head and he makes a hocus pocus-like motion, like he's trying to make a person disappear.

"It's not like that," I say. My knees lose their strength and they buckle together. My ass and my back hit the floor of the apartment and Peter rushes to my aid.

He stands above me and slaps my face. "Teddy?" he asks. "Are you alright?"

I have to blink three times before there is only one Peter left in my vision.

"Here," he says. Peter's shadow leaves me and disappears behind the shades. From where I'm lying, all I can see is the darkened white ceiling of the apartment. It's dominated by one giant ceiling fan, a cheap brass one with four light bulbs covered in cheesy translucent flowers as covers. Two of them are darkened and probably burned out, but I use it to focus my attention, anyway. But the more I focus, the more I swear that it's been moving around on me. Waving around in counter-clockwise circles, if I was pressed for an answer. The blades aren't moving, but the lights and the lamp part this is only held there by a thin metal pole, it looks like it moves and responds to the movement of the room.

I know Peter is getting closer to me when the lights move faster, but still subtle. All of this compounds to making me want to vomit right here on the floor.

"Where's the gun?" I say.

"I hid it, don't worry," he says. "Drink this."

He hands me a glass of water, and I hold it still for a moment before I realize I am going to need to stand up if I'm going to drink this. Not sitting up will result in a much-needed, but ill-timed shower.

"Help?" I ask. Peter grabs my hand and pulls me up and to the left so I'm leaning up against his bed. My brain must still be twirling about in my head. The room is thankfully staying in one place, but my body feels like it's on a merry-go-round.

My dry lips soak up the water that touches them. What does eventually go down freezes my throat and I have to swallow my own spit to warm it back up again.

"Thank you," I say.

Peter sits down on the bed away from me.

"Why would you use it on me?" he says. "I thought you loved me. Do you not trust me? Are you hiding something?" he asks.

They are all good questions, but I can't answer a damned thing right now. I shrug, and Peter sighs, looks away and rubs his hands through his hair. The soft undersides of his arms were holding me just a minute ago. Now they seem so far away.

"I got carried away," I say. "I did make the people in the school leave. I think. Shane," I say, looking for the right words, "was also my fault."

Peter's head turns to look at me. The front of his bangs looks light brown and the edges glow with a dark red from the lighting from behind him.

"I think I might have hurt my sister, and my mom is terrified of me," I say. These words come out nice and slow and deliberate. I'm in the middle of a tense situation here.

"Why your family?" he says. "Why are you hurting everyone?"

"Fuck," I say to, well, anyone in the room other than Peter, which I guess is me. "I didn't mean to. It just happened because I got greedy. Life didn't want me to be happy," I say.

"Excuses, excuses," he says. "And why aren't you owning up to any of this?"

"I don't want to lose you," I say.

"You may have already lost me," he says. "You did that yourself." Peter stands up and my mind starts to wander.

Peter's feet stop in mid step and he says, "Let me go."

"You need to listen to me first," I tell him. "Then I'll let you go."

"You'll only let me go if I decide to stay with you," he says. "That's a trap."

"I promise, I'll let you go if you just listen to me," I say. "Listen to what I have to say." Peter's heavy breathing is the only sound he makes. His head is cocked away from. He never did well with confrontations.

"Fine," I say. I take a drink from the water glass and rest it next to me. "You win. I admit. It was all my fault. I made all of these things happen because I guess deep down I wanted to. I know it's not a good reason, and that probably makes me a bad person, but I care a lot about you, Peter. I don't want to lose you. You are the reason why I didn't die, and you are the reason why I came back here. You can help me."

Peter shakes his head and says, "I" but stops. "Continue," he says.

"I know it makes me a bad person, and maybe even a scary person, but I swear I'll never hurt you. Please, please, please believe me. I'm not a monster," I say, beg, and plead.

"Why can't you just turn everything back and undo it?" he says.

"I'm afraid," I say. "Nothing goes right. Everything I do, something bad happens, too, that just causes more and more problems."

"So you can't just go and make everyone forget and bring other people back from the dead?" he says.

"That's what happened at the party," I say. "Bridgette came back, but she was still suffocating and couldn't die."

Peter keeps his commentary to himself. When he thinks I'm not paying attention, his body pulls to one side to see if his legs are loosened up yet.

I blink and focus on his legs, thinking the word "freedom."

"You can move now," I say.

The worst part is, "My sister is probably dead and my mom is trapped in the room with her."

"Jesus Christ," says Peter, but his body tightens up and he stands upright when he sees my glance at him.

"And I told my dad to go to hell when we left the mall, so he's dead, too," I say. When the laundry list of details is spread out like this, it's easy to see why Life and Mother Nature hate my stupid ass so much.

Peter turns around and looks me in the eyes. He looks at my hair. My eyes. My face. He says, "So why can you do this?"

I shake my head. "I don't know." Peter sighs. "I know it's not a good answer," I tell him, "but it's all that I have. Maybe I'm some superhero or a mutant." Peter's lips almost make a smile, but fail. "Maybe I'm an anomaly. I was supposed to be dead when I was born."

Peter's head cocks to one side.

"When I was born, I was stillborn. I wasn't breathing or moving." Peter holds his breath and sits down on the bed.

"I'm sorry," he says.

"It's not your fault," I say in something like a laugh and a moan. "My mom cried over my body. When my mom gave me over to the nurse, I started breathing. Weird shit has been happening to me ever since."

"So what are you going to do about it?" he says. I reach a hand out for Peter's, but he pulls away, standing up and shoving both of his hands into his pockets. When he does this, his shoulders rise up around his cheeks, and he looks as adorable as ever.

"Don't do that," I say.

"Do what?" he says.

"Do this," I say, pointing at the way he's standing. My hand traces the sides of his body shape. "Doing this and looking so adorable."

"Teddy," says Peter. His voice trails off into thought and he looks at me, sad. "What are we going to do?"

"We can go," I tell him. "We should just run, run off and go somewhere and build a place where we can be together and not worry about anyone or anything."

"And where would we do that?" he says. Always trying to be the logical one.

"Who cares?" I say. "We'll know it when we see it. Maybe some small town somewhere, maybe near Columbia, or Charleston. Maybe up north, maybe out west," I say. The possibilities become endless in my mind. I see us strolling down the sidewalks of Los Angeles or West Hollywood. "Wherever we go, we can make it into whatever we want." I pull myself up using the mattress to balance my weight. "Whatever we want, I can make it happen."

"And what if you screw up again," he says. Peter's smile smirks at me, challenging me and doubting me.

"I can't fail, Peter." I grab his hands with both of mine. "I can't fail with you."

Peter tries to slip his hands out of my grip, but my thoughts command him to stand still and relax. Peter sighs, but stops struggling.

"What do you say?" I ask.

"Sounds good," Peter says.

"I thought you would be more excited," I say. "Just think, we can build a haven for gays and nerds and the outcasts of society. We can create the perfect world where no one is treated poorly for whatever reason."

Peter doesn't understand. He doesn't understand any of this, but he will. He has to. My will be done.

"We should pack!" I say. My mind commands that there be suitcases in his closet and I pull them out. They are large, black leathery ones that will be perfect for collecting all of Peter's clothes. "What do you want to pack?" I ask.

Peter's body relaxes suddenly as my mind lets him begin packing.

Peter says nothing as he grabs a handful of boxers and socks and shoves them into the suitcase.

"Do you have gas?" I ask.

"Yes, I think so," says Peter, "but we can't get very far."

"Don't worry," I say. "I got that."

As Peter goes back and forth, packing a few of his belongings, I sit on the bed and watch Peter's body move back and forth. From this perfect view, I can see the muscles in his arms flex and move as he grabs and lets go and organizes. The way his ass looks in the jeans he's wearing, the way they hug each of his perfectly tight cheeks, it's easy to start thinking other, more distracting thoughts.

"We need to go," I say. "We can get more money later," I say. "We're in this together now," I say, "just the way it should be."

I stand up and grab Peter's waist and pull it closer to mine. My lips kiss his cheek, then his neck and I whisper, "I love you."

Peter, that ingrate bastard, says nothing back to me.

"You do know that if I go down for anything, I will take you down, too," I say.

From this close to Peter's body, I feel his heartbeat pick up and his body tenses up. I can only imagine the thoughts that are clawing their way around in his head. None of them matter right now. I have a plan, and it needs to go this way. I need him and though Peter doesn't know it, he needs me.

He'll see it eventually. I know he will, and when he does, we'll be happy and so glad that he came along for the ride.

"We're a great team, me and you," I say.

Peter says, "We need to finish packing." His feet try to move away from me, but his gently waits for me to finish hugging him. His body smells like sweat and cologne, the same cologne that so attractively caught my attention the first day we met.

Due to a severe lack of judgment, I let my penis do more of the thinking.

I think "love" and "sex" and Peter's hands are grabbing my torso. Slow and graceful, he peels my shirt off of my body and unzips my pants. They fall to the floor, heavy with my wallet and keys answering to the laws of gravity.

Peter's lips find mine and his hands go to his own clothes. Peter says, "You should take a shower and clean up," he says. "If we go anywhere with you looking like that, you'll turn people's heads."

Peter tosses my shirt back at me and smiles. He kisses me, sucking hard on my bottom lip and pushes me away, gentle.

I think "stay" and "here". His words, he better not leave.

The shower starts in a sputter, then finally to a full stream. Peter uses regular body soap for both his body and his hair.

Beggars can't be choosers right now.

The water runs dark, then light red and finally clear as I just stand in the stream, letting the beads of water beat down on my skin.

I can't take too much time because I don't know what will happen while I'm away.

Peter won't leave me, will he? Can he?

"Pete?" I shout from inside the shower. My words echo back into me, followed by a muted knock and then Peter's adorable little head creeping in through the opening of the doorway.

"Yes, dear?" he says.

"Where are your towels?" I ask.

Peter points against the wall, where the rack is, "Right here."

"Right," I say. "I didn't see that."

False. I saw that the first time. Just checking on you, my dear.

When I get out of the shower, Peter is still packing things up, but looks at my wet shirtless body and searches through the suitcase.

"Here," he says and tosses me a white T-shirt.

The way his bathroom is structured, his bathroom is actually directly across from the closet. Peter hasn't packed everything, so I rummage through what is right in front of me and I grab a blue and white striped buttoned shirt to keep me warmer.

On my command, Peter zips up the suitcase and brings it to the front door, where he waits for me. I check my pockets for everything that I need, my wallet and keys.

Wait, I won't need the keys. I pull on the key ring and toss them onto the ground. "I won't need them anymore."

We leave the apartment and Peter hands me the suitcase. "Can you bring this to the car and I'll lock up?"

I nod and kiss him on the cheek. The opportunities are endless and this escape is exactly what I need, I tell myself. This is exactly what I deserve. A fresh start in a new place with the one I love.

My family, they won't miss me if they stay alive. I won't be there to mess up their lives. It's hard to miss someone who has been nothing but a burden, an accident that will kill or hurt you. I can't hurt anyone else if I'm far, far away from them.

No, they can't find out where we are. They can't know what happened to me. It is for the best.

No one else will be harmed. For now, only good things will happen. This is my command. My will be done.

Peter's doors aren't open and I turn around to see if he's coming soon. The crackle of sneakers on gravel sounds out behind me and I turn to see who it is.

Something hits me hard on the head, so hard I see colors in shades of red and orange and yellow. My feet give out underneath me. And even though I try to catch my hands on the car to keep me up, they slip on the paint. My nails scratch along the dried up, twenty-year-old paint job and once again, I'm on the floor writhing. The pain radiates from the back corner of my head, where my hair parts. It travels down my face and neck in waves of heat and pain, blood rushing to the area. Even now, the skin feels tighter as blood rushes to the area to build a nice, big bruise.

At my face is a pair of white leather tennis shoes, Pete's shoes.

You traitorous bastard. "Pete?" I say or whisper, I'm not sure because my ears are still ringing.

Another sharp strike to my head makes me see black and I close my eyes and fall asleep.

32

The tunnel I dug up above me his just barely big enough to let my whole body stand up. The nice thing about cheap wooden coffins is, once they being to fall apart, the rest of the wood becomes easier to tear away.

This, by the way, is the only way to make enough legroom to stand up in a coffin. It's not easy to go from a completely seated position to crouching so to get your feet up under you. Just saying.

Peter's digging got me about six feet under, I figure, and since I'm standing, I have only about a six inches of dirt to actually dig through. As I dig and claw through the top layer of dirt, more and more of it loosens up and falls on my face. If it weren't for the shirt wrapped up around my face, I'd be eating worms and rocks right about now.

I try not to focus on not having enough air to breathe. Not easy when your brain reminds you that you're lightheaded and slowly suffocating to death. Asphyxiation, I think they call it.

Maybe it's the shirt over my face, maybe it's the complete darkness, or the lack of oxygen going to my brain, but it's next to impossible to know if I'm standing up or spinning around. With every dig and every pull, I swear I must be swaying back and forth.

I try to keep my fingers together completely to make sure that they work as shovels and not rakes. Ever try digging a hole with a rake? Not easy.

My hands pull dirt from the walls and my earthy ceiling to the ground below me, every few digs I lift my legs up and try to stand on the new ground I'm building in the coffin.

And finally, my right hand breaks through the ground and I'm met with the cool air that hits my fingertips. I feel like I've plunged my hands into ice-cold water, and never before has being this cold felt this good.

This new hole invites new life-giving oxygen into my grave and my lungs thank me with more energy and an eagerness to work harder and faster to get out.

You're almost there, Teddy. Almost there.

And you're almost dead, Peter.

God damn you, why do all the cute ones want to kill you?

My hands grip the grassy mound of dirt above me and I pull more dirt in. My fingers claw at the sides to make the hole bigger to let my shoulders and hips and stomach through to the surface.

My knees and feet, they dig into the sides and try to inch my body up, inch by inch, breath by breath. A few inches up, and my whole hand is enveloped in the crisp cold nighttime air. My hands grab the closest chunk of rock I can feel for, and grabs with dear life.

I pull. And as my biceps begin to burn with fatigue, I wish I had paid more attention to P.E. and tried harder in those Presidential fitness tests. I mean, in retrospect, one more pull up would not have killed me.

Actually, it sounds like this is one of those rare times when it could have saved my life. Damn you, P.E.

My hands claw at the sides and my feet kick to dig deep and create pockets for the tips of my shoes to keep and hold me still. And this tunnel is too dark for me to tell if I'm actually going anywhere. The only sign of effort and success comes to me in the form of crisp oxygen and shivering of my forearms.

I take the first long deep breath in what seems like forever when my head finally breaks above the surface. Fresh sunlight creeps in through the threads of fabric in my shirt. My shoulders crack and stretch when I'm grasping for everything in my path that will help me climb out. This must be what it feels like to break out of jail.

With a shirt wrapped over your head, all you see in random shapes and colors. Nothing clearly defined, just there and fuzzy like watching television through a Tupperware container.

My hands reach around, slapping the grass and dirt and rocks that surround me. As carefully as I can, I turn around, moving my feet inch by careful inch to rotate my direction. And though I only see in blurry shapes, there is something in front of me, something big, so I grab it with my hands.

What I feel is leather with cloth stripes running crisscross along the top.

I really was hoping he would have left by now.

"I was really hoping you would have stayed down there," says the male voice, Peter's voice.

"I was hoping you wouldn't have tried to bury me alive, you asshole." I grab hold of his pants and pull myself up. The leg cuffs of his pants nearly give under my pull until Peter's feet kick my hands away.

It doesn't matter. At this point, I'm almost high enough to pull myself out, so I rest on my elbows and try to pull my body up and out.

The shirt still on my head, I must look like a full on moron.

"How about we just call it a truce?" I say. I throw my hands up into the sky like I'm being held up at gunpoint. The way I feel, nearly completely almost blind, I'm hoping Peter just lets me go and I can run off on my own.

Clearly, Plan A is a no-go.

"How about you stop trying to kill everyone?" he says. "How about you stop trying to manipulate everyone? How about I get the Teddy back that I used to know?"

"I don't know how to go back to that," I say. "I've tried, and it just doesn't work out."

"You can do whatever you want, right?" he says. His blurry legs take a few steps backwards.

"Can I, please?" I say and my hands point to my shirt, still wrapped up like a bag over my head. I don't hear anything, so I take that is a silent, "yes." I fold down the sleeves of my shirt and slowly pull everything down.

And there he is, just so right there in all of his glory. Even when he's trying to kill me, he looks adorable as hell.

"I don't know how to put things back to where they were," I say. "I tried and I'm scared."

"That's bullshit, and you know it!" he says.

With my shirt finally back down around my waist, I can see the dark green needles of the pine trees that cluster nearby. Where we are, is the local cemetery, somewhere near the middle of the plots. This one is surrounded by large statues of angels in medieval battle gear, breastplates and swords and shields. Every grave around my plot has the same looking headstone, flat and long with a basic last name chiseled in the same Times New Roman font. SMITH and ROBERTS and RODRIGUES surround me to the north, west, and east of me.

Peter worked here, I'm guessing.

"You had this plot ready for me?" I say.

"It was the last thing I was working on," he says, "before we started dating."

"So you fucking bury me?" I shout at him. My eyes still blur and want to close. My forehead feels tense, but this time, it feels different. The setting sun's rays are needles, poking and prodding into my eyes. It's painful to look at Peter without shielding with my eyes first.

"I had to do something!" says Peter. His hands are folded behind him, and he looks calm and cool and collected. "You're out of control, Teddy!"

"I am not out of control!" I say. The ground beneath us changes from soft, grass and sod-ridden sand to hard solid marble and black, shiny obsidian rock. "Okay, maybe I need a little help," I say. I take a few steps toward Peter, but he takes a few steps backwards. "I need a little help from you, Peter. Please help me."

"What can I do?" he says.

"You can run away with me. You can love me, promise to be with me," I say. This is what word vomit feels like.

Peter pulls his arms from behind him to his front, putting them up in front of him to ward me off.

"I can't love you," he says. "I can't love someone who threatens me if I do something wrong." Peter takes another step backwards. "You can't threaten someone into loving you."

I smile. I think "happy" and "love me," but Peter doesn't respond. He takes more steps backward until the back of his legs run into a headstone marked for a Mr. Henry Berlin. Peter's eyes peer downward, and he sidesteps it, but stays still.

"You can be by my side," I say. "We can have anything you want. All you have to do is ask."

"Even you can't control your own," Peter stops, searching for the words, "for whatever this is."

"I can learn to control it," I say. "I have already learned so much," I say. I point my hand over to Henry Berlin's headstone to draw Peter's eyes there. "Watch," and I think "pink" and "wood".

The headstone morphs and changes before our eyes, turning into a pink headstone, carved out of wood.

"I can do that so easily," I say. "I'm learning to use this."

"And what about your mom? What about your sister?" Peter runs his hand through his hair and looks up at the trees above him. His eyes close, forcing tears out onto his face. "What about everyone at school?" he shouts at me. Peter's hands fall to his side, his shoulders slouch, and he reaches behind him again, this time drawing a gun out and pointing it at me. "What about that?"

My eyes see the round threat of the gun barrel pointing at my chest, then my head, then my shoulders. Peter's frightened shaking keeps the gun from being steady. I don't know if this is more or less threatening. A wrong move and he might show his itchy trigger finger.

"Peter, put the gun down," I say. "Please." I wave my hands down, signaling for him to put it away. "I won't hurt you."

"You're dangerous," says Peter. "You're dangerous and you need to be stopped."

For an instant, I envision Mother Nature in her big grassy goddessness, stomping her green heel into my forehead and smearing me on the ground the way you scrape gum off your shoe.

"I'm not going to hurt you," I say. "Jesus Christ, why won't you understand that?" I take a single step forward, and the gun in Peter's hand clicks and stays steady, following my motions.

"Stop right there," he shouts.

"We both know this doesn't work, Peter." I take another step forward to him. "I can't die."

"You can't die when you try to kill yourself," he says. "Let's see what happens when someone else tries to kill you."

Well played, asshole. Remind me to haunt you from hell, Peter.

"Put it down," I say. "Let's make a deal." Peter's hands quiver more the closer I get. His face tries to remain still, but his top lip quivers then flattens out, pressing hard against the lower lip to remain still. "How about you let me live, and I leave? Just me, no one else." I swallow my tears at the bitter thought. "You can stay here."

"And you'll leave me alone?" he says. "You'll leave everyone alone?"

"Deal," I say. I hold my foot forward, about to take a step. I'm probably only about eight or ten feet away from him. I'm close enough to be threatening if he decides to shoot me.

True confession? I'm not sure I will come back this time.

"Please?" I say. My elbows feel tired and my hands are beginning to feel numb from holding them elevated higher than my heart.

Peter's left hand loosens on the grip of the gun, his fingers twitching, before his shoulders drop and he rests his arms at his side. "Leave, now," he says.

"Good bye, Peter." I take my foot and spin around. The road that takes us to the highway interstate is only a short block away. I can catch that and maybe hitch a ride somewhere. Or steal a car. Or create my own car.

The possibilities are endless.

My feet squeak on the wet, slippery grass. The sprinkler system must have been running while I was buried no less than a half hour ago. In this part of the country, the humidity makes everything feel wet and soggy. Because of this, I couldn't tell you if I'm sweating because the air is so humid, or if I'm so nervous that I've lost my first love.

"I'm sorry," Peter says from behind me.

I don't know why I do, but I turn around to say something. As quickly as the words enter my brain, they are lost, pouring out of my head at the speed of blood. My entire skull burns and I'm reminded that this pain, all of it, is actually from the skin and muscles that surround my brain. The brain itself, despite being the source of all nerve endings, does not actually have any nerve endings itself.

It feels no pain, and I suddenly feel jealous.

Splashes of sprinkler water from the grass coat my cheek and forehead. The heels of Peter's feet turn toward me and they walk, slowly, then stop just a few inches or centimeters or whatever away from me.

What I want to say is, I don't remember. What I want is, well, it escapes me now.

Having nothing else to do or say, my lips smile just a little. The words, "I deserve this" and "finally" flash and then fade before my eyes.

My mouth gasps for air in short bursts until I cannot act or do anything.

Because the muscles that control my eyelids are voluntary, I blink. I watch Peter walk toward me and blink. My ears think they hear a sniffle, maybe some crying but I could not tell you for sure. My last thought, well, it's

ABOUT THE AUTHOR

David Gearing is an educator and author of over 30 novels across multiple genres and pen names. He specializes in fiction with an LGBTQ twist and supernatural edges.

His psychology degree helps him delve deep into the anima and animus of the human mind, where he loves to stare off into the shadows. He doesn't mind when the shadows stare back.

He lives in the Pacific Northwest, but has lived all over the United States, but is mostly inspired by the Southern Gothic stories of the Deep South.

You can sign up for David's newsletter here and visit him at his website, davidgearingbooks.com, or his Publisher's website.

facebook.com/davidgearing
twitter.com/dgearingwrites

ALSO BY DAVID GEARING

Akusai Publishing specializes in LGBTQ centric stories, often with a supernatural edge.

Do Ya Like Dark Fantasy or Godpunk horror?

Join Hermes and Heracles in the **War of the Gods** series

Exiled from Hell (Book 1)

Reign from Heaven (Book 2)

Across the Realms (Book 3)

A Jono Grey Dark Fantasy Mystery

Apocalypse Nigh

Psychological Horror

Savior

Gifted

Mad Maddy

House of Braddock

Echoes

Mr. White

Wannabe

Like Sci-Fi?

For the Republic

Reset

LGBTQ

Just a Thing

Pride and Glass Unicorns

Like Thrillers?

Patient Zero

Tartarus

Short Stories

Unwanted

Touched

Evaluation

Writing as KD Johnson

The Shattering Series

Sword of Stone (Book 1)

Shapes of Clay (Book 2)

Halls of Shadows (Book 3)

Ray of Light (Book 4)

Man of Fire (Book 5)

Orb of Light (Book 6)

Omnibus 1: Collection of Books 1 - 3

Young Adult

Method Acting

www.ingramcontent.com/pod-product-compliance
Lightning Source LLC
Chambersburg PA
CBHW031025260626
47153CB00017B/2183